IMAGINE THE SCIENTIFIC GENIUS OF IT ALL...

George Marland was amazed at Barton Wiley's startling discovery—the creation of a new kind of matter that was able to cancel out the effects of its own gravity. This soon led to Wiley's creation of something even more phenomenal—a revolutionary spacecraft, capable of deep space flight and landing on other planets. It wasn't long before Marland and Wiley were headed toward Earth's nearest celestial neighbor...the moon!

But when they landed on the barren Lunar surface they were astonished to find that they were not alone. A secret outpost had been established there by a team of Earth scientists several years earlier. The outpost was headed by perhaps the most brilliant man alive, an odd-looking scientist named Forscher, whose dream to reach out to the other planets would soon become a reality...

FOR A SECOND COMPLETE NOVEL, TURN TO PAGE 165

CAST OF CHARACTERS

GEORGE MARLAND
This down-on-his-luck journalist saw his luck turn from bad to good—starting when he smashed his car into a telephone pole!

BARTON WILEY
His discovery was amazing—the creation of matter that nullified the effects of its own gravity, thus making space travel feasible.

DR. FORSCHER
He wasn't much to look at, but his brilliant mind had created something previously unthinkable, a secret outpost on the moon!

THORNTON QUAILE
When given a job working with the biggest telescope ever made, he was literally in heaven. Its location…the moon.

LAFOURCHETTE
This genial Frenchman was a high maintenance space traveler for sure. He proved that when he exited a moving spaceship!

DR. ERNST
Aboard a long flight into deep space there was a need for someone with a calming influence—Ernst was that kind of man.

DALTON
He was thrilled to be part of long space voyage, but being held by murderous alien thugs wasn't quite what he had in mind.

THE ALIEN INTERPRETER
He looked like a big carrot with fish-like skin. He had a simple request…send mercenaries from Earth to help wage war!

OUTPOST ON THE MOON

By
JOSLYN MAXWELL

ARMCHAIR FICTION
PO Box 4369, Medford, Oregon 97504

For more information about Armchair Books and products, visit our website at…

www.armchairfiction.com

Or email us at…

armchairfiction@yahoo.com

CHAPTER ONE

IT was late on a Sunday afternoon in early spring. Impelled by a feeling of restless loneliness, I had taken my little secondhand roadster for a drive, wandering at random over the highways, far from the city. The day had been deceivingly mild, and I had left my overcoat at home; now the lowering sun and a chilling breeze forced me to head for my little third-floor room in the heart of the great metropolis. The numbness of my fingers and toes influenced me to discard the caution that crowded roads and hurrying cars require; my foot rested more and more heavily on the accelerator, until I was passing the traffic wherever an opening in the line of closely-packed cars presented itself.

The falling darkness brought with it a light rain, which rendered the highways increasingly slippery, and as the approaching cars turned on their headlights one by one, the driving became very difficult. The pace I was taking was the height of folly, but I was cold to the marrow, and reason was swept aside in my hurry to reach the warmth that waited. I rushed heedlessly past a sign that read "SHARP CURVE" and swung over to the left-hand side of the road in order to pass the car ahead of me. Too late I saw the coupe rounding the curve toward me. I could not drop back into line, there was not time to pass the car ahead; I must leave the road or crash. Instantly I chose the former alternative, swung my wheel hard to the left and jammed on my brakes. There was a moment of jarring over rough earth, a violent shock, and I was lying on the seat behind the twisted steering wheel.

It was one of those freak wrecks. The car was completely demolished, yet I had escaped without a scratch. I found myself unable to get out of the machine, which had hit a telephone pole and was so bent out of shape as to be almost unrecognizable. Pieces of glass lay all about me, yet not one had touched my skin. In fact, the only injury I could discover outside of a severe shaking up was a slight bruise on my left elbow.

While I was debating the best method of escape, I heard voices close to the car, and presently a head appeared through an opening in the wreckage of the top.

"Are you alive?" the owner of the head asked excitedly, and a bit timidly.

"Quite all right, thanks, but I can't get out," I replied. The head disappeared, and I heard a murmur of voices, people passing the news along to the constantly growing crowd: "he's all right," "nobody's hurt." Presently the man who had first spoken re-appeared with a fence rail which he used as a crow-bar, prying open a hole large enough for me to get through; albeit with some damage to my clothes.

I found myself in the midst of a circle of curious passersby, most of whom, to judge by their expressions, thought that I had got no more than I deserved. Perhaps they were right, but I hoped that at least one of them would forget his prejudice to the extent of offering me a ride back to the city. It was in looking over the crowd that my glance fell on a familiar figure. I recognized him almost immediately as Barton Wiley, a prominent physicist, who during my attendance at the City College had been a young instructor. That institution had now grown to the proportions of a good-sized university, though still retaining its original name; and with its rise Wiley had attained considerable fame through his ex-periments in electricity. He was now Professor of Physics. After thanking the man who had liberated me, I spoke to him.

"Do you remember me, Professor Wiley? George Marland—I was a graduate student at the City College nine years ago."

"Yes indeed, Marland," he replied. "So it was you! Apparently the laws of man do not appeal to you as much as those of nature!" He laughed. "May I give you a ride back to town? I see you were in a bit of a hurry to get there." He indicated with a wave of his hand one of the autos parked alongside the road, and noting gratefully that it was a closed car, I accepted.

We climbed in, and he headed the car for the city. On passing through a nearby village, I made arrangements with the local garage-owner to collect such of my car as was worth salvaging and dispose of it to a junk-dealer for what it would bring.

As we proceeded toward the city, there was little conversation between us, the professor being intent on watching the road, and I had an opportunity to reflect on my acquaintance with him in the past. During my graduate work, I had come in contact with him often, and a friendship had grown up between us. He had urged me to accept a position as instructor at the college, but I had preferred to try my luck in the commercial world.

He had remained to watch the growth of the College; and after an unsuccessful attempt to find work in the laboratory of some large corporation, I had drifted into the newspaper business.

My chief success in that line had been the writing of near-scientific articles for the Sunday supplements; but I had wearied of the job, and tried my hand at one thing and another. The intervening nine years had passed quickly, and found me no nearer to fame and fortune than when I had graduated. Perhaps if I had followed his advice I should now be in a position comparable to his own. He was highly regarded in scientific circles for his research work in the field of electricity, and had made less known, though perhaps even more startling discoveries regarding the structure of the atom. Of his methods I knew little, but his results had often been published.

He had succeeded in repeating the experiments of Rutherford, in which atoms of nitrogen were broken down into helium and hydrogen; and it was rumored that he was working on the ever-fascinating problem of getting energy out of atoms. I welcomed an opportunity to talk over some of these matters with him, as presented by our present accidental meeting.

As though my thoughts had suggested themselves to him, the professor turned to me.

"How about having dinner with me?" he asked. "Why not spend the evening? You must have had some experiences during the years since you left the College that would interest a man like myself, who never gets out of the laboratory except to teach classes."

I told him I would be delighted, but that I was much more anxious to hear more about his work than to talk of my own fruitless efforts.

Accordingly we dined at a neat little restaurant close to the City College, near which he maintained his residence. Our conversation ran to pleasantries and topics of current public interest; by common consent we deferred deeper subjects until we had finished the meal.

When we reached the professor's comfortable little apartment, and had lighted cigarettes and settled ourselves comfortably, I again broached the subject of his work. He said nothing for a moment, apparently lost in reflection.

He looked much the same as when I had seen him conducting classes; a tall man, of rather slight build, with regular features too large to be called handsome. His hair, now graying slightly, was, as always, perfectly combed; and in spite of his shell-rimmed spectacles and slight stoop, his appearance suggested the distinguished man of leisure much more so than the scholar.

I was startled out of my contemplations by his voice, mild and slow, yet with great carrying power.

"I understand, Marland, that you are connected with a news agency, and if I remember rightly you have been the author of a number of articles purporting to describe the discoveries of research workers."

I nodded assent.

He continued, "In that case I should ordinarily have nothing to say. But since I take it that your question has been prompted more by a personal interest than by a desire for news, and provided that you give me your word that you will publish nothing of what I tell you without my express permission, I shall be glad to talk over some of my experiments with you."

I assured him that whatever he said would be held as strictly confidential, and that my interest was purely that of a student of science in the work of a successful researcher. He smiled.

"I can hardly be called successful," he said. "For the most part I have merely done what others have done before me. There was considerable comment in scientific journals, I believe, over my attempts to change the structure of the nitrogen atom, which were in part successful. As you doubtless recall, the atom consists of a number of charges of positive and negative electricity. These normally neutralize each other; but occasionally a change in the number of negative charges, or electrons, as they are called, takes place in the outer limits of the atom; one or more electrons may be picked up or lost, and the atom becomes an ion. This is of course familiar to you, but I am merely restating it in order that you may be prepared for what I am about to say.

"With the single exception of experiments like those I have recently performed, no one has been able to redistribute the protons, or positive charges. Of course, in the very heavy metals, such as uranium, radium, and the whole class of radioactive elements, this goes on spontaneously—the nuclei of helium atoms being liberated in the form of alpha rays, and electrons in the beta rays. But to do it artificially to any of the other elements, or to even speed up the spontaneous processes of radioactivity, is at present impossible."

I nodded, leaning forward interestedly. He continued. "Even were this accomplished, it would not necessarily result in the liberation of energy. That is not the end to which my efforts have been directed, contrary to certain reports. The aim of the modern alchemist—that of transmuting one element into another, such as mercury into gold—has been my field. As I say, I have as yet been unsuccessful.

"But let us suppose that one could, at his desire, separate the protons and electrons of an atom, and recombine them. It would he possible for such a person to make at will any element or chemical compound he wished from any other; or perhaps to create a substance as yet unknown to us—a metal whose atomic weight was greater than that of uranium, for example. Such an element would probably he highly radioactive, if we may judge from the behavior of those radioactive substances already known."

"You mean," I asked, "that it would be possible in that manner to liberate the latent energy of the "atom?"

"No," he returned, "that is not what I had in mind. But a substance so unbalanced in structure might easily be a storage battery, so to speak, of vast quantities of energy, which could he built up slowly and liberated quickly."

Less Than Nothing!

HE was silent for a moment, and I took the opportunity to ask, "What of your experiments in electricity?"

"That has been more of a hobby with me than a subject of real research," he replied. "The two fields are closely related, however. We know that electric charges are merely unbalanced proportions of electrons and protons, and that an electric current is nothing more than a stream of moving electrons." Again he paused for a moment, looking at me intently.

"Marland," he said, "if I remember rightly, you once remarked on the similarity of the behavior of astronomical bodies to that of electric charges of opposite sign, and asked whether it might not he possible to discover same sort of 'negative' gravity, which would repel, and be repelled by, matter as we know it. I answered you, I believe, by saying that the resemblance was merely superficial; and to prove my point I called your attention to the fact that when two charged bodies approach one another there is a redistribution of the electrons, which repel each other and consequently are driven to the far sides of their respective bodies; while no such redistribution takes place when two bodies are placed each within the gravitational field of the other. Since our discussion Einstein has brought out his theory on the interchangeability of gravity and electricity; and I have found, in the laboratory, definite corroboration of his views…"

He stopped; but I remained silent, knowing that he had not yet finished. Presently he resumed: "We believe that an atom—say of hydrogen, since it's the simplest of all—consists of a positive charge at the center, and a moving negative charge. We've assigned a pretty definite size and weight to the negative charge—the electron. But the hydrogen atom weighs nearly two thousand times as much as this electron, so we say that the difference must he in the proton; and to make it agree with our theories we say it has the same charge as the electron, but is much smaller. I know it sounds rather contradictory to say that the smaller body has the greater weight, but that's all covered in the electromagnetic theory of mass, some of which has been developed since your time.

"I fell to speculating on what would happen if the negative charge could he made smaller, and therefore heavier, or the proton larger and lighter. I devised some experiments along that line, and with rather startling results, I assure you. For when I succeeded in exchanging the weight of the proton and the electron I found that I had actually created a 'negative element.' One which weighed less than nothing! Continuing along this line, I made another curious discovery—that when a proton and an electron of the *same* weight are combined, their weight disappears entirely—though not their inertia—and furthermore, they absorb the force of gravity, so that matter made up of these charges, which I have called 'equi-protons' and 'equi-electrons', *weighs nothing, and is a perfect insulator against gravity!"*

"Like Cavorite!" I exclaimed. H. G. Wells' famous story, "The First Man in the Moon," flashed into my mind. Here was the very sort of thing that had enabled his heroes to make their voyage to our satellite. Why shouldn't his dream become a reality?

"No, not Cavorite." Professor Wiley's amused face brought me back to earth with a flush. "Wells' imaginary compound, if you will remember, was made into shutters fastened on the outside of his glass space-car. But, unfortunately, you can't make a gas into shutters. And that is what I have been experimenting with—hydrogen gas!"

I experienced a feeling of bitter disappointment. Stories of trips through interplanetary space, independent of the attraction of the heavenly bodies as well as that of the Earth, had always excited my imagination; and in the brief flight of fancy that I had just experienced, I had hoped to actually witness the accomplishment of this dream.

At length my thoughts returned to Wiley's remarks. I was curious to know something of the method by which he accomplished this wonderful thing. The explanation that he gave I shall not reproduce in detail for many reasons; primarily because the process is not protected by patent; and also because the mathematics involved would be meaningless to the average reader. Let it suffice, then, that the procedure consisted in passing hydrogen ions through electric and magnetic fields of such intensity as had not been produced anywhere else on Earth; and that, in the end, the dimensions of the proton were expanded to those of the electron. Then, their charges being equal and opposite, the respective weights became likewise. Wiley offered no explanation of the absorption of the force of gravity; he confessed frankly that it was beyond his ability to explain at present.

WHEN he had finished speaking, I asked him whether he had tried the process on any substance other than hydrogen ions. He replied that he didn't believe it would work with any others, but that he intended experimenting with helium shortly.

"You see," he explained, "there are electrons and protons bound together in the nucleus of the atom; and you can't very well affect one without affecting the others." However, he said, he proposed to run the test on a number of common elements, including some of the lighter solids. In response to my eager questions, he admitted that should one of these last behave in the same manner as hydrogen he would indeed have a substance similar to Cavorite.

"But," said Wiley, "if it should turn out to be true, I'd have to keep it quiet, else some idiot would want to start right off on a trip to Mars. Of course, no one with sense enough to know the danger would think of it; and it would take a man who realizes the danger and who understands astronomy to carry it through successfully. Yet there's always some fool ready to try it. He'd undoubtedly be lost, thereby giving the hopes of those who might be competent a severe setback."

"Not necessarily," I exclaimed. "Why, I'd be glad to undertake the trip. I've studied astronomy enough to plot my course."

"You!" exclaimed Wiley.

"And why not?" I demanded, a hint of a smile on my face. "After all, I've been enough of a failure at everything else to deserve a chance at success in this. And I've no connections, no property—nothing at all to tie me here to the Earth."

Wiley regarded me steadily for perhaps a minute, before speaking.

"Well," he said at length, "we've let our fancies run away with us, since the success of the vital element hasn't been tested yet. Our gravitation-screen is merely an idea so far." This was obviously intended to discourage me and divert my attention from the question of a trans-ethereal flight. His next words, however, assured me that he expected success.

"If I were you," he said, "I should let the matter drop. In time it will be accomplished, but one is foolhardy to anticipate developments. The first aviator didn't set off for Paris; he left that to a man better trained, and with the equipment and experience developed through a quarter of a century."

"True enough," I answered. "The Wright brothers didn't set off for Paris; but they flew as far as they could. A flight to Mars would perhaps be too much at present; but why not a trip to the moon—only a two-hundredth part of the distance?"

"What would be the object of that?" asked Wiley.

"What was the object of the Wrights in flying their few miles?" I retorted. "To show the world that it could be done, and to encourage others to try it."

"Perhaps you're right," he said slowly. "But I must have your promise to say absolutely nothing of what we have discussed tonight."

"Promise given—on condition that you keep me informed of your progress in your experiments," I replied.

We agreed, and I departed exultantly, for I knew from his manner that he would be successful if he made the attempt to produce the gravity-resisting solid; and I knew also that he would never allow the opportunity for such a discovery to escape him.

But my thoughts were turned away from Wiley and his experiments in an unforeseen manner. When I reached my residence I found a call from the chief of my news bureau. There were reports that China had declared war on Russia; the Washington office was short-handed, and I was ordered to catch the first train there to cover developments. I hastily packed a suitcase, caught the midnight train, and reported for duty shortly before nine the next morning.

During the next two weeks I found plenty to occupy my mind. I was new at the task of reporting political news; consequently I spent hours where more experienced men would have taken minutes, searching in vain through the dark halls and airy rooms of the big State, War, and Navy building for someone with both authority and inclination to speak; attending conferences at the White House in company with a dozen or more representatives of rival press agencies; or waiting in the ante-room of the State Department's press bureau for a mimeographed "handout" radioed from the Consul General at Shanghai.

News is no respecter of the clock, and coming as it did from the other side of the world, it happened as often as not that the most important developments were reported to the national capital in the small hours of the morning. Time and again my slumber was broken by phone calls from the indefatigable chief of the Press Bureau, informing me that a statement was being prepared.

It was after such a night, spent in trying to beat rival reporters to the wire, that I returned to my room and found a letter bearing Wiley's name above the return address. I tore it open and read it at a glance:

Dear Marland:

After trying unsuccessfully several times to reach you by phone, I was informed by your office that you were in Washington covering the Russo-Chinese outbreak and were apt to be there for some time. I had hoped to see you soon; but I trust you will communicate with me immediately upon your return.

Referring to our spirited conversation of the other night, if you will come to my laboratory at your earliest convenience I may be able to show you something of interest.

Cordially,
Barton Wiley

He had succeeded!

CHAPTER TWO
Success!

WILEY'S letter filled me with an immense impatience to see him at once. A leave of absence from my duties at this time was out of the question; the only remaining alternative was to resign. I gave notice, and waited with what patience I could muster until a man had been found to fill my place, meanwhile notifying Wiley of my intentions.

Upon being relieved from duty, I caught the first train and hastened to the laboratories of the City College. I found my friend making preparations for another of his innumerable experiments, but on seeing me he dropped everything and, dismissing his assistant, led me to a corner of the room where there lay a heavy box, apparently fastened firmly to the floor. I could feel a strong draft of air rising about it, and as he unlocked it, the lid flew back apparently of its own volition. Observing my surprise, Wiley explained these phenomena.

"As you probably surmised," he said, "I have been successful. I have in this box a plate that is perfectly impervious to the force of gravity. Nothing above it has any weight; hence the vertical air-current and the lightness of the lid."

He reached into the box and brought out what appeared to be a square of blackness, and laid it on the table. Do not misunderstand me; it did not in the least resemble a piece of black wood or metal; there was no reflected gloss, no appearance of solidity; it was as though I was looking into a bottomless hole in the laboratory table, and the effect was heightened by the strong upward draft, I commented on this, and again Wiley satisfied my curiosity with a simple explanation.

"The color of this substance differs from what we ordinarily refer to as 'black' in that it absorbs practically all of the light which strikes it," he said. "Ordinarily black paint reflects enough light to make it visible, but the human eye is unable to detect any reflection from this. There is no visible surface, and therefore nothing from which to judge its location. The effect is the same as that of looking into an unlighted hole."

I was struck by another thought: "If the air above it has no weight," I said, "won't it escape into space?"

"I hardly think so," he answered. "This plate is six inches square, and removes the influence of gravity from a column also that large directly over it. However, as the air arises, it expands equally in all directions, and the greater part by far is forced out over the ground again. There are probably strong currents high in the atmosphere that blow the rising air out of line with this gravity-resister. Then, too, think what an infinitesimal portion of the globe it covers; all the rest is free to attract the air after it gets a little way up."

"One more question," I said. "Why doesn't the plate itself fly upward?"

"I took the precaution to cement it to a sheet of iron, on the under side," said Wiley.

For a few moments he demonstrated the peculiar properties of his discovery; holding objects above it and allowing them to rise until stopped by the ceiling, where they remained until he slid the black plate from beneath them, or juggling them up and down by passing it back and forth, allowing the force of gravity to act intermittently. At length he returned the plate to its box, pushed down the lid and fastened it. Then he faced me.

"Marland," he said gravely, "think of the possibilities of this discovery as applied to aviation." He paused to let his words take effect; then he continued: "Suppose an airplane were equipped with enough of this material to make its weight practically nothing. The wings could be reduced to a size sufficient to direct its flight upward or downward, such as the ailerons at present employed. The air resistance would be cut down enormously and the motive power could be increased almost indefinitely, since the weight of the engine would cut no figure. Think of the great airliners it will be possible to build! Ships carrying thousands of passengers, tons of freight, around the world—anywhere!"

It was a glowing picture he painted. Carried away by his own thoughts, he enlarged on the idea...

"A plane could rise high into the thin atmosphere many miles above the Earth, and there attain such a speed as would carry it across the Pacific in a few hours!"

These words brought forward again the idea that had lingered in my mind since our previous talk.

"What's to prevent such a plane from heading straight up and flying off through outer space to the moon?" I asked. Wiley's face became grave, and he considered for some time before answering.

"Nothing," he said finally. "I could depend on you to think of that again," he added, smiling. "But there are practical objections to the idea. Suppose you did head straight up and leave the Earth; how would you steer so that you would land on the moon?"

"A matter of starting in the right direction," I replied. "After leaving the atmosphere the plane would continue in a straight line until stopped by some other force."

"Such as collision with the surface of the moon?" asked Wiley.

"Exactly," I replied, "though the contact should not be violent enough to cause a wreck."

"And to avoid a wreck you must either slow down before landing or start at a low enough speed so that a direct collision would not injure the plane. I am not an astronomer, but I do know that the moon's atmosphere, if any, is so thin as to go undetected by any means known yet. Too thin to slow down in at any rate. If you adopt the other alternative—start at a speed of, say, five miles an hour—how long would it take you to make the journey?"

"About 48,000 hours; that is, 2,000 days, or roughly five and a half years," I said, calculating mentally.

"RATHER a tedious journey," commented Wiley. "And when you had landed, how would you return, with no atmosphere to start in?" He smiled. "Better stick to the Earth, Marland, and leave your interstellar voyages to the future."

"But we haven't exhausted the possibilities yet," I protested. "There are other means of motive power than a gasoline engine and screw-propeller. For instance, suppose the plane were built like a rocket, with discharging explosives to drive it. It would be possible to start and stop in a vacuum then."

"Perhaps so," agreed Wiley. "It would require a considerable amount of gunpowder to give you much initial velocity, though, and the same amount to stop. Then to go back you would require still more."

"Only half as much as you think," I replied. "To start off, it would only be necessary to interpose the gravity screen between the Earth and yourself; the centrifugal force of the Earth's rotation would do the rest. At the equator you could start off with a velocity of a thousand miles an hour, and less as you liked from a higher latitude. Returning with the same velocity you need only turn the gravity screen toward the Earth, and the atmosphere would soon stop you. The discharge would be necessary only on the moon."

"Right again," said Wiley. "You know, Marland, you're beginning to convince me of the practicability of this idea of yours. The other factors are not insurmountable: light, heat, air, and food. They've been worked out by submarine builders."

He arose and paced the floor nervously, then faced me.

"Do you really mean you'd care to try it?" he demanded.

"Wiley," I said, "there'd be no better man for the job. I've been a failure so far. I've nobody to care what becomes of me if I shouldn't come back, and it would be a great help to science if I succeed. I'll start the instant you give your consent."

He shook his head doubtfully. "I couldn't let the credit go to someone outside the College," he said. My hopes fell as he continued, "After all I made the trip possible, and I ought to take charge of it." He regarded me quizzically. "But I'll need an assistant who knows astronomy. I can make a job for you in the Physics Department— Cosmic Research shall we call it? You'd have to teach a couple of classes. What do you say?"

"Accepted!" I exclaimed. "I could ask nothing better. When do we start?"

"We start, if ever, when I have convinced the Trustees of the College of the advisability of financing us," was the reply. "We can't build our machine on knowledge and hopes. But your first duties will be to make complete specifications for the machine and a map of our course. I haven't the time, and your knowledge of Astronomy is much better than mine. I'll leave it to you."

Wiley had put it up to me squarely to get the plan into presentable form, and I resolved to do my utmost. The first problem was to determine the course we must take in order to reach the moon. To the layman it might appear to be a simple matter of waiting until our satellite was directly overhead and starting off, leaving the rest to gravitation. But such a course would probably have ended in our being reduced to gaseous elements in the sun, or freezing and starvation as we drifted further and further away from the solar system.

The centrifugal force which would set us free would send us in a direction tangent to the Earth's surface. To an observer beneath us at the moment of our departure we would appear to rise nearly vertically for a time, drifting more and more to the west; and if he were to follow us with a telescope we would disappear below the western horizon, or "set", as does the sun. Twenty-four hours after our departure he would find us almost due east of himself, several thousand miles away.

Supposing that we started from our own latitudes, our initial velocity would be approximately seven hundred miles per hour. Our course would be bent slightly upwards—that is, away from the Earth's surface—by the buoyant force of the atmosphere on our weightless car, but once free of the air our course would be a straight line. My problem, then, was to determine our ultimate direction, and time our departure so that we would meet the moon at whatever point on its orbit we might choose. The journey would require a little over fourteen days.

Patient Plans

I NEXT turned my mind to the design of the car in which we would travel. The first consideration was its shape. The gravity screen was difficult and expensive to make, so that the smallest surface possible was desirable. This of course suggested a sphere with its surface covered by the gravity-opaque substance. It was necessary to remove the screen at times, in order to land; hence the screen was to be divided into hemispheres, one of which could be slipped above the other.

A second requisite was that the hull of the car must be strong enough to withstand the shock of the innumerable tiny meteorites that fall with great velocity near the Earth, and are destroyed by the atmosphere, but which would strike our craft when free of the protecting air. High-grade armor steel seemed suitable.

Next, we must have a means of swinging the moving half of the gravity screen from beneath us, such as an electric motor; and we must have light and heat. Storage batteries seemed desirable as a source of energy, as their weight was no objection. Then there must be a means of keeping the air breathable. This could be accomplished by driving the stale air through limewater, and heating potassium chlorate to liberate its oxygen from combination.

Then there must be the means of stopping. By storing hydrogen and oxygen at high pressure and burning them in the right proportions, steam under tremendous pressure would be generated; and this, directed as desired by nozzles, would stop the car by the recoil of its departure. I determined on hydrogen and oxygen as an explosive mixture because of the convenience of storing large quantities and the relatively great energy of their combustion. Last of all there was the matter of storing sufficient food and water to last us during the trip. In addition to the four weeks in making the journey, we would spend some time in exploring the surface of the moon, and the return.

I had entered on my duties as assistant instructor, which consisted of taking charge of a few laboratory and recitation classes each week. The remainder of my time was spent in the physics laboratories, surrounded by drawing instruments, reference books, and reams of paper with calculations, drawing up plans and specifications, mapping our course and compiling data to present to the Board of Trustees. During several weeks I scarcely ate or slept, and when at length the task was finished, I showed the results of my work to Wiley with considerable satisfaction.

In their final form, the plans called for a steel shell twenty-five feet in diameter, lined with asbestos. Inside this was to be a second shell, with the space between the two allotted to the storage of the hydrogen and oxygen. The inner shell was also to be lined with asbestos, and have fastened to it the storage batteries and tanks of water, compressed air, and purifying chemicals. Inside these were to be cupboards for food and such equipment as we took along.

All this occupied a considerable portion of the interior of the shell, leaving us only a small living space, but with the idea of economy I had purposely made the machine as small as possible. I had included in my plans a sort of "diving apparatus" with which to leave the car through an airlock that provided the only means of entrance and exit. In the outer door of the airlock was the one glass porthole, I had allowed. More than this I had not deemed advisable because of the possibility of their being broken by meteors. It could be covered with a steel cap and need be exposed only for the time necessary to make observations. The inner door of the airlock could be left open when the porthole was in use.

Wiley went over my drawings carefully. "You certainly seem to have considered everything," he remarked. "I see you're quite an astronomer; your explanation of our course would be clear to anyone. This data will help me to put the proposition up to the Trustees in a convincing manner." He put the sheaf of papers and drawings in his desk, adding: "From now on it's up to me to put it across. I've been talking to the head of the Physics Department, Dr. Willson, and he'll back us. Heftner can't see it at all, but you know how these old-time astronomers are. He predicts that we'll land on the sun, if we ever leave the Earth, and he's refused to give us any help in the matter. But we don't need him, as Radner has agreed to check your calculations, if necessary, and give us any information we want regarding the position of the planets."

"The positions of the planets has been allowed for," I replied, "though I'd be glad to have him go over my figures. But do you think it's a good idea to talk about this plan to so many people? Don't you think it would be better to keep it a secret, at least until we're reasonably sure of success?"

"I haven't mentioned it to anyone outside the faculty," replied Wiley, "and I meant to caution you not to either. By all means we must keep it dark. Too many men have become the laughing stock of the world over their fruitless attempts to plan to do what we plan, and publicity would only bring ridicule."

During the ensuing days I waited with considerable impatience for the meeting of the Board of Trustees. I devised, in my mind, a thousand plans for financing our trip independently should the Board turn us down, mentally resorting even to speculation in the stock market and bank robbery; but the more I thought on the matter, the more obvious was the conclusion that we must be backed by the College or not at all. You may imagine with what eagerness I waited for news from Wiley when, on the second of April, he went before the Board of Trustees with our plan. During my morning quiz I found my thoughts miles away from the classroom, and twice caught myself marking "A" opposite the name of a student who reported himself unprepared. At length I dismissed the class early, and waited in the office of the Physics Department for a phone call from Wiley.

It was an hour before the bell rang; but even as Wiley spoke my name, I knew the outcome.

"Marland, *we win!*" And he banged up the receiver.

CHAPTER THREE
First Flights

OF THE bustle and feverish activity of the next few weeks I remember few details. Wiley and I spent most of our time in the laboratory making the gravity screen, as we would not trust the precious formula to anyone else. The contract for the outer steel was signed, and arriving in due time it was subjected to every test the Physics Department could devise. Occasionally Wiley or I took time to supervise some detail of the installation of tanks, batteries, and such equipment. There were many delays. A whole shipment of plates for the batteries was defective and had to be replaced; the cement that we had ordered to fasten together the plates of the gravity screen, was lost in transit; and the plate glass porthole had to be trimmed down to fit the frame. An unforeseen difficulty, due to our lack of knowledge of diving apparatus, arose when we tested out the special suits in a vacuum chamber. They enabled us to breathe as we had expected; but the pressure of nearly fifteen pounds per square inch stiffened out the fabric so that we could not move—the difficulty being solved by placing metal joints at the shoulders, hips, elbows, and knees.

The school year was over and it was early summer before the car was completely assembled. Neither Wiley nor I taught any classes in summer school, so our entire time was devoted to the examining and testing of the car. I was impatient to begin our trip at once, but Wiley more prudently planned to make a series of test trips, cruising above the atmosphere for awhile in order to determine the behavior of the ship while actually free in space, and to make observations on the number and size of tiny meteors encountered.

Our first trial trip nearly resulted in disaster. The car had been carried to a field outside of town, and after a final inspection we entered, closed the airlock, and put the gravity screen in position. The sensations were exactly opposite to what one might expect after having ridden in high-speed elevators, for with the force of gravity suddenly cut off from beneath us we felt as though we were dropping rapidly an immense distance, there being only the slight acceleration caused by the buoyancy of the car to hold us to the floor.

We promptly opened the porthole and found ourselves already some distance above the ground (as we could tell only by the proximity of the clouds, since our view below was cut off). We quickly passed through these, and by the blackening of the sky above us we realized that the air was becoming extremely thin.

Soon some of the brighter stars were visible. Almost overhead I recognized Capella, the twinkling diamond of our winter nights, and well to the east, nearly lost in the sun's glare, was Mercury, the most elusive of the planets, whom many die without seeing.

As the diffusion of light by the air grew less and less, the sky was soon studded with stars, and by reference to our watches we saw that we were nearing the upper limits of the atmosphere. Presently we began to hear occasional light taps on the shell of the car—falling meteors of minute dimensions which had not yet penetrated the protecting blanket of air far enough to be burned by the heat of their passage. We closed the cover of the porthole for safety and listened to the slowly increasing patter of these wandering particles of metal and volcanic rock. Occasionally one, louder than the rest, denoted our collision with a stone of appreciable dimensions, and once a loud crack and noticeable jolt accompanied the fall of a fair-sized meteor.

At length Wiley decided that we need go no further from the Earth, and reached for the switch that rotated the moving half of the gravity screen from its position beneath us. Hardly had he made the contact, however, when the car lurched violently to one side and capsized, throwing us into a heap with all the movable objects in the car in one corner.

For a moment I thought we had been struck by a large meteor, but presently I realized what had happened. Imagine that you have a ball balanced on one finger. If you move your finger to one side, the ball promptly tips to the other side and falls off. That was what had happened to us. The lower half of our spherical screen had been moved, and the moment the force of gravity took hold of the edge of the car, it drew that side down sharply, upsetting the car and turning everything in it upside down. We were diving headfirst toward the Earth.

I scarcely had time to be grateful that there were some fifty miles between us and the ground when a new danger presented itself. The interior of the car was becoming uncomfortably warm, due to the friction of the air as we passed through it with increasing speed. The mental picture of us landing on the Earth—reduced to cinders in the midst of a blazing steel meteor—galvanized me into action. I reached for the switch with the idea of turning the gravity screen into position, but the futility of that soon became apparent. The shock of the upset must have jammed it open. Then I remembered the tanks of hydrogen and oxygen. Shutting off the current from the motors that controlled the gravity screen, I reached for the valves, turned the gas into the nozzles beneath us and shot an electric spark across them. There was a sharp report, a roar, and I was again precipitated to the bottom of the car as the recoil of the burning gases checked our fall.

We were saved from destruction-by-falling or death-by-incineration, but there was still a difficulty. Where, and on what, would we land? I could see only one way to answer this question. After we had dropped slowly for several miles, I shut off the gas and opened the porthole for a look. All I could see, however, was a bank of clouds brilliantly illuminated by the sun. I must wait until we were nearer the ground. Accordingly, I again opened the gas valves, braced myself and touched the igniting button.

WE fell several miles more, slowly passing through rarer layers of the atmosphere, until I estimated we were close enough so that I could see where we were. Moving as quickly as possible I cut off the gas and opened the porthole. By pressing my face close to the glass I could see the city several miles to the east, with the silver thread of the river winding close to it. This offered an idea; if I could maneuver the car to a position over the water and drop into it, there would be little danger. I closed the porthole and started the gas, this time from the nozzles to the west as well as below me.

My next observation showed that we were nearly over the river and about a mile high. I allowed the car to descend slowly until it was only a few feet above the water, then shut off the gas entirely. There was a shock as we hit the surface of the river. Then, after all motion had subsided, I opened the porthole once more and the darkness outside told me that we were resting on the bottom.

During our headlong descent I had not had time for more than a glance at Wiley. He had been lying amidst the pile of loose objects—which had tumbled about the car on the way down—quite unconscious. I found a large bruise on the back of his head, but apparently he was only stunned, as his respiration and heart action were normal. I found some water in one of the tanks and bathed his head. Presently he came around and sat up, rather unsteadily.

"Still alive, at any rate," he observed dryly. "What happened? Did we hit a meteor?"

I explained briefly. He nodded and made a hasty inspection. Apparently satisfied, he turned to the switchboard again with a warning to "hang on." By means of the gas jets he again capsized the car so that the gravity screen was beneath us—and with the aid of more gas we burst through the surface of the water and into the sunlight.

We effected a safe landing on the field—this much to the surprise of the few mechanics and assistants waiting for us, who had witnessed our drop into the river. That night found us again in the laboratories of the College, bruised and shaken but still full of impatience to undertake the journey.

Before making any further trips it was apparent that we must change the design of the gravity screen. The simplest solution appeared to be that of making it in the form of four quarter-spherical surface, mounted on common bearings, so that they might he manipulated to expose any portion of the car in any direction. They could now be moved apart separately from the lowest portion of the car so as to expose equal portions on either side of the center of gravity. This design possessed the added advantage of stable equilibrium, since if the car should turn to either side, more of that side would be covered by the gravity screen and tend to rise.

The new screen was completed and put in position on the car. Thereafter on our test trips we met no more mishaps from this or any other source, nor did we discover any injurious effect from drifting for hours free of the Earth's gravitation. At length we were satisfied that our car would make the trip without mishap, and there remained only to load it and wait for the moon to reach its proper position. We had decided that the most advantageous time for a Lunar landing would be during the cycle of the full moon. Our tests were completed in late August; and since we would require two weeks to reach the moon's surface, we must start our journey at the next new phase. During the two weeks that remained we busied ourselves in stocking the cupboards with every imaginable kind of canned and condensed food, reading matter, and similar supplies.

Finally all was in readiness. Toward sunset of a clear autumn afternoon, Wiley and I bade farewell to those few of the College faculty who were in town. We then proceeded to the field where the space-traveling sphere awaited us. Wiley appeared as calm as though he were about to take a Sunday afternoon drive, but I must confess that I felt considerable nervousness. We had regulated our chronometer to a fraction of a second, and as the orange disc of the setting sun touched the horizon we entered the car and bolted the airlock fast. Wiley took his position by the switchboard, while I kept watch on the chronometer. At seventeen minutes, thirty-two seconds after sunset he closed the switch that sent us on our way, with that now familiar sensation of dropping.

We kept the porthole open until we had left the atmosphere in order to verify our direction; then, when the slowly-passing stars had shown that we were headed for the position the moon would take two weeks hence, we closed the steel cap over the glass and resigned ourselves to hours of reading and sleeping, punctuated by occasional meals and observations of the stars. We agreed that one of us should always remain awake, though for what purpose it would be hard to say, since there was no navigating to be done.

We had provided ourselves with shoes having magnetized steel soles in order that we might have some footing, for being insulated from the attraction of all the heavenly bodies, there was not even enough gravity to hold water in a glass. Because of this, an amusing spectacle presented itself when either of us went to sleep. Following our terrestrial habits, we lay down to rest on whatever surface of the car appealed to us, but the slightest movement was sufficient to send our heads away from the wall of the car while our feet, anchored by the magnetic shoes, held fast. One was apt to find himself in fantastic positions when he awoke. The sight of the waking person was even more grotesque, especially if he happened to be on the opposite side of the car, for then the sleeper apparently hung head down in peaceful repose. We had brought along a camera and a supply of films, and I used several of these making time exposures of Wiley in various positions, none of which, unfortunately, turned out well.

Nearing the Moon

TEN days dragged by—marked only by the hands of the clock—before the first event of real interest occurred. We now left the porthole open, continuously, since the danger from small meteors was low, due to their lesser velocity at this distance from the Earth, and while looking through it at the stars as Wiley slept, I noticed a thin crescent of light on the outer edge of the steel frame of the glass—the rays of the moon! By a simple triangulation I computed its position with respect to our own, and knowing our respective velocities, verified my expectation that we would cross its orbit as it reached the full moon phase.

From then on, Wiley and I watched the progress of the reflected rays down the frame of the glass until, by pressing our faces close to the opening, we could see the edge of the sunlit Lunar surface. It resembled the moonrise on a dusty evening, its color being a dirty orange, and the disc was much larger than as seen from Earth. It was already nearly full, but since we saw it from a different angle than terrestrial observers, only a little over half the surface visible to us was lighted by the sun. The mountain ranges near the terminator (the dividing line between sunlight and darkness) were plainly visible, as they are seen from Earth through small field glasses. By employing the powerful binoculars we had brought, we reduced its apparent distance to about thirteen hundred miles.

Because of the small size of the glass porthole we were forced to take turns observing the moon through it, and while Wiley was using the binoculars I checked our position. We were about forty thousand miles from the moon and had completed five-sixths of our journey. At this point the attraction of the moon would overcome that of the Earth, and we would fall toward it unless we turned the gravity screen to that side of the car. This would of course cut off our view of the moon, except for an occasional necessary glimpse while landing, when the screen would have to be opened for a moment.

I was about to call Wiley's attention to this when he uttered an exclamation.

"Marland, come have a look," he called. I hurried to the glass and he moved aside, handing me the binoculars. I examined the visible portion of the moon's surface but could see nothing out of the ordinary, I was about to say as much, when he directed: "Look on the dark side, near the south pole."

I turned my glasses toward the lower portion of the globe. There, perhaps a sixth of the distance from the equator to the pole and almost on the terminator was a tiny speck of light, barely distinguishable even to my excellent eyes, and all but lost in the glare of the sunlight on nearby mountain peaks. At first I though it might be an illusion in the glass, but I was struck by the peculiar color of the light—blue, or blue-green, with perhaps a slight yellow tinge; but entirely out of keeping with the surroundings. Even as I looked more closely, it faded into the line of sunlight and was invisible.

"Did you see it?" asked Wiley.

"I did," I replied, "but it's gone."

"Gone out!" he exclaimed.

"No," I returned, "it crossed the terminator and was lost in the sunlight."

"Impossible!" exclaimed Wiley. "How could it have crossed the terminator? It was miles away when I saw it. Besides, how could a volcano move?"

"Volcano!" I exclaimed. "Do you really think it was a volcano?"

"What else could it be?" he demanded.

"Then why hasn't it been previously seen from Earth?" I asked.

"Plenty of reasons," he returned. "In the first place it was so faint as to be almost invisible, although we have no atmosphere between it and ourselves. The distortion produced by the Earth's atmosphere would make it invisible. If not, it might easily be hidden by a range of mountains. You forget that we see the moon from a different angle now. And finally, it may not have existed before now…"

He seized the glasses and went to the porthole for another look, but after several minutes of close scrutiny he gave up, unable to locate the light again.

I suddenly recalled that it was high time that the gravity screen was closed, and mentioned it to Wiley. He gave up his position reluctantly, and I closed the steel cap over the porthole and set in motion the motors to shift the screen. Wiley returned the binoculars to their case on the wall and remarked, musing:

"What do you suppose could cause a volcano to stop erupting like that?"

"It's probably still going, but you can't see it because of the sunlight," I suggested.

"No," he objected, "it was too far from the terminator when I saw it. The sunrise doesn't move that fast."

"It might have been on a gentle slope," I said. "The sunlight would travel down the slope pretty rapidly."

FOR answer Wiley went to one of the shelves in which were stored, among other things, a number of maps of the moon's surface, together with a number of photographs. From these he extracted a view of the section we had just been discussing that, though seen from a different angle, was still fairly recognizable. We examined the map closely for some such formation as I had suggested, but failed to find any which might meet the conditions. Then we tried to recall the location of the point as we had seen it.

Wiley indicated by a dot the place where he had last seen it, and I indicated where it had crossed the terminator. We looked at each other in considerable amazement, for not only did our estimates as to the distance from the edge of the shadow differ, but my point was considerably further north than his! Nor could we reconcile our views. By reference to surrounding landmarks it was possible to set limits to our possible errors in observation, and we enclosed each of our points in a circle that made the maximum possible allowance for such errors. Yet our two circles were a quarter of an inch apart at their nearest point! Wiley insisted that the light had been well clear of the terminator, while I was equally certain that it had crossed the terminator.

Allowing for the motion of the sunlight itself while we had changed places—which was, in fact, almost negligible, since the terminator travels on the moon at about nine miles per hour—we had still a difference of some fifty miles in our points. There was only one inference: the light had moved!

A further examination of the scant data we had on the subject showed even more startling results. At the very least, the source of the light had moved fifty miles in five minutes or less from the time Wiley had first called my attention to it until the time I had located it just as it crossed the border of the shadow. In other words, it must have been traveling at a rate of six hundred miles an hour!

In the face of such figures we were both inclined to question our minds as to the certainty of the positron of the light. But the facts remained unquestionable. Wiley had seen it well in the shadow and I had seen it pass into the light. It had moved, and it seemed likely that its motion had been very rapid.

The subject of this mysterious traveling point of light occupied our minds for the greater part of the remaining journey. We pored over maps and photographs of the moon's surface, speculated on the nature of such a high-speed body, and thought of every possibility—so it seemed to us—even going so far as to raise the question of intelligent inhabitants, living perhaps on the interior of the satellite, or even a form of life that was not dependent on air for existence.

The thought intrigued us, yet I must confess that my interest was not unmixed with apprehension. A people sufficiently intelligent to maintain their existence in spite of the evident lack of air or water on the surface of the moon must necessarily be far in advance of the human race in mental development. We should probably be looked on much as are the rats that invade our homes in their own selfish interest, just as we were at present bent on invading the moon. The prospect had, at least, its questionable angles.

Wiley, too, was evidently thinking deeply on the matter. He had put away the maps and photographs and was sitting (insofar as it is possible to sit without the aid of gravitation) on the opposite side of the car, his hands clasped around his knees, his toes stuck under a projecting valve to anchor himself, gazing into nothingness. Presently he spoke, as if addressing himself to his thoughts rather than to me.

"Let's see what we've got," he said. "First, I saw a light. Then you saw the same light cross the terminator. We have only estimates of the distance it moved, but we agree that it was too far for the sunlight to travel so as to cover a stationary point. The best estimate gives it a velocity of six hundred miles an hour. Suppose we're wrong by half that…it still moves faster than anything on Earth except bullets and some airplanes. The question is, what was it? A machine driven by some living being? What sort of being could live on the moon? There is no air—no water. Even supposing there was a creature with super-intelligence and that had conquered moon's uninhabitable surface, how did it develop? The moon must have lost its atmosphere and water long before the surface solidified. It could never have been a habitable globe like Earth. Then either the creature, supposing there is one, has a body radically different from our own; or else he is an immigrant from some other planet. But if the former, why has he never come, to the Earth? And if the latter, why go to the moon at all?"

Wiley sat huddled, motionless, his eyes half closed, and presently he appeared to have fallen asleep. I got out paper and pencil and was about to re-compute our position, as I was constantly doing in order to discover any deviation from our intended course, when he uttered an exclamation.

"Of course!" he cried. "Nothing simpler! Marland, what a pair of idiots we are! Super-beings—life without air—tommyrot!"

I wondered what was the cause of this outburst, but was quickly enlightened.

"We have been fortunate enough to find a new member of the solar system," he said smiling. "What we saw, Marland, was probably a sub-satellite—the moon's moon. A little globe revolving around it at a distance of a few thousand miles— probably not far from where we are; hence the apparent rapid motion. It passed between us and the dark part of the moon, then across to the bright side and was outshone by the reflected light of the moon. Too dim to have been detected from the Earth because of the atmospheric refraction."

This simple and logical explanation of the phenomenon presented such an easy solution to the problem that we were both surprised we had not thought of it before. Wiley and I were both anxious to take a further observation in order to determine the size and behavior of this lunar satellite, but this was out of the question at present. Indeed, it was quite a problem to get enough data to check our position, as we had to do frequently without unduly exposing ourselves to the attraction of the moon.

CHAPTER FOUR
Journey's End!

AS THE hours passed, we drew closer and closer to the end of our journey. We remained awake constantly now, and nearly all of our time was spent in calculating the exact moment and spot of our arrival, from the latest observation. We found that we should arrive somewhat to the south of the equator, on the "sunrise" side—that is, the portion on which the sun had been shining for less than half of the two-weeks-long day. This section of the moon's surface was more thickly covered with mountains than some, but there were a reasonable number of level spaces, and it was in this quarter that some of the most interesting features of the globe were to be found, such as the giant craters Tycho and Copernicus with their radiating streaks.

At length there remained only a thousand miles or so between the moon and us. At our present rate we should reach it in somewhat more than an hour. We spent the remaining time in arranging the loose articles in the car—such as dishes, bottles, reading matter, and similar debris—so that they would not pile up on the downward side of the car when we landed and opened the gravity screen.

The amount of junk that we had amassed was tremendous; we had not bothered more than once or twice to make use of the airlock to throw out our trash, and there were empty meat cans, bottles and such stuff that were of no use to us whatsoever. Wiley suggested that we pile them into the airlock so that they would be out of the way and could be thrown out as soon as we landed. We began this at once, but the action immediately called our attention to another fact; the airlock was turned toward the moon, and was covered by the gravity screen, since we had been looking through its glass porthole. It would be down when we landed and would make it impossible to leave the car. This gave us a moment's worry, until we recalled our former startling success in turning the car upside down during our first trial trip. Accordingly we took our final observation of position when we were but a few miles from the surface, over one of the great plains, termed "seas" by the early observers because of their darker color.

This one was known as "Mare Nubium" (the sea of clouds), and we were approaching the center of it. We quickly calculated our velocity from two observations a few minutes apart, then closed the porthole for the last time until landing and turned the gravity screen until the car rotated through 180 degrees under the influence of gravity; then closed it entirely, shutting ourselves off once more from all attraction. Then we opened the valve controlling the flow of gas into the jets that were pointed toward the moon and touched the electric spark.

Having become accustomed during our two weeks' journey to move about the car as we pleased with no regard to the relative directions of "up and down," we had neglected to hold on while doing this, and we found ourselves in rather laughable circumstances as a consequence. However, the acceleration of the gas was not sufficient to throw us very violently to the bottom of the car, and the situation was more humorous than unpleasant. We had just picked ourselves up and endeavored to become accustomed to the strange sensation of direction once more, when there was a moderate jar announcing our landing. Wiley jumped to shut off the gas while I opened the gravity-screen. The jar was repeated, the car having "bounced" a little from the surface, but it promptly settled down on an even keel—and we were on the moon!

So far our journey had been carefully planned, but now that we had reached our objective we were rather at a loss as to our next step. "Exploration" had been vaguely mentioned, but we had outlined no route. However, our bodies had been cramped in the small interior of the car long enough to desire action, so with one accord we unpacked our "diving suits" (the term is poorly applied, but we never gave them any other name) and put them on. They were unwieldy things, but with the slight gravity of the moon we managed them quite well.

I was ready first, and released the fastenings of the inner door of the airlock. As I lowered this, I was showered by the refuse that had been hastily piled into the opening and forgotten in the excitement of our landing. I took an armload with me—leaving Wiley to bring as much as possible with him—and climbed into the airlock.

The doors to this could he fastened from inside or out, so as to remove the necessity of an operator inside the car. Once inside the lock with the airtight doors bolted fast, a pump exhausted as much of the air as possible into the interior of the car, in order to conserve our not over-abundant supply of the vital gases. I had crowded into the small space, fastened the door, and soon afterward the swelling of my suit to its interior pressure told of the pump at work. I waited with as much patience as I could muster until the air was thinned out to a near vacuum, and released the catches to the outer door.

A blaze of sunlight such as I had never seen before met my eyes, I wore dark glasses, but even so the brilliant light reflected from the rocky plain about me was almost intolerable. I stepped out onto the top of the spherical machine, re-closed the door, and after kicking the rubbish over the edge began to survey the surrounding territory while waiting for Wiley.

WE were situated approximately in the center of a vast plain extending in all directions to the horizon, broken here and there by the lower elevations of craters. The smaller, closer ones presented an appearance suggesting the crater formation familiar to those who have seen the moon through a telescope, while those in the distance resembled lines of jagged cliffs, being too remote and too high to be seen in their true form. The floor of the plain resembled a mud flat from which the water has receded, leaving its surface dried and cracked by the sun. Indeed, we soon found out that it was much like that, the surface rock being split and checkered by ages of boiling heat followed by cold unknown to the Earth.

The sky was even more remarkable—jet-black, with thousands of stars blazing with a splendor beyond description. The sun was dazzling, even more so than on Earth. By peeping over my arm I could see the corona and a red spot that might be a huge prominence. The Earth was faintly discernible as a pale circle of light close to the sun, visible only by the light refracted through its atmosphere.

My observations were interrupted when Wiley's head appeared through the airlock, and after blinking from the sunlight he stepped out beside me. We had no method of communication other than gestures, supplemented by what lip-reading we could do through the glass of our helmets, but he presently made me understand that he wished to descend and explore the plain about us. We made our way cautiously along the curving surface of the sphere to the ladder that extended up the outside. I started to climb awkwardly down, but Wiley made a flying leap from the twenty-foot height on which we stood. I turned in startled amazement, having forgotten the slight attraction of the moon, and watched him float as if on a parachute, landing with perfect ease on the ground.

I followed his example, but with less grace, landing on my hands and knees, but with no discomfort. We started off at a brisk walk, but, our first step lifted us clear of the ground and we coasted several feet before touching. Our muscles, accustomed to Earth-travel, instinctively exerted enough pressure to bear our normal weight, but meeting with little resistance lifted us clear off the ground. We experimented a bit and found that by leaning slightly forward we could travel at a fast trot with practically no effort.

We set off in this manner toward the nearest of the little craters. We must have resembled a slow motion picture of a pair of sprinters, so leisurely were our movements. Our feet raised clouds of the fine dust that covered everything, but like everything else on the moon, this dust behaved in a strange manner. It rose to a greater height than on Earth; then, instead of remaining suspended, large and small particles alike fell to the ground, leaving not the slightest haze behind us.

Until now I had been so absorbed in the new sensations that surrounded me that I had not noticed a growing sense of discomfort, but suddenly I realized that it was becoming intolerably hot inside my protecting suit. The temperature increased as I went a few steps further, and I realized that if I did not find shelter from the sunlight soon I would suffocate. I tapped Wiley's arm and started for the shadow of the nearest rock. It was some distance away, and I realized that I was rapidly losing consciousness when I stumbled headfirst from the glare into the blackness of night and fell to the ground.

My exhaustion perhaps saved my life. I had barely gotten into the inky-black shadow of the rock and lay with my face only a few inches from its edge. As I recovered my faculties I saw that the glass of my helmet had become coated with frost condensed from my breath. The temperature around me was many degrees below zero; the effect of extreme changes of heat on glass is well known. No doubt the heat reflected from the sunlit ground a few inches away had saved my glass from cracking and letting out the air.

A few moments' cooling sufficed to set my teeth chattering, and Wiley and I set off once more, being careful to stop in a shadow once in a while. We reached the little crater toward which we had been walking and skipped up its side as easily as two mountain goats. It was perhaps one hundred feet high; the sides sloping at an angle of about sixty degrees. The rim was jagged and split by many fissures, while pieces of rock had scaled off and slid into the interior. From where we stood we had a good view of the entire crater. It was about five hundred feet in diameter, and the floor was studded with tiny replicas of the crater itself, a few feet in diameter, while in the center was a small cone, rising to a height of some thirty feet.

A Puzzling Phenomenon

As we stood looking at the crater, an odd thought ran through my mind. "Pancakes," I said to myself. Pancakes were one of my weaknesses, and I had had ample opportunity to make them during our trip. The interior of the crater resembled a vast pancake on the griddle. Bubbles of escaping gas had burst, leaving holes as the surface stiffened and solidified. Perhaps the crater itself was such a bubble left by a larger up-rush of gas.

We descended into the crater and examined the formations more closely. Everything seemed to bear out my idea. As the surface of the moon had cooled, gas had formed in spots under the hardening crust, and presently burst through, piling up the semi-solid lava in a circle around the eruption. Later, as the cooling proceeded, the crust of the interior of the crater, being thinner, was more easily broken; hence the many small pits. All this activity had long since ceased and the dust of ages of exposure to heat and cold covered everything.

At length we started back to the car, for despite the ease of travel we found the heat quite enervating and the need of rest and a meal was pressing. We had been gone several hours, and we could not be sure just how long the air in our suits would last. We hurried along, going from rock to rock, resting a few minutes in the shadow of each and taking a slightly different route on our way back.

We had covered perhaps half the distance to our machine when I felt Wiley touch my arm. Looking in the direction he indicated, I saw that not far to our right there were evidences of the all-pervading dust having been disturbed. We walked in that direction and came to a patch of bare rock some fifty yards across. The dust had been swept clean, piling up around the edges of the bare spot as if a circular windstorm had blown it away. But that obviously was not the cause of this phenomenon, as we well know. What could have caused it? As I turned the matter over in my mind, the thought of meteorites occurred to me, so I started for the center of the space to look for traces of meteoric stone. I examined the ground closely, but found nothing whatsoever except a few scars on the rock itself, as if it had been melted by some tremendous heat. They seemed fresh, and might possibly have been caused by the fall of a meteor.

We continued our journey with no further events, and presently were once more within the car with a meal cooking on the electric stove. Neither of us referred to the events of our trip until we had finished eating and settled down to enjoy a smoke. Then Wiley spoke...

"What do you make of that bare spot?"

"Probably the mark of a meteor," I replied. "It looks quite recent."

"Recent, yes," He paused. "But why haven't we noticed any more meteors?"

I thought for a moment before answering: "Perhaps the Earth gets most of them—its superior gravity, you know, and so close. They would have to be headed just right to get here," He nodded.

"But why didn't we find the meteor itself?" after a moment.

"It probably hit hard enough to be heated to gas," I answered.

"It would take considerable speed," he observed. "By the way, what velocity would a meteor have, landing here?"

"If you assume certainly factors about distance, it would be going a mile and a quarter a second," I said.

"The Big Berthas did better than that during the war," he remarked. "Ever hear of a shell turning to gas when it hit?"

"No. But the meteor might have exploded like a shell."

"Not likely," he said, "but it's possible, I grant you. Perhaps our friends at the City College are dropping us a note," With which remark he ended the discussion; but long after I lay down for a sleep he sat up, engrossed in his thoughts.

I was awakened by the smell of food, and found I had a prodigious appetite.

"About time to get going, old timer," said Wiley. "You've slept the clock around and then some."

We quickly dispatched the meal, donned our "diving" outfits, and were soon out on the surface of the moon. Despite the passing of more than twelve hours since we had last seen it, the sun had moved but little, and everything was much the same. This time we set out in a different direction toward another of the small craters. This one was more distant and somewhat larger than the first, but we made better time in reaching it and climbing its steep sides, having become more accustomed to the strange mode of travel. We spent a little time exploring its interior, which was much the same as that of the other crater and presently made for the little cone which so often is found in these formations in the center of the circular hollow. Its sides were steep, and on the summit we found a vent extending down inside to an unknown depth. The sunlight penetrated a few yards, in which the walls narrowed slightly, suggesting a funnel; beyond this we could see nothing.

Wiley motioned me to follow him and started to pick his way cautiously down the steep side of the funnel. I followed to the edge of the sunlight, and we stood for a moment trying to fathom the inky depths. Presently our eyes became more accustomed to the darkness and we could see the faint gleams reflected from footholds just below us. We took a few steps downward and were surrounded, by darkness.

Suddenly I was startled to see the side of the pit opposite me illuminated. I looked for the source of the light, and discovered that Wiley had succeeded in withdrawing his arm from its covering into his suit, and had taken a flashlight from his pocket and directed it through the glass of his helmet. He turned it into my face, then away, and I could see that he was laughing at my surprised look. Then he turned the light below him and led the way further into the depths.

We descended for perhaps another hundred feet, the walls of the funnel narrowing until we could brace our feet against one side and our backs on the other. We paused, and Wiley turned the light downward. The shaft continued toward the center of the moon, no one could say how far, without becoming much narrower. I would have liked to continue, but it was inadvisable, as we had quite a climb back to the surface and must consider our air supply.

I looked up. The funnel framed a circular patch of sky above us, in which the brighter stars blazed with brilliant splendor, on a jet-black background powdered with other stars too small to be distinguished one from another.

It was now some twenty-four hours since we had landed, and for the first time I saw the surface of our mother Earth. Not very much, to be sure, only a thin sliver of light was visible, like a huge day-old moon. The crescent shone with a brilliance far surpassing everything in the heavens except the sun. I wondered what it would be like when it was full, when the sun would have set on our side of the moon.

One moment I was looking at the silver thread of the Earth, the next I was blinded by a glare of light sweeping across my field of vision. The heavens were obscured by a broad fan-tail of flame, blue, or blue-green, with a tinge of yellow in it, I closed my eyes for a moment to let the dancing spots on my overtaxed retinas fade and looked again, but it was gone. Whatever it was had seemed to be moving southward. I thought I could detect a glow on the northern side of the funnel above me, but my eyes were still too blinded to be certain.

I felt Wiley pushing me upward urgently, and with as much speed as possible I scrambled up the side of the pit. It required perhaps five minutes to reach the top. We faced south with one accord, and there, over the rim of the crater, far in the distance, could be seen a faint blue-yellow glow. It did not strike me as strange at the moment, but Wiley pointed out its meaning later.

We had retraced our steps to the car and were discussing the appearance of the light.

"Did you notice the afterglow?" he asked, and as I nodded he said, "Do you realize what that means? Gas, Marland. There must have been gas. You know that light cannot be diffused in a vacuum. The air does it on Earth, but we have no air here. There must have been a body of gas attached to that light, or the light gave off gas, which glowed. Now what could be liberating glowing gas so near the moon?"

We sat silent for many minutes. Finally Wiley answered his own question, in part, "It may have been a small comet," he suggested, and made haste to bury himself in a book. Obviously he did not wish me to point out that the comet—if indeed it was a comet—had passed between the Earth and the moon at a velocity heretofore unheard of.

I must have fallen asleep, for presently I had a sensation of motion, and awoke to find Wiley manipulating the controls. He answered my questioning look with a single phrase: "Heading south," Further explanation was unnecessary. I knew he had closed the gravity screen and given the car a start to the southward; we were drifting under our momentum in the direction of the light that we had seen, once before landing and later over the nearby crater, cruising about the southern section of the moon's surface.

CHAPTER FIVE
An Awesome Sight!

WILEY had inverted the car so as to take an occasional look at the moon through the porthole. I left running it up to him and caught up on my notes on the two trips we had made. We traveled for eighteen hours in this manner. There was no way of telling our exact speed, but Wiley estimated it in the neighborhood of a hundred miles an hour. This increased from time to time slightly, due to our changing course to meet the curvature of the moon. If we had continued on our original course we would have left the surface on a tangent and continued in a straight line, but our views below served the double purpose of giving us our bearings and allowing us to fall toward the surface enough to maintain an altitude of three to five miles. The velocity of our fall was in part added to our speed of travel.

Thus we arrived over the moon's south pole, which could be located from the appearance of the terminator beneath us, beyond which the sunlight did not reach. Here Wiley brought the car to a stop and descended gently to the interior of a fair-sized crater. It was, his purpose, he said, to remain there for half a month, when the other side of the moon would be illuminated. Then we would continue our search for the mysterious light.

The spot had been ideally chosen, for here the sun never completely set, never showed more than part of its disc above the horizon. The extremes of heat and cold were therefore less evident. Our car rested on a little knoll where the rays of the sun seldom struck it directly but were always reflected from a nearby rock. The Earth, part of which showed above the mountaintops, was nearing its "first quarter", and added to the illumination. The stars of the southern sky showed brilliantly overhead. Neither of us was much inclined to exploration, preferring to spend our time reading or lolling about the car, smoking and meditating. We settled ourselves comfortably for a two weeks' stay.

Our living quarters were given a much needed overhauling, and put in perfect order. We checked our supplies of food, gas and air, tested the storage batteries, and satisfied ourselves that everything was shipshape. Then we caught up on our sleeping and eating. Thus we passed the hours serenely, awaiting the sunrise on the hidden half of the moon.

Five terrestrial days had passed since our first arrival. Wiley was immersed in a book and I was peeling potatoes, preparatory to getting a meal, when the walls were flooded with a bluish-yellow glare from the porthole, I jumped erect, but Wiley was at the glass first.

"It's coming down," he shouted, making a rush for his diving suit. I climbed into mine as he disappeared into the airlock and waited impatiently for the pump to stop, signifying that he was out. I followed as quickly as I could, but by the time I emerged he was already a quarter of a mile away, going at a fast trot toward a bright glow beyond the mountains. When we had gone a mile or more it faded out gradually, but we had located it well enough to be sure of finding its source. We reached the wall of the crater and climbed quickly up, Wiley several yards in the lead. He reached the summit and passed out of my sight, while I paused from exhaustion.

When at length I resumed my climb and reached the summit, I was first too startled, then too horror-stricken to move. For at the foot of the slope, two hundred yards from me, sat an awesome and marvelous object. It was in the shape of a cone with a fifty-foot base and a somewhat greater height, with circular windows around the sides and particularly at the top; while from the base, which was pierced at regular intervals by semi-circular vents resembling culverts, there issued a cloud of luminous gas, bluish-yellow in color.

This much I saw in a swift glance. Then I discovered that Wiley was running down the slope toward it. Suddenly from the apex of the cone there issued a jagged flash that struck Wiley as he ran, tumbling him headlong onto the rocks. I shouted in an agony of horror and apprehension, and in a futile rage seized a fragment of rock and hurled it at the unknown thing. This evidently drew attention to me, for it emitted another flash which seemed to burst into myriads of stars; there was a crash, and blackness.

TO MY mind the oddest feature of complete insensibility is one's total ignorance of the passage of time. My sensations on awakening followed immediately upon the flash that had stunned me, yet when I was able to talk I discovered that over fifty hours had elapsed and my life had once been despaired of.

I was alone with Wiley, who was fully dressed but minus his diving suit. I was lying in an amazingly comfortable bed, in a small but attractive room such as one may find in many American hotels.

The walls were painted in a solid color that was restful to the eyes. There were no pictures, and the room was devoid of useless decorations, but contained many conveniences. The furniture was of metal, attractively upholstered and colored. A shaded electric lamp shed a remarkably good counterfeit of sunlight, and though there were no windows the whole effect was inviting and cheerful.

Wiley spoke to me: "Glad to see you're awake again, old man. You had a rather tough time. The doctor had a pulmotor on you for an hour, and would have given up if I hadn't kept after him."

"Doctor?" I echoed, dazed. "Pulmotor? Where are we?"

"This is the headquarters of those fellows in the flying-machine," he replied. "They knocked us out with a high-tension spark, I came around in a few minutes, but you had broken the glass on your helmet, and they had a nice time getting air back into your system and teaching you to breathe again. They're prepared for such things, but you were a pretty bad case."

"Who are 'they'?" I asked.

"I don't know much about them," he answered. "I talked to the doctor some, but he keeps his mouth shut. It seems there are a lot of them here, and they've been here for years. A man who calls himself 'Forscher,' meaning 'searcher,' is the guiding spirit. I'm to have a talk with him soon. The two of them are human of course, from Earth. They came here in machines like the one you saw— quite an ingenious bit of machinery, by the way.

"I had a chance to look it over after they'd finished working on you. It gives off gases at a tremendous velocity, and the recoil drives it. Same principle as the gas jets on our car, but much more powerful. Apparently they haven't any gravity screens, but the force of the discharge from their machine is sufficient alone to lift it free of the ground, and they get it up to some pretty big velocities. We're two thousand miles from the pole, yet they got here in three hours."

"What are they doing here?" I asked.

"I couldn't say," replied Wiley. "The crew that picked us up was sent out to do just that. They found our machine on one of their trips and reported it. We saw the mark of their landing— where your 'meteor' had blown away the dust. They got orders to bring us back, and here we are. That's all they've told me, and apparently it's all we're to know until I talk to Dr. Forscher."

As he finished speaking, the door opened and a man in a white coat entered. He was perhaps forty, tall, with close-cropped blond hair, and wore rimless spectacles. From the bag he carried, I judged he was the doctor Wiley had referred to. He nodded pleasantly to Wiley, and turned to me.

"I am pleased to see that you are again conscious," he said. His slight accent confirmed my impression that he was of German birth. He produced a stethoscope and set about an examination of my heart and lungs, which was as rapid as it was thorough.

"There will be no danger," he announced presently. "Some food will taste good—is it not so? Then a long sleep, and you will be as good as before."

His prescription suited me perfectly. He took his departure, and in the course of a few minutes a dapper Frenchman appeared carrying a tray of food.

"Pour le malade," he said, indicating me; then to Wiley, "Monsieur will follow me to the dining hall?"

"I'll see you after you've had some sleep," said Wiley, as he departed.

I turned to the dinner that had been brought to me. There were dishes I had not seen for weeks—fresh green vegetables, fresh meat, butter, milk! Evidently there were farms and dairies on the moon. I attacked the meal with considerable appetite and made a respectable impression on it; then, more comfortable and very tired, I fell asleep.

When I awoke Wiley had returned. His face shone with a smile of satisfaction, and I was filled with curiosity.

"Have you seen Dr. Forscher?" I asked. He nodded.

"I have," he replied, "and a good deal besides. I had dinner with some of the higher-ups and was shown around a bit. Then I talked to the Doctor and found out some more. We're scheduled to be guests of honor here for awhile, to get acquainted with the place. I don't know what will happen then, but you may be sure that we're quite welcome, much more so than when we first arrived. I didn't mention it to you, but we were considered as interlopers and weren't very popular at first.

"You see, this Dr. Forscher is a rather reclusive sort, and while he supposed that someday someone would succeed in reaching the moon, he hoped it wouldn't be until after he had finished his business here and passed on. But he was much relieved to find out that we weren't the advance guard of a sizable expedition, and that no one knows the secret of the machine except ourselves." Wiley paused to light a cigarette, then continued: "They picked up the old space traveler and brought it here to find out what makes it work. But they can't, unless I help them, and the Doctor knows it by now. So they're keeping it for us—to make sure we don't run away before he's ready to let us."

"What sort of a man is he?" I asked. "And why is he here?"

"As to the latter, I don't know," replied Wiley. "Nobody seems willing to tell me, and I can't guess. But as for the doctor, he's quite an odd sort. Not very attractive physically—about five-foot-two, as a guess, with a head all out of proportion. He just sits like a statue while he talks to you, but I really believe he can look right into your mind. He has the most marvelous intellect I've ever seen."

This, from Wiley, was a real tribute, for the world can count on one hand the men with minds equal to his.

"He's what you might call a super-scientist," he continued. "He knows more physics than the whole department at the City College; the world's best chemists are mere tyros compared to him. As a physician or surgeon he could have made a fortune on Earth. The science of psychology is mere A-B-C to him; and he can solve problems in mathematics without putting a mark on paper that would take me an hour or more. That is by no means a comprehensive list of his achievements. He had specialized in none of the sciences, but he knows them all, and better than any man on Earth. Everything in this colony is the product of his mind; he conceived it, engineered it, built it, and now he rules it.

Many Wonders

"I'VE seen enough of the place to appreciate what a man he is. For instance, there's the air. Perhaps you've noticed its freshness. It should be fresh—it was made a few hours ago! He makes the oxygen and nitrogen right out of the rocks around us. There's plenty of oxygen to be found in the quartz but its hard to get out, and there's little, if any, nitrogen to be found in any form. Nevertheless, he makes both of them, by a kind of atomic chemistry. He gave me a general idea of the process. He uses high temperatures and strong electric and magnetic fields to break up the atoms of some elements and then recombines them into others. Silicon seems to suit the purpose well, and there's plenty of it, in combination with oxygen, all around us in the form of sand and quartz.

"He uses the same principle, indirectly, in driving those flying machines, which they call tractors. Do you remember our talk, the night you wrecked your car, when I mentioned that if anyone could find a way to build up a radioactive atom more complex than uranium he would have a storage battery for unlimited power? It's a substance like that, that drives the tractors. It takes millions of horsepower to make a pound of it, but the power all comes out again as it's wanted.

"Did you enjoy your dinner? Perhaps you're interested in knowing where it came from. There are acres and acres of artificial soil where plants and animals live under quartz-glass roofs, receiving light from the sun and from arc lamps. The cattle, hogs and chickens he raises would be the despair of our best farmers, and the 'tall corn from Iowa' can't be compared to the crops he harvests the year around. Marland, that man has everything there is to be found on Earth, and he's gone nature one better in every way.

"I found out, too, where the power comes from. The most obvious source, the sun—and very simply. From sunrise to sunset there are hundreds of boilers heated by huge burning glasses, which generate electric energy. Part of it is stored in batteries for the dark period.

"This colony lives underground, in a system of excavations and tunnels that extend for several miles around. There are hundreds of men, but no women or children. I don't know how he intends to replenish his labor supply when age and accident take a hand. They've been here eleven years, building and digging. There are corps of scientists who are the Doctor's assistants and share his confidence to a considerable extent. The rest are mechanics, artisans, and laborers. One of them told me where they all came from. There are French, Germans, Belgians, English, Austrians—almost every white nationality on Earth. They have enough to do, but never too much, and enough variety to make it interesting. They've provided with facilities for recreation, comfortable quarters, and plenty of food. They seem contented with their lot, and indeed they may well enough be.

"Some of this the Doctor told me, and some I found out from other men. But the most interesting thing of all—the reason for this tremendous establishment so far from the Earth—no one has mentioned. He wants us to become acquainted, and then he's going to have a talk with both of us. Meanwhile there's nothing much to do but make ourselves at home."

He sat in silence for a time, while my head whirled from the multitude of wonders he had described. But I was anxious to be up again, and see for myself this strange, subterranean world of humans a quarter of a million miles from their birthplace, I set about exploring our apartment and found a completely equipped bathroom with facilities for shaving and a shower-bath. I immediately availed myself of these, and once more dressed and moving about, I found that my appetite had returned. In answer to my question, Wiley informed me that there would be a meal in the dining hall in half an hour or so. Meanwhile, he suggested that we take a stroll around the hallways, which suited me perfectly.

I found that the corridors formed a large H, with the laboratories and farms opening from the parallel passages and the living quarters, dining hall, etc., along the connecting corridor. The doors in most instances bore only numbers, though a few had legends in many languages over them. One of these was the dining room, to which we presently returned.

We were led to a table at which there were several men of various nationalities who, Wiley told me, were Dr. Forscher's scientific assistants. The Doctor himself preferred to eat alone, seldom joining the others in the dining hall. Wiley introduced me to each of the men at the table. They were for the most part unknown to me, though in a few I recognized men whose names had once been familiar on Earth.

They had best remain anonymous, for reasons that will presently be understood. There was also the Chief Engineer, whom I shall call Dr. Langley, who stood highly in the estimation of Dr. Forscher, and who had been partly responsible for the feats of construction at which we marveled. During the meal he told of the many difficulties that had been overcome, and of some since their arrival. It seems that he had come in company with Dr. Forscher and some of the scientific staff, together with a part of their present labor force, some eleven or twelve years before. They had established a small headquarters, digging a cave into the rock, fitting it with an airlock, setting a small power plant in operation, and converting the cave into a workshop.

With this as a starting point they had designed and constructed the vast subterranean labyrinth that formed the present dwelling of the colony, increasing the power plant as necessary. At present there were accommodations for nearly twice as many inhabitants as it now held, and no more construction was under way, their activities being directed into other channels. Here he stopped, as if fearful of having said too much, and we could learn nothing more.

THAT there was some purpose to this organization as yet unfulfilled, we had no doubt, but every time the subject came up we ran into a blind wall. Wiley and I had made conjectures as we explored the corridors, but we could arrive at no reasonable supposition. Nearly all the sciences were represented by the list of lab directors, yet none seemed to predominate. These scientists had all come of their own volition in spite of greater opportunity for fame on Earth, where there were far greater facilities. Why had they chosen an existence on this barren satellite, so inaccessible, so cut off from communication, so fraught with danger? For solitude? It hardly seemed likely. In fact, one might find comparatively greater privacy on Earth than here, pent up with a few hundred fellow-beings whose daily association was unavoidable. There must be some more powerful motive, which was so far wrapped in secrecy and guarded by the trusted few who surrounded Wiley and myself at the dinner table.

The repast was finished, and at Dr. Langley's suggestion we adjourned with him to his own apartment. We settled ourselves for a chat and discussed further the work of constructing the colony. He told us in detail how the air-plant operated, leaving out only the vital principle that enabled Dr. Forscher to destroy and reconstruct atoms, which he confessed was known only to the doctor, the head of the physics laboratory, and a few others. He described also how a continuous circulation of water was maintained, the sewage being filtered and boiled so as to render it pure again. It was of course simple to supply more—uniting hydrogen and oxygen by combustion—but it was seldom necessary.

We found out many other interesting things: how, after the glass covered pastures had been made for them, a few cattle, sheep, hogs, etc. had been brought from Earth and allowed to multiply to the present herds; how it had been necessary—for the first year or so—to live almost entirely on synthetic food, made there in the workshop; and how they managed to procure the materials for their work. Some minerals, he told us, they found it easier to mine, as they were found in large quantities about the moon. Iron was one—they had several iron mines. They were reached by flying machines, and maintained separate power, air, and water plants.

Some substances too, could not be found on the moon, and were too difficult of manufacture, notably organic substances. Chief among these was wood. Dr. Forscher projected the planting of a forest of timber in the near future, but it would take many years to reach maturity. In most cases a more durable substitute had been found—metal for furniture, doors, etc.; also concrete stairs and floors. The indispensable materials of this sort had been brought from Earth and used as sparingly as possible, but at some future time it would doubtless be necessary to renew the supply.

Dr. Langley added, too, that the need for occasional communication with the Earth was growing increasingly evident, as a greater labor force was needed, especially since time and accident had contrived to materially reduce its original numbers.

At this point we were interrupted by the ringing of the wall phone, and Dr. Langley answered it. We gathered from his re-marks that something was amiss. As he hung up we prepared to take our departure but he detained us.

"Would you care to take a trip to one of the mines?" he asked. "The air plant has broken down, and I must go there to supervise repairs and of course remove the men."

Wiley turned to me. "How about it, Marland," he asked. "Have you energy enough, after your siege?"

"Try to count me out!" I exclaimed. Dr. Langley nodded his approval and turned to the phone again. Getting in touch with the Transportation Chief, he ordered two tractors made ready for flight; then he gave directions to a corps of mechanics, and finally signified his readiness. We followed him to one of the corridors near the center of the main tunnel, and for some distance along this to a storeroom. He took out three of their "air-envelopes," which served the same purpose as our diving suits, and illustrated the method of donning them. We found them largely better than our own. Besides greater ease of movement, each had a small radio apparatus consisting of microphone and miniature loudspeaker, having a range of a half a mile or more, so that conversation was easily carried on. They were also heat-insulated to guard against the unpleasantness that we had experienced, and the helmets were entirely of colored glass, which permitted greater ranges of vision, yet prevented possible sun blindness.

CHAPTER SIX
A Tragedy!

DR. Langley now conducted us through the smaller of two doors into a cylindrical chamber that served the double purpose of airlock and elevator. The doors, when closed, were hermetically sealed, and by touching a button we were carried rapidly a hundred feet or so to the surface. Meanwhile a pump had been exhausting the air in the chamber, and we now stood in a nearly, perfect vacuum, with only another airtight door between ourselves and the exterior of the moon. On stepping out we saw before us two of the huge conical flying machines, each with a wisp of vapor issuing from the semi-circular openings at the base. Following Langley, we approached the nearer, and I was startled to hear his voice, loud as a gunshot, from the radio speaker: "Aboard the tractor! Open up!"

"Yes sir!" came a response, and in a moment a door opened in the side just above the ground. Passing through another door to the right to the interior of the machine, we found ourselves in a circular runway extending entirely around the base of the machine. A tall man might have had difficulty standing erect in it, as there was little more than six feet headroom. The sides slanted toward the apex of the machine at slightly different angles, the inner more nearly vertical. The floor was approximately ten feet wide, and the roof somewhat less. On our left, directly outside the air lock door, was a ladder leading to compartments above. We mounted through two more compartments differing from the first only in that they were continuous, having no airlock.

Dr. Langley mentioned in passing that they served as cargo space or as accommodations for passengers. The ladder continued up to a trapdoor in the floor of the fourth compartment. This was open, and we climbed into the engine room of the tractor. Here we removed the air-envelopes, and Dr. Langley showed us through the room, explaining the driving principle and the apparatus in the engine room. It was much larger than those below, and jammed with machinery that nevertheless occupied a minimum of space, so well was it arranged. There were eight huge generators, covered with aluminum cases, which served the double purpose of protecting the occupants from injury and preventing possible leakage of air, as the machinery was driven by turbines which connected with the interior conical well of the car. It was through this interior well that the gas, which we had seen, escaped, being given off by the driving element.

It has often been said that there is nothing new under the sun; but the author of this famous saying had never heard of Dr. Forscher. The driving element was literally new; not in the sense that it consisted of a hitherto unknown substance, nor of a new combination of old substances. It was entirely a new element, above uranium in the periodic system. It was appropriately called "synthium," being a manufactured element—the ultimate achievement of Dr. Forscher's dexterity in atomic physics. Not content with changing the elements one into another, he had added protons and electrons to the uranium atom, and created synthium. Undisturbed, its half-life period was a matter of minutes only, but if kept at an extremely low temperature its activity was greatly reduced. It was necessary to cool it constantly, as its very activity resulted in heat, and heat bringing more activity, it gathered speed like a rolling snowball, and was quite as apt to wreak havoc. Kept under control by electric refrigeration, however, it was a willing and mighty slave. It gave off molecules of gas, which glowed, with the heat of their liberation. They were given off in all directions equally, but those that encountered the walls of the conical container rebounded outwards. So great was the recoil of their departure that they easily lifted the huge tractor.

The method of driving was simplicity itself, the chief difficulty being to retain the liberated energy within controllable limits. The synthium was allowed to attain a temperature of some three hundred degrees-centigrade, and here it was maintained by the eight generators, which supplied current to a system of electric cooling. These generators were driven by turbines in the path of the escaping gas. When the tractor was to be brought down, more current was supplied, the resulting lessened discharge, which also affected the turbines, being compensated by the opening of valves which at full power diverted all but a fraction of the stream from the vanes. At rest, a slight discharge continued, which served merely to run the cooling system. When the machines were returned to their hangars, the driving element was removed to cold storage far beneath the ground.

There were also in the engine room the gyroscopic balancers, and the necessary apparatus for renewing the air, which need not be further described. Above the engine room, at the apex of the cone, was the pilothouse. It was practically soundproof, and darkened save for hooded lamps over instruments that indicated the temperature of the driving element, the acceleration of the tractor, condition of the air, etc. A little to one side of the center was the tube of a small refracting telescope, which was used in long flights away from the moon to examine the path of the tractor and reveal possible obstructions.

We stayed but a moment, for the pilothouse was sacred to its occupant, and since the corps of mechanics were now on board it was time to depart.

A GONG rang sharply in the engine room. Four attendants took their places quickly, each beside a pair of the generators. In turn they called a series of readings from instruments before them through speaking tubes to the pilothouse. This, Langley told us, was a check on the pilot's instruments. The gong sounded twice; the generators slackened their speed, and for a second quiet reigned. Then there was a hissing from the interior well, which rose to a shriek; the tractor quivered, and from the increased pressure of my feet on the floor I knew we were off. Looking through a window at our backs we saw the jagged surface of the moon sinking rapidly below us. We gained speed upward for several seconds; then the hum of the generators increased as the rising temperature of the synthium was checked. We were now traveling upward at some thirty miles an hour; it took us but a couple of minutes to reach an elevation of a mile or more.

A new sound directed our attention to two great gyroscopes, which tilted, through an angle of thirty degrees, inclining the tractor to one side. We now started off in this direction, gaining speed constantly until, even at our elevation, the ground slipped by at an amazing rate.

Our window was a little off the direct line of flight, but we had a good view of the path before us. Many miles ahead we caught a glimpse of that telltale blue-yellow light from the other tractor, which had started off ahead of us. We were rapidly overhauling it, gaining speed continually, for there was nothing to retard our progress and the discharge gave us a constant acceleration. Presently we came up with the other machine and passed it, spouting its trail of glowing gas, a mile or two on our left. Its pilot was taking his time, having slanted the machine less than ours. It dropped back and presently was lost to our view.

Estimating our acceleration, I calculated that we were now traveling at nearly seven hundred miles per hour. We passed over a range of mountains whose tops were within a few hundred feet of our elevation; and I began speculating as to the consequence of a collision with them. Perhaps the pilot entertained similar thoughts, because at that moment the gyroscopes began to swing back to vertical. It was mistaken, however, as they continued their motion, including at an angle of thirty degrees in the opposite direction.

We must he halfway to the mine, and in the absence of friction, as much energy would be required to stop as to reach our present velocity.

Looking out the window again, we saw the ground below us, now tilted at a different angle. It was difficult to dismiss the idea that we were climbing. Looking down we saw the cloud of gas from the synthium preceding us and obscuring the ground immediately below us. As we continued, slackening our speed constantly, I wondered how a landing could be made with the view thus obstructed. I did not wonder long, however, so when our velocity had been reduced to about twenty miles an hour the hum of the generators rose, the roar of the gas became less violent, and we began to descend. A moment later the gyroscopes turned vertical, and we drifted slowly forward under momentum, dropping rapidly.

We could now see the airlocks to the mine, projecting above the ground a short distance ahead. The rate of our fall increased, until it seemed to me that the machine must be shattered. The ground was alarmingly close; the gas cloud had already begun to flatten out along the rocky plain. Then, at the last moment, our speed was checked and we drifted at a snail's pace a few feet above the ground. The surface itself was invisible, but its nearness could be seen in the behavior of the gas.

We descended gently the last few feet, landing with hardly a quiver.

Langley and Wiley had already begun to put on their air-envelopes, and I quickly followed suit. It now struck me that although my helmet was soundproof, the hum of the generators was plainly audible. Their note was the characteristic whine of electrical machinery, faithfully reproduced by my radio receiver.

We hurried down through the empty compartment below and onto the surface of the moon. The airlocks lay a short distance before us and the mechanics were already on their way there. As we approached, a crowd of men in air envelopes came out of the larger airlock, pushing wheelbarrows full of iron for the colony's foundries. We stood by until the loading was finished. Meanwhile the second tractor appeared, dropping slowly from the inky sky. It nestled down near the first, which had now received its cargo and was preparing to take off. Even at our distance the note of the generators was quite evident, and its lessened volume foretold the blinding rush of gas. As it took off it rose more and more rapidly to a great height; there was the faint rising whine of the current as it tilted over to begin its return journey. Meanwhile the second tractor had taken the men aboard, and it too rose in a burst of blue-yellow flames. Higher and, higher, faster and faster, it went, as if hellbent on overtaking its companion. Its path through the sky was an irregular, crazy corkscrew.

I heard Langley mutter, "Why doesn't the fool straighten out?" Then the generators hummed again, faint and low at first, but higher and higher as they took up their load. Louder, higher, they whined. Langley watched, anxiety written in his face. Suddenly they were silent. Langley waved his arms, shouting: "He's overloaded them! He's burned them out! My God, *he can't stop!*"

Fascinated, I watched the machine, growing brighter, receding further, climbing into the pitiless sky. It was a tiny dot now, changing color; turning red, then white—the color of molten metal!

I turned away, unable to watch longer. Langley muttered, "Twenty men, and one fool pilot!"

Slowly we turned to the airlock. The mechanics were huddled around the outside. They were eyeing us—some fearfully, some questioning, a few defiantly—all no doubt mindful of the return trip. For my part I was half inclined to risk walking back. The tragedy had affected us all and it was a silent and morose group that followed Langley to the air plant.

An Audience with Forscher

A BRIEF inspection was sufficient to determine the nature of the breakdown. A valve leading from the mixer to the storage tanks had jammed, allowing the freshly generated air to escape into the mine, while the storage supply also leaked out, leaving no reserve. The repairs necessitated a complete shutting down of the plant, and while this would not have been dangerous at the main colony because of its airtight construction, the character of the mining operations rendered it risky here. A deposit of iron was being worked; and while some of the ore lay on the surface, it was the practice to sink a shaft beneath the ore and work up. It was manifestly impractical to give the ore a substantial air-proof covering, and the jar of the mining operations might open up a crack in the rock through which the air would escape. For this reason the miners were shut off by an air lock, through which they could escape to safety in case of an accident.

The air-making machine was so compactly built that the dismantling of the valve exposed quite a bit of the inner works, and we were able to see how it operated. On the surface of the moon there lay large quantities of quartz, the common dioxide of silicon. This was placed in a container in the center of which was a small piece of synthium. The tremendous heat it generated, probably aided by a catalyst, liberated the oxygen, which escaped upward into a cooling tank. The residual silicon was subjected to further heating, while a blast of helium particles from the radioactive synthium passed through it and disintegrated each atom of silicon into two of nitrogen.

The results of this operation were to convert silica into equal parts of oxygen and nitrogen. The oxygen was far in excess of the amount required to produce the proportion of one part oxygen to four of nitrogen existing in the air. The remaining oxygen, however, went to replenish the supply in the atmosphere of the mine, oxygen and nitrogen in normal proportions being mixed and stored to compensate leakage. Impurities in the air, such as carbon dioxide and smoke, were removed by well-known processes.

The task of repairing the valve was nearing completion, having occupied the time we had spent in examining the machine. While the work of reassembling was going on, Langley notified headquarters that we would shortly be ready to return. The machine arrived by the time the job was finished and was waiting for us.

The return trip was made without incident, though each changing sound in the machinery of the tractor sent shivers up my spine, and we arrived in due course at the main colony. The news of the loss of the tractor had spread rapidly, making a profound effect. Throughout the course of my second meal in the dining hall it formed the main topic of conversation and led to discussions of its probable cause. The men at our table reviewed the possibilities of mechanical defects, talked of margins of safety and of overloading; while from time to time a stray phrase from another table voiced the opinion that the machines were unreliable, or that the pilot's recklessness was to blame. Langley, who knew more about it than anyone present, said nothing. He was scheduled for a conference with Dr. Forscher after the meal, and reserved his opinions.

Finally the gathering broke up into groups and sauntered from the dining hall. Wiley and I found our way to our quarters and were grateful for the relaxation of comfortable chairs and strong tobacco. We remained silent for the most part, for though there was much to talk over, it was tacitly understood that rest was at present more important. Wiley had had no sleep since we reached the establishment of Dr. Forscher, and I was still weakened from the effects of my long spell of unconsciousness. Our smoke finished, we bade one another goodnight—Wiley remarking that two weeks of darkness would suit him well—and in ten minutes I was oblivious of moon, Earth, and the entire cosmos.

My watch showed that eight hours had passed when the telephone rang sharply. Wiley had heard it sooner, and was at the instrument when I reached the living room. I could make nothing of his conversation, but presently he turned to me with a grin.

"The boss is interested in us with a vengeance," he said. "I'm next on the conference list, and he wants me in a hurry..." He bounded into his bedroom, shouting at me as he dressed and shaved. I was astounded at the speed with which he made himself presentable, but the cause of his excitement remained a mystery for the time. He promised me full details on his return, and was off in such a rush as I had not seen for days.

As I bathed, shaved, and dressed I gradually came fully awake; my dazed wonder at Wiley's tumultuous departure gave place to an intense excitement. I found diversion for a time in wheedling some breakfast from the chef—a German to whom a breach of routine was a supreme sacrilege. But, returning to the apartment, a sense of anticipation grew on me. Eagerly I awaited Wiley's return, pacing the floor, smoking the air blue, and wearing my watch pocket threadbare. I tried to read, but there was nothing I hadn't thumbed through half-a-dozen times. I contemplated a trip of exploration, only to dismiss it immediately for fear of missing Wiley. Minutes dragged. Twelve o'clock became half-past, then one, two, three…

After a seemingly unbearable amount of time, Wiley suddenly burst into the room and hit me with such a thump on my back that I was unable to do more than gasp.

He exclaimed breathlessly, "You're next, old man! Don't let him bluff you! Tell him you know your stuff! We'll have the world by the tail…" And he gave me a push that sent me flying into the corridor. Shouting a room number after me, he slammed the door.

MORE bewildered than ever, I set out in search of the room. It proved to be the office of Dr. Forscher, and I was immediately ushered into his presence by a silent secretary.

I had formed little conception of what the man might be like, other than that he must possess such an intelligence as I have never before encountered. But I was not disappointed. From behind a low desk a pair of eyes regarded me fixedly—eyes that seemed to look through me, to search out my very thoughts. They were sheltered by shaggy brows, yet seemed to protrude from beneath a massive forehead which might have contained all the knowledge of the ages. A fringe of grayish hair, close cropped, surrounded the dome of his head; large, well-formed ears indicated an acute sense of hearing. His nose was long, thin, and, rather out of keeping with the rest of his features. A wide mouth, thin lips compressed into a line indicating determination rather than hardness, surmounted a jaw like that of the Heidelberg Giant. He spoke in a resonant bass, which rose from the barrel-like chest of his short, squat body.

"George Marland?" he asked. "I had not had the pleasure of your acquaintance before. However, your colleague, Wiley, has told me about you. I regret the slight inconvenience to which you were subjected a short while ago—" referring to the electric spark which had nearly ended my life. "We had no knowledge of your intentions, and thought it best to have the first word. I trust you will pardon it."

I nodded politely.

He continued. "I had intended to allow you to become more acquainted with our establishment before having this talk with you.

Recent developments make it imperative, however, that we come to an understanding.

"No doubt you wonder...as did Mr. Wiley...why we are here. A fair question: why should a group of scientists voluntarily give up the comforts of Earth for such a confined existence as we lead? It will take a bit of explaining. Let me say, however, that my assistants followed me here of their own volition. I only provided the opportunity. They, and I, are here solely to benefit mankind.

"The driving ambition of my life has been the advancement of human welfare, I came early to the conclusion that this was to be realized only through knowledge; or, as some put it, science. Hence I studied science in all its branches. I specialized in none. For with the burning ambition of youth, I hoped some day to know all there was to know. I mastered the practice of medicine, and its right-hand assistant, chemistry. I studied the laws and phenomena of physics, mathematics, and astronomy. I delved into psychology, biology, philosophy, and more.

"It was while a student in Berlin that the first event occurred that led me to my present situation. Looking through my open window, I saw a meteor fall from the sky; not such a meteor as we frequently notice on clear fall evenings, but a most unusual meteor. While still high in the air, it burst into brilliant blue flame and scattered into a thousand pieces that hurtled downward, finally disappearing close to the ground. Shortly after, the breeze brought to my nostrils a faint odor, almost indistinguishable, yet unmistakable—the odor of burning sulfur."

"It must have occurred very close to the Earth's surface," I interjected.

"Actually no. I'll explain in a moment. I was so struck with the peculiar behavior of this meteor that I called it to the attention of Dr. Steinle, my professor of astronomy in Berlin. He agreed with me that the phenomenon was unprecedented, and concluded to ask for reports on it from other observers.

"The results of his inquiries brought forth a singular coincidence. No more data was forthcoming about our meteor, but twenty-nine days before, a meteor behaving exactly like it had been observed near San Francisco. The two were identical, except that the odor of sulfur dioxide had not been noticed. Its color, however, was that of rapidly burning sulfur. Furthermore, it had come from the same section of the sky—in the plane of the ecliptic, on the side away from the sun. We now broadcast the description of these two meteors, asking for further information regarding them or others like them, and set about searching the sky in that neighborhood for some strange body.

"Our search brought out another peculiar fact. The meteors had been seen for many miles around the points where they landed; they must have burst into flame not too long after entering the Earth's atmosphere. Yet, to our knowledge, there was not enough oxygen at that altitude to support combustion. They must have contained large quantities of it within themselves to produce such a brilliant flame; and indeed, their fierce light suggested combustion in pure oxygen.

"However, we were unable to locate any possible source of the peculiar bodies. On the nights in question, the moon, the stars of the constellations Libra, Scorpio, and Sagittarius, and three of the planets—Mars, Jupiter, and Neptune—occupied that part of the heavens, but no comets or other strange bodies could be found.

A Strange Bombardment

"ON the fourteenth day after our search began, newspapers from the United States reported that a meteor similar to the first two had fallen over North Dakota, probably in the neighborhood of Devil's Lake. We could find nothing definite about the direction from which it had come; but twenty-eight days later we received a cablegram from an amateur astronomer in Cairo named Zirkle, reporting a fourth, in whose light he had detected the spectrum lines of sulfur."

"Sulfur appears to have been the connecting clue," I commented.

"Yes, that's what I thought, too. But let me go on. The absence of any comet or other source of this meteoric shower, together with their remarkable composition, began to suggest to me some design behind their appearance. There was a certain regularity about their arrival; the two longer intervals were exactly double the fourteen-day period and it was easy to imagine that others might have fallen unnoticed to make this period exact. But they were obviously not of Earthly origin—they were too widely distributed. Were they then the work of intelligent beings somewhere out in space?

"Reasoning from that basis, I set out to discover, if possible, what sort of beings they were, where they might be, and their intentions in bombarding the Earth. Considering the last item I concluded that the meteors were harmless; they had in no instance reached the surface of the Earth, and while sulfur dioxide in sufficient quantities is poisonous, the relatively small amount which they liberated had no effect whatsoever. The brilliant light, however, was bound to attract attention, and I believed that this was the sole aim of the meteors. But why attempt to attract the attention of us Earth creatures, unless to lead us to their source? And who, other than beings possessing an intelligence comparable to our own, would wish to draw attention to themselves?"

I shook my head. "I have no idea. Obviously men or creatures from some other world."

"Make no mistake; I did not assume they were *men*. Our physical form is merely the product of our environment, and without surroundings paralleling ours in great detail, it is extremely unlikely that the process of evolution would have produced an animal even generally resembling us on another planet. However, they must have some things in common with us. To begin with, they were not greatly inferior to us mentally, nor could they be much further advanced than ourselves, else they must look on us as lower animals unworthy of attention.

"Furthermore, their science of chemistry, physics, astronomy and psychology must be akin to ours, as was proved by their knowledge, or suspicion at least, that intelligent life existed on our planet; their ability to direct a meteor, as we fire a gunshot, to a small target across empty space; their knowledge of the common meteorite, and ability to produce one so totally unlike it as to attract attention; and finally the expectation that this attention would lead to man's slow realization that he had been contacted from beyond Earth."

I raised my eyebrows slightly at this. "Intelligent beings from another world," I half-whispered.

Forscher nodded solemnly, then continued, "Furthermore, they must possess the ability to perceive light-vibrations. This does not mean they necessarily have eyes, but at least some method of distinguishing the same rays, or a part of the same rays, as we do, and to distinguish one color from another. There was, then, considerable ground in common on which we might build a basis for communication.

"But to communicate with them, we must know their location. Unfortunately, we did not know the exact direction from which the meteors had come; nor would we have been much better off if we had, for the attraction of the sun and other members of the solar system might have caused them to deviate considerably from their original course. But by noting the portion of the sky from which they appeared, we had computed their original direction approximately. Their being in the plane of the ecliptic suggested the probability that they came from some body in the solar system, and this at once narrowed the possibilities to Mars, Jupiter, Neptune, their satellites, and the asteroids."

I smiled and said, "A visit from our next door neighbors."

"That's a congenial way of putting it, but yes. So having gotten this far, I needed more, data. Nothing more could be discovered from the meteors already fallen; closer observation of later ones was necessary.

"The next meteor somewhat upset my calculations, however, arriving on the northwestern shore of North America three weeks later, where it was seen from both Prince Rupert, British Columbia, and Juneau, Alaska. The fourteen-day period was now destroyed, but I saw almost immediately that the intervals were all multiples of seven days. It might be that my unknown creatures had a knowledge of our calendar and were timing their shots to come once a week, but it seemed far more likely that they were fired at a regularly recurring time when the greatest accuracy was possible; that is, when some point on their planet was in line with the Earth. Working on this assumption, I plotted the points of arrival on a terrestrial globe, and found confirmation of my theory. Each location pointed to the same spot in the sky; each was two, three, or four times fifty-six degrees of longitude west of the preceding one; and furthermore, supposing that one had fallen every seven days, the intermediate spots were so little frequented that the fall must have gone unrecorded. The interval of longitude must correspond to a fraction over seven days—just less than four hours, in fact—in which the unknown globe completed its orbit.

"I projected my path of arrival into the future, and predicted the arrival of the next four. The first two, in Siberia and Asia Minor, would probably be missed, but the third should be visible from Paris. It came three weeks later, bursting almost over the city and causing no little excitement, I made bold to announce publicly that the fourth could be seen from Newfoundland, and when the consul at St. John's reported its arrival at 2:00 am. I considered my theory established. I had only to name a body in the solar system near the point from which the meteors had come, which completed its orbit in a fraction over seven days, and the abode of the beings was found.

"I published my analysis of the data, but the scientific world was loath to place credence in the work of an undergraduate. They pointed out that I had overlooked the simple fact that life as we know it could not exist where I said it did. They then shrugged their shoulders and forgot me. To add to my discomfiture, the fall of the meteors abruptly ceased, and my intelligent creatures assumed a place alongside the fabled engineers of Mars as the creation of a mind that saw only what it wanted to see.

CHAPTER SEVEN
A Gigantic Plan

"I WAS amazed at the hail of criticism which fell upon me, I became a nine days' wonder through the efforts of the newspapers; I was besieged by reporters, photographers, and the like, seeking interviews the better to deride me publicly. In short, my life became a veritable hell and I was forced to abandon my studies and seek refuge for a time in solitude.

"The power of the Press," I added.

"Exactly—and it was almost unbearable. However, my faith in my conclusions was unshaken, but one such experience was enough. I resolved never again to mention my planet and its inhabitants until I could lay before the world unquestionable proofs. Henceforth I devoted my life to obtaining evidence with which to convince mankind that I was right. But how to obtain these proofs? I must demonstrate that life was possible on the aliens' home planet, and it seemed as though I could never do so.

"As you know, there are several conditions that are indispensable to any form of life we know. Foremost among these is an atmosphere containing a large portion of free oxygen. This is equally indispensable to life in the sea, for it is the pressure of the air that prevents the water from evaporating entirely, and the fish receive their oxygen from that which is dissolved in water. It is equally important that the climate must be moderate; that is, the temperature must not be so high as to injure the delicate chemical compounds of living bodies, nor yet low enough to prevent their functioning. Likewise there must be an abundance of water, without which the processes of life cannot go on. These conditions are not sufficient by themselves, but if they are met, in all probability the situation will be favorable to the growth and development of some form of life.

"Whether or not they do exist on that planet is a question for the telescope and the spectroscope. If they are there, their presence will be betrayed in the spectra of water vapor, oxygen and carbon dioxide in its atmosphere.

"But accurate spectroscopic measurements with the instruments then available on Earth were impossible. The entire planet could be seen in the largest of telescopes only as a minute globe, the size of a pea. I wanted to see it a hundred times larger; but this would require a telescope with a magnifying power of 60,000 to 100,000 diameters.

"Manifestly this was impossible; even though such a tremendous instrument could be built, it would be worthless. With the telescope then in use, the motion of the air was sufficiently magnified so that the heavens were seen as through a stream of water a foot or more deep; the practical limit was fast being approached. Unless I could find a way to get rid of the disturbing air currents, there was little use in building a telescope any larger than that which has no doubt been completed for the Kingsley Observatory in the United States; and even its 200-inch mirror would be hopelessly inadequately for my purpose."

I looked at him, a knowing smile on my face. "So you came here," I said almost under my breath.

He smiled back. "Yes. A solution, fantastic yet intriguing, suggested itself; and indeed you now know that our object in being here—in establishing this outpost on the moon—is to build a telescope, where there is no air, where objects weigh only one-sixth as much as on Earth, where the rotation is much slower, where celestial objects are visible whether the sun shines or not; where conditions ideal for astronomical observation prevail hour after hour, year after year, with no interruption from clouds, winds, or what you will.

"And of course anything seems easier in retrospect than before it is accomplished. I will not bore you with the details of my coming; let it suffice that I spent forty years seeking the means of getting here; that I found it at last in my new element, synthium.

"But to return to the telescope, I mentioned that I would require a magnification one hundred times greater than that of any telescope used on Earth. It is a well-known fact that the most efficient eyepiece for looking at extended surfaces has an enlargement of about twenty-five times for each inch of aperture, though greater powers are sometimes used. Sir Benjamin Wright had, at the time of which I speak, built a reflecting telescope one hundred inches across; hence his best eyepieces possessed powers of enlargement more than 2500 times. To get the magnification I required, my instrument must then have an aperture of four hundred feet! However, there are factors that reduce this figure materially. To begin with, the Earth's atmosphere absorbs six-tenths of the light from the stars; here on the moon we get it all. Then, too, photographic plates may be used to accumulate light from faint objects by long exposure. In short, a telescope on the moon one hundred feet across would give the results I desired.

"I recruited my little band of scientists and my force of laborers, built the tractors, and came here, eleven years ago. Eleven years is not too much time for the construction of so great an instrument; it is just nearing completion, and will be ready for the great test in a few months. And it will stand thereafter, a monument to science, a source of invaluable information, long after I have seen my theory proven. My only regret is that I cannot live as long as it lives and see with my own eyes the secrets of the heavens unfolded.

"However, I am an old man. Though still vigorous, I am past seventy and can hope for but a few more years of active life. Yet the work I have begun must go on; the greatest benefactors of humanity are those men who have given to succeeding generations better tools with which to add to their store of knowledge. And so it is that I now seek a successor, to begin where I must leave off.

"THIS successor must he an exceptional person. He must be a trained scientist of the highest order; must he possessed of a brilliant mentality, great courage, and the ability to endure hardships; and above all he must have the patience and the endurance to devote his life to his work, as I have done.

"I say, without egotism but as a statement of fact, that I know of no one man who possesses all these requirements. There are many who have a few, some who possess most of them; but none who can take over all of the responsibilities that must be assumed. Therefore, I have decided to pass on the management of this colony to a *group* of men, who, taken together, have all these qualities.

"Your colleague Wiley is a remarkable man; I hold him in the utmost respect. His attainments in the field of physics surpass my own in some respects. He is young, vigorous, and brave to the point of recklessness. He is a man suited in many ways to undertake the task of carrying on my work. But unfortunately he is not an astronomer, and after all it is in that field that the greatest good will come from this outpost of science. Nevertheless, as a lieutenant to an able astronomer. Wiley will be invaluable. I have suggested it to him, and he is most enthusiastic.

"With him will be Dr. Langley, a hardheaded, practical engineer, who will be a useful counterbalance to Wiley's impetuosity. These two, and a third, will be the leaders of this colony when I retire.

"The third man will be an astronomer. He is not here; he knows nothing of this enterprise. In fact, I do not know yet who he will be. I have considered the men on Earth whose ability I know, and have selected from them three possibilities. All were men of promise when I knew them; any of them is capable of doing the astronomical work. But I know little of them personally. Before I select one of them I must know whether he possesses the qualities I have mentioned, and whether he is in a position to abandon the Earth for such a life as we lead here.

"I cannot go personally to interview these men. I shall send someone who can take months, if necessary, to become personally acquainted with them, and sound them out making any proposition. It will require diplomacy, patience, and resourcefulness. Moreover it will require an up-to-date knowledge of the events of the world.

"I should also like to maintain more or less regular contact with the Earth hereafter, for various reasons. I need more laborers; there are doubtless scientific developments that should prove useful to me; and from time to time I shall want materials that are not readily procurable here.

"I have taken an hour of your time and mine to lay before you in some detail our situation, so that you may be prepared to answer the question I wish to ask you. It is this: Are you willing to be my intermediary between the moon and the Earth?"

I had come for this interview expecting almost anything; yet I was utterly dumfounded at the doctor's last words. I controlled an impulse to question my ability, for I paid him the compliment of knowing men, and I felt sure that he would never have offered me the post without first making sure of my qualifications. Therefore I collected my thoughts and considered for a moment, I had no reason ever to return permanently to Earth, and if Wiley was to remain here and eventually come into a controlling position, there was every incentive for me to remain and see the thing through.

The doctor was sitting patiently awaiting my reply. His face was expressionless, yet those piercing eyes of his seemed to penetrate my mind and expose the thoughts there. He smiled slightly, even before I spoke, as though he had already read the words that came:

"I shall be very glad to accept!"

It was some forty-eight hours later than Wiley and I had our first glimpse of the nearly completed telescope. It was truly a monstrous thing. Build on the reflecting principle, it measured one hundred feet across, and fully six hundred to the top of the "tube", which was a criss-cross framework of steel girders built to support the smaller mirror, which deflected the beam of light toward its focus on the side of the instrument. On this tube was also a small platform on which the photographic apparatus was mounted, and which could be used for direct observation if desirable.

The instrument was housed in a dome similar to that of the ordinary terrestrial observatory, save that it was insulated against heat and equipped with an apparatus to maintain the temperature within a small range. This eliminated all deformation and possible cracking of the mirror due to heat and cold. The observatory was located exactly at the lunar equator, so that every star in the sky was visible at some time or other. The twenty-eight day period of the moon made possible much longer periods of observation of one body than on Earth, where the duration of the night and changing conditions of weather often made it necessary in photographing faint objects to expose the same plate on several nights.

As I stood at the base of this greatest of scientific instruments, I sensed some of the gratification that the man who had made it possible must feel. I no longer wondered that he could shut himself away for so long a time, for I was becoming imbued with the enthusiasm that all these men here must feel, knowing that some day soon this great inquisitive eye would be turned on the heavens to search out its greatest secret—the whereabouts of other equally intelligent and curious creatures. Although realizing full well that it was a matter of months to the completion of the telescope, and after that many more months of careful research work before the theories of Dr. Forscher could be proven or discredited, nevertheless, as I stood near the axis of the cradle which held that hundred foot mirror, a feeling of restlessness, of expectation, came over me. I could not help but feel that we were on the verge of some great event; that the story that the telescope was soon to tell would be not only the answer to a question for which a great man had spent his life, but the beginning of a new era in science and the history of mankind.

On Earth Again!

My opportunities to watch the progress of the construction were few, however. I set to work at once to master the running of the synthium tractors. For days I rode in the pilothouse, silently watching the man at the helm as he sent the machine hurtling above the ground at terrific speeds; later I guided its course with my own hands under his watchful eye. I circumnavigated the whole moon in less than a day, seeing the rocky plains and jagged peaks of the hemisphere which had been forever hidden from my Earthbound fellows, taking short jaunts directly away from the ground into the weird, mottled sky.

At length my instructor pronounced me competent to start out for the Earth in search of an astronomer to collaborate with Dr. Forscher and complete the controlling triumvirate, which was to succeed him. Time had passed quickly in our little underground world; I could hardly believe that six weeks had passed since my arrival. But the hour was at hand when I must return to my native planet. Dr. Forscher, Wiley, and a few others were on hand to see me off, and after a brief exchange of farewells I climbed aboard with a small crew of engineers and a relief pilot.

The journey took only about two days, and there was little novelty in it. Once free of the moon's attraction we cut down the force of the discharging gas so that we gained speed at the rate of only one-sixth of a foot per second, each second; yet at the end of twenty-four hours we were shooting through space at the terrific pace—better than a hundred and fifty miles a minute. The telescope in the pilothouse occasionally picked up a tiny dot of light that revealed itself as a chunk of meteoric rock, and only a quick shift of the gyroscopes saved our rocketing tractor from being split from top to bottom.

We turned its base toward the Earth and began to slow down. We must travel blind now, yet we were safe. The fierce blast of gas from the driving synthium blew obstructions from our path like chips in a hurricane, leaving us nothing to do but make plans for our sojourn on the Earth.

At length we sighted the rim of its night-shrouded face stretching away beneath us. Our speed was reduced to a hundred miles an hour—a snail's pace to us—and we dropped into the rare layer of hydrogen that marks the upper limit of the atmosphere. Below us was the gentle sheen of the Atlantic, glimmering in the pale light of the moon—a moon that had inspired volumes of poetry. Distance indeed lent enchantment to its jagged, blazing face.

Our immediate destination was the City College. Accordingly I turned the tractor westward, and at a now constant velocity we sped across the ocean. Day was breaking when we dropped gently to earth on the outskirts of the great city I had left less than two months before.

Two months! Was it possible that in so short a space of time my life could have changed so radically, so strangely? It seemed ages since I had said goodbye to a little group of scholars near the spot where we now rested. And how much more strongly must these sentiments have affected the others of the party, who had not trod the earth, seen trees and grass, nor watched the coming of the day in a dozen years!

We burst forth reeling and stumbling like drunken men, so unused were we to the strong pull of gravity. The tractor lay off the traveled highways, so we fastened its outer door with little fear that it would be molested. I led the way to a trolley line half a mile distant, thanking Wiley's foresight in taking along a fair sum of American money for our return. Dr. Forscher had provided a quantity of gold bullion to defray my expenses, but I could imagine the astonishment of a trolley-car conductor on being offered a ten-kilogram bar as fare.

We left the trolley at a downtown hotel, where I engaged rooms for the others. Then, after a hasty breakfast, we set out in search of presentable clothes, for those we had worn on the moon were designed for service alone. My credit was still good, and we presently sauntered forth in unimpeachable garments.

I promised to arrange for living expenses for the crew for a couple of months, and bade them goodbye for the present after exacting solemn promises to keep in touch with me and to be on hand for the return trip. They set off en masse in search of excitement, and I headed for the City College alone.

Dr. Willson had not yet arrived when I reached the Physics Building. His secretary ushered me into his private office, where I made myself at home. I had not been waiting long when he entered, stopping in his tracks as if facing a ghost.

"Marland!" he exclaimed. "We believed you dead! When did you get back? Where's Wiley?" His questions rushed in a torrent.

I answered the last.

"Up there," I said, indicating vaguely.

"On the moon?" He demanded. "He isn't—?"

"No," I replied. "Alive and well, and among friends."

He apparently thought me demented, and I added, "It's a long story, but I'll tell you about it."

I recounted briefly the facts of our being picked up by the lunar colony, of the remarkable works of science that had been done there, and of Dr. Forscher's purpose. When I reached this point Dr. Willson interrupted.

"What planet is this that he believes supports life?" he asked.

"He didn't name it," I said, "but I can hazard a guess. He described it as being at a great distance from the Earth and having a period of seven days and four hours or a little less."

"That doesn't sound like a planet," commented Dr. Willson. "More likely one of the satellites—Saturn's, or Jupiter's."

"Ganymede," I affirmed. "The third of the satellites discovered by Galileo. Its period is seven days, three hours and forty odd minutes. About 3,300 miles in diameter—quite a fair-sized world."

"But life there isn't possible!" he protested. "The sun gives it only one-twenty-seventh as much heat as the Earth receives. Measurements have been made to show that the surface temperature is 220 degrees below zero."

"Dr. Forscher does not contest that," I replied. "He merely states that the evidence of the meteors is conclusive. However, the question will be settled soon." And I went on to explain my present mission.

"And you're to find the astronomer, eh?" commented Dr. Willson. "Did he specify anyone?"

"He named three for me to choose between," I replied. "Though I haven't any idea where to find them now. That was one object in coming here—I thought perhaps you might help me."

"I'll be glad to," he agreed. "Who are they? I'll get in touch with the Astronomy Department—they'd be most apt to know." The names of the men were in a letter among the other documents I had brought with me. After a moment's search I found them.

"Bradley, Rondeau and Quaile," I said. "Bradley took his degree at Chicago, and was with the Lick Observatory for awhile. Rondeau was at Paris, and Quaile at Greenwich, I believe. But that was twelve years ago; there's no telling where they are now, of course."

"No," he agreed, "but I'll see if Radner knows anything of them."

He turned to his phone and was connected with the Astronomy Department. After a few minutes' conversation, he reported:

"Bradley is in Africa, getting ready for the next solar eclipse. He's in charge of an expedition somewhere in the jungle, and it would take months to reach him. Rondeau died in 1924— pneumonia. They say he would have been a great man, too; it's a pity. Thornton Quaile is in this country—at Flagstaff in fact, doing research on the planets." He paused suddenly. "By the way, did you know—or of course you don't—that he has published a book recently on the conditions of the planets? He's become quite an authority on the Solar System. He'd be a good man to look up, I'd say."

"I'd like to read the book," I declared. "Have you a copy of it at the College?"

"At the library."

"I'll go there immediately," I said. "Much obliged for your assistance."

"Be sure and keep in touch with me until you go," he said.

"Of course."

At the library I obtained a copy of Thornton Quaile's treatise, "Life on Other Planets," and settled down to peruse it. The author tried to point out the folly of definite assertions about the matter. Referring to Mars, he observed that the popular theory of its "canals" must stand or fall on the question of whether its atmosphere contained water and oxygen, for without water vapor in the air there could evidently be none on the ground, and without oxygen no life could exist. Then he presented contrasting results obtained by different observers who had tried to settle that question without success.

"The very fact that we can live on the Earth interferes with our attempts to find out about other worlds," said the book. "In taking pictures of the spectrum of Mars, in which the dark lines of oxygen and water appear, we are also photographing the air above us, which contains these same lines. We can only guess how much of the spectrum on our plates belongs to Mars and how much to the Earth. The water band, particularly, is subject to wide changes in a few hours, when a shift in the wind brings quantities of moisture to the air above us. Thus in the same night photographs may give results which differ by two or three hundred percent."

In a later chapter I found: "Venus, too, guards her secrets as closely as the Queen of Beauty for whom she is named. Two capable astronomers may point their telescopes at her clouded face. One announces that the length of her day is twenty-three hours; the other says six weeks."

"In the face of such conflicting data," the book summed up, "who are we to say there is, or there is not life elsewhere in the solar system? If you were to ask me: 'how shall we find out?' I should reply 'let us take our telescopes somewhere where there is no air to annoy us; or better still, let us go and see for ourselves!' "

I closed the book and sat wrapped in pleasant thought. Unless I was greatly mistaken Thornton Quaile's wish would soon be fulfilled.

CHAPTER EIGHT
Quaile

I left the City College about noon, and hiring an auto, drove alone to the resting place of the tractor. The last mile or so was over a bumpy cart track, almost unused; and it was not easy to drive the car to the tractor's base. I set about removing my few belongings to the auto, together with the gold, which was to defray my expenses. This last was a job that taxed my strength to the limit, but finally it was done, and I returned to the city. Here I deposited the gold at a bank, purchased a suitcase and some more clothes, and bought a railroad ticket to Flagstaff, Arizona.

The journey was long and monotonous. I bought a periodical from a newsstand and read until the jiggling print made my eyes hurt. After a dinner of underdone beefsteak in the diner, I wandered back to the observation platform and watched the rails chase each other into the distance. As darkness fell I grew drowsy and presently fell asleep.

I imagined I was floating through space above a tiny world, no larger than a pea. It grew in size to a globe just big enough to stand on and I set one foot gingerly on its surface. Then I became aware of another man standing before me. He was trying to communicate with me, as I could see from his gestures, but I could make nothing of them. At length—angered at my stupidity—he picked up an enormous ball of glowing sulfur and hurled it in my face where it burst with a terrific roar. I awoke to find a switch engine coupled to the rear of the train, its headlight illuminating the platform.

The other chairs were deserted except for the one next to mine, where there sat one of those talkative travelers who are always ready to start a conversation, given the slightest opportunity. He was somewhat amused at my startled awakening.

"Where you going, friend?" he roared above the exhaust of the locomotive.

"Ganymede!" I roared back.

"Never heard of it!" he shouted. "Little place?"

"Bigger than North America," I answered. He looked at me, puzzled; then, apparently thinking I was trying to make a fool of him, he arose in a huff and went inside. I followed after a few minutes, and finding my berth made up, I went to bed.

During the next day I speculated as to how I should approach Quaile in order to gain his confidence without disclosing my object. At length I decided to represent myself as an amateur astronomer and lead him into conversation about life on the planets.

After a change of trains I arrived at Flagstaff on the third day, and set out at once to locate Quaile. The observatory was some distance from the town, and it was well after dark when I arrived there. The big telescope was already pointed to the heavens, where Mars was visible in the western sky. Quaile was not in the observatory dome, however. I found him with a fellow scientist, puffing an enormous pipe and discussing the respective merits of refracting and reflecting telescopes. His accent stamped him at once as being British. He was about average height, partly bald, and wore a tiny blonde moustache. I judged he had recently turned forty. He was a jolly, lively person, and I felt at once that I liked him.

"Y'see," he was saying, "they can't make these lenses big enough. Give me the reflectors—they get so much more light from the planets. Now, if I could just take that big fellow at Mount Wilson up about fifty miles where there's no air, I'd show you some jolly good photographs."

I felt an impulse to tell him that his wish would be more than granted if he went with me to the moon; but I must not be too hasty. I apologized for interrupting their conversation, and introduced myself. The other man excused himself, saying he had work to do. Quaile seemed surprised that I should come all the way to Arizona merely to talk with him, and not a little pleased that I considered him the foremost authority on the planets. I told him that I had a theory regarding one of Jupiter's satellites, and would like to talk it over with him when he had the time.

"NO time like the present," he said promptly. "Let's make ourselves comfortable, and you tell me about it." He settled back in his chair, still puffing his huge pipe, and listened with interest as I explained that I believed Ganymede might be the abode of life. I suggested that the satellite might receive enough heat from Jupiter to make it habitable; but I was forced to omit Dr. Forscher's most convincing arguments, and my reasons lacked force. Instead of laughing at me, however, he heard me through. When I had finished, he explained the opinion of present day astronomers.

"Y'see," he said, "there have been a few measurements of Jupiter's temperature, which indicate that it's pretty cold there—say a hundred and forty Centigrade below zero. There's nothing in the way of plant or animal life that could live at such a temperature. We don't know of any reason why the satellites should be warmer, so that just about lets out the possibility of men being there."

However, my insistence on the point aroused a spark of interest in his mind and he suggested that I stay around until the present series of measurements on Mars were finished. By that time Jupiter would be in a favorable position for observation early in the mornings, and he promised to try to find out something about Ganymede.

I found accommodations in Flagstaff, and spent much time in Quaile's company. He was passionately devoted to his work, and had no other interest except music. He was a capable performer on the violin, and often whiled away his leisure hours entertaining small audiences with the dreamy tones from his skillful bow. I secretly rejoiced to learn that he had no family ties, since this removed the greatest obstacle to his going to the moon. I found him an excellent fellow, and enjoyed spending hours with him at the observatory as he sat at the eyepiece of the telescope, motionless as a statue, following the path of the "Red Planet" across the firmament. We exchanged few words during such times, yet a considerable friendship grew up between us. I bided my time, waiting for an opportunity to broach the subject uppermost in my mind.

It came one night a month or so later. The spectroscopic work on Mars was suspended for the time being, and we went one night to the observatory to train the telescope on Jupiter and its satellites. The planet did not rise until two o'clock in the morning, and was still low on the horizon when we turned the dome to the eastward and focused the eyepiece. In the field of view we could see the disc of the great planet, streaked with belts about the middle. Near one edge was a grayish blot, the remnant of the "Great Red Spot" that caused much comment among astronomers half a century before.

Scattered across the field like so many stars save for their slightly greater size, were three dots of light, one almost touching the planet's edge, the others farther away on the opposite side. These were Europa, Ganymede, and Callisto—the second, third, and fourth of the satellites first seen by Galileo. Io, the first, was eclipsed by Jupiter's great shadow.

We brought Ganymede to the center of the field and applied a higher-powered eyepiece. It now appeared about the size of a large piece of buckshot, a tiny disc of light that wavered slightly, that swelled and contracted, as the trembling atmosphere above us distorted the beam of light that reached the great lens. We could see nothing of its surface characteristics; it was like looking at the entire map of Asia drawn on a pea, I imagined looking at it through

Dr. Forscher's giant telescope, making it appear a hundred times larger. What would we see then—oceans and continents, clouds, or a barren waste of ice?

I resigned the eyepiece to Quaile, and he peered through it intently for a moment. Then he shook his head with a sigh.

"Bad seeing," he said. "The thing jumps around like a cricket." He climbed down from the observer's station on the stepladder beneath the telescope. "Y'know," he observed, "if we could find a way to get rid of that motion we'd be able to find out a lot more than we can now. It's bad tonight, but it's always there."

Quaile Decides

I DECIDED to spring my proposition. "When I first saw you," I began, "you were saying that you'd like to take the Mount Wilson telescope up above the atmosphere." He smiled. I drew a breath and plunged ahead. "What would you say if I told you where there was a bigger telescope on solid ground, with no air above it at all?"

"You mean, someone's put one on top of Mount Everest?" he asked, puzzled.

"Better than that," I replied. "There's a telescope ready for use now, waiting for the man to handle it, and it's better than a dozen of the Mount Wilson telescopes."

"Y'know, you interest me," he said. "Go on."

"The mirror of this telescope is one hundred feet in diameter," I said. "It can be used with eyepieces magnifying up to 100,000 diameters. And there's absolutely no atmosphere around it."

"Where?" he demanded.

"On the moon," I said.

"I say," he exploded. "Joking is fine,, but you carry it a bit far."

"No joking about this," I said. "And you needn't have any fears as to my sanity. I can prove every word I say. I've seen that telescope with my own eyes; and there are men within our reach who will back up my statements. Say the word, and I'll take you there. In fact, that's the reason I'm here…"

Quaile was thunderstruck, naturally enough. He pulled out his handkerchief and wiped his forehead.

"Well!" he said, and again. "Well!" After a moment he asked, "But how the devil does one get to the moon?"

"Two men have done it independently by different means," I replied. "I can take you there—if you're interested."

"Interested? Well, rather. But y'know, it's somewhat of a knock, all this about a telescope on the moon, and men going there. How can one live there, without any air!"

"There are several hundred men living there now," I said. "Making their own air."

This was the last straw for Quaile. I saw that he regarded me as a raving maniac.

"Yes, of course, old fellow," he said placating. "But let's not bother with it. What say to a cup of tea, and we turn in?"

"It suits me," I agreed. "But do me a favor. Perhaps you've heard of Dr. Willson, the physicist?" He nodded. "Send him a wire—ask him whether my story is true."

Quaile seemed doubtful, but I pressed him, and finally he agreed to do as I asked. I accompanied him to the telegraph office where he dispatched a wire to Dr. Willson, asking for a prompt reply. Then he went to bed. For day was breaking and the astronomer, like the owl, seeks his home during the daylight hours.

When we woke the following afternoon, Dr. Willson's telegram was at the observatory:

"MARLAND'S STORY REGARDING TELESCOPE UNDOUBTEDLY TRUE, STOP, HE HAS MY COMPLETE CONFIDENCE—WILLSON"

Quaile was impressed, but I saw that he still regarded the affair as a hoax. Nevertheless I followed up my advantage.

"If I can show you a machine which will take us to the moon, will you go with me?" I asked.

"Seems like a fair proposition," he assented. "You won't mind, of course, if we don't say anything about this to the men here?"

"Not at all," I assured him. Obviously he did not want to be made a laughingstock in case this should turn out to be a fool's errand.

WE packed our baggage and took the train east a few days later. Quaile was a jolly traveling companion, and despite his not entirely unjust suspicion of me, the trip was enjoyable. However, as we neared our destination, a doubt assailed me: During the entire month of my sojourn at Flagstaff I had not heard a word from the crew of the tractor. What if they had deserted me? I could not very well manage the machine alone for the return journey, and I could not find another crew. With this in mind, I set out at once for the spot where I had left the machine, Quaile going with me.

The tractor had been screened from the roads by a grove of trees, and it was with mingled elation and fear that I led the way to its resting-place. However, I was in no way prepared for the sight that met my eyes. I recognized the trees, the surrounding knolls, the exact spot—but there was not a sign of the tractor!

"It's gone!" I exclaimed, rushing forward. There was no doubt that this was the right place. There was a patch of bare ground, where the discharge had burned away the grass. "Gone!" I repeated.

"Yes," observed Quaile, "it seems to be take leave of one, eh?" His face wore a knowing smile. He thought his suspicions were confirmed, and that I was crazy beyond a doubt.

"Quaile," I said fervently, "on my word of honor, that machine was here. "I'm going to take you to Dr. Willson and let you hear from him the facts about this. Whatever has become of the machine, I am going to prove to you that I am neither a liar nor a lunatic!"

In a fit of hopelessness I turned toward the city; but we had not gone ten paces when I heard my name called. I turned, and saw a man hurrying towards me over the nearest hillock.

"Mr. Marland!" he called. We stopped, and he caught up with us, out of breath. It was the relief pilot!

"I was afraid I'd miss you, Mr. Marland," he panted. "The machine's in a field a couple of miles from here. Some picnickers found it and got curious, and we had to move it. One of us had been on the lookout for you all the time. We thought you never would come!" he added.

I was too relieved to ask any questions. The pilot led the way over the hill to where a tent was pitched beside a battered car. The crew had established a camp here and kept a lookout night and day for my return. We took down the tent, bundled it into the car, and the three of us climbed in. The pilot drove up off into the country, to a bare, unsettled spot. There, in the hollow between two knolls, lay the tractor. The pilot blew the horn of the decrepit auto, and the rest of the crew, lacking only one man, came tumbling out to greet us. My amazement knew no bounds. With their first opportunity to visit their homeland in twelve years, these men had elected to live right in the tractor!

CHAPTER NINE
A Leak!

THE pilot, acting as spokesman, explained the situation.

"We all went off to look up our families and friends," he said. "They thought we were dead, and had made heroes of us. When we showed up, hardly able to walk on account of the gravity, and not knowing anything about what's happened on Earth, they didn't know what to make of it. And when we said we'd been on the moon, they thought we were crazy. Our wives and sweethearts have all married other men, and our friends didn't know us. We tried to get work, and couldn't hold a decent man's job. Nobody wants us here; we've got friends on the moon. We want to go back…"

Quaile was convinced. After answering a plethora of his questions, he made last minute communications with his people in Flagstaff informing them of his indefinite leave of absence. Then there was nothing left but to load our baggage and start for the moon. I checked over the supplies of food, water, and air in the machine, and made a list of the things we would need. Then we went back to the city, leaving the crew to care for the tractor until our return. On the morrow we visited Dr. Willson, purchased our supplies and picked up our baggage. Loading it into the car, which we had borrowed for the occasion, we drove out to the tractor. The crew assisted in loading, and in short order we were ready to start off.

I climbed to the pilothouse, rang the warning gong, and sent the gas roaring through the central well. I paid no attention to the position of the moon, preferring to set the course after we were free of the Earth. We climbed slowly at first, not wishing to overload the machine, which must exert a tremendous force merely to overcome the Earth's pull. It took us upwards of an hour to reach a point sufficiently far away to neglect its gravity. Then we turned in a great circle toward the moon, which was visible over the edge of the globe to the west, toward the sun. The tractor gained speed rapidly, and we were soon far away from the Earth in the midst of the airless expanse of the solar system.

Quaile was immensely excited at the strangeness of his surroundings. He remained for a long time at one of the windows, his eyes glued to the glass, giving vent from time to time to exclamations of amazement. I could hardly restrain him from turning the telescope in the pilothouse on the planets, and he was filled with impatience when I told him that it would take two days to reach the moon. He explored the tractor from end to end, asking innumerable questions about its construction, source of power and the like. When my shift in the pilothouse was over he bombarded me with queries about the colony on the moon, which he had up to now regarded as a figment of my imagination.

I told him what I could of the way it had been built, the principles which made it possible, and the work done there; but I was hard put to satisfy his curiosity. It was with the greatest difficulty that I persuaded him to take some sleep, and only got him to do so by pointing out that the time of our trip would seem shorter if he did not remain awake so much.

By the time we had reached the halfway point and turned the tractor about, however, he lost some of his impatience. He got out his violin and played to us for an hour or more. He was really an excellent musician and had a remarkable repertoire. His taste ran more to dreamy, soothing melodies and those of lighter character, and between numbers he kept up a running fire of talk, recounting the history of each of his selections and explaining his interpretation of them. He had an excellent ear and possessed the sense of absolute pitch to a high degree. There was no doubt that, had he chosen to do so, he could have become a famous artist.

During the rendition of "Liebestraum" he suddenly put down his bow and began tuning the strings. I had noticed nothing wrong, but he said with a grimace:

"The thing's deuced sharp. Must be that the air's very dry here." He picked up the bow and continued playing, but he had gone only a few bars when he again stopped.

"Really," he exclaimed, "it's most astounding! I never heard an instrument get off pitch so quickly. The air has a remarkable effect!"

Suddenly a thought flashed into my mind: Sounds are higher-pitched in thin air!

"The pressure!" I shouted. "Get into your air-envelopes quick!" I dashed for the suits hanging along the wall, noting the air-gauge as I pulled on the nearest. The pressure was only twelve pounds, and as I watched, it fell lower. I rushed up to the engine room to warn the men on duty, while others who had put on their envelopes followed to relieve them. Then when we were all protected, we set out to hunt for the leak. By closing the airtight doors between the compartments and noting the air pressure in each we quickly located it in the lowest section. The glass windows were all intact; but after fifteen minutes' search we found a small break, clean as a bullet hole, in the outside wall.

The tractor had two walls. The outer was built to withstand the impact of meteorites too small to be seen in the telescope. It was not air tight; as soon as the machine left the atmosphere all the air between the outer and inner walls escaped, leaving a perfect vacuum that prevented loss of heat by convection. The inner wall was lighter, of air proof construction, and was coated with asbestos. Just before reversing the tractor, when we were at the peak of our velocity, we must have encountered a small object of extreme hardness, which had punctured both inner and outer walls.

We closed off this section of the interior, welded a plug into the hole, and brought the pressure up to normal from the reserve tanks. Then out of curiosity we began a search for the meteorite that had caused the trouble. Quaile spied it, in a corner near the air lock. He brought it to the light where we examined it. It was perhaps half an inch in diameter, with a rough surface under which a tiny glitter of fire could be seen. Quaile rubbed it sharply against the steel partition, making a deep scratch.

"A diamond!" he exclaimed. "A diamond flying through space!"

There could be no doubt as to the correctness of his assertion. The characteristic hardness, the fiery sparkle—it was the rarest of meteoric stones, which had struck our tractor by the barest chance.

Quaile pocketed the stone as a souvenir.

"Y'know," he said, "I like this space-flying, what with picking up diamonds and all. But I hope we don't meet them much bigger!"

A little over two days' travel brought us close to the moon. We circled rapidly around its surface to the spot on the equator where Dr. Forscher's outpost was located. Quaile never ceased to enthuse over the wild, rugged landscape beneath us, eyeing it with binoculars for many minutes. He seemed amazed that none of us had taken the time to explore it mile by mile, or examine the character of the rocks and the depths of the fissures. This had been left to the geologists of the colony, and none of us was acquainted with the results of their work.

The Great Telescope

WHEN we sighted the airlocks of the entrance near the enclosure where the tractors were stored, Quaile's excitement knew no bounds. The chief of transportation was on hand to greet us, and as we donned the radio-equipped air envelopes his voice could be plainly heard, giving directions to the mechanics who were to overhaul our tractor. We descended the elevator in the airlock shaft, and were met by Dr. Langley in the corridor inside. I introduced Quaile to him. Langley immediately escorted him to the quarters that had been prepared for him. I departed for the apartment that I shared with Wiley, and found him there. He jumped to his feet as I entered, his face beaming.

"Welcome back, old man!" he shouted. "What news from Earth?"

I told him of my visit to Dr. Willson, and recounted my adventures while in America. He listened eagerly, interjecting questions about his colleagues at the City College. I could tell him little of them, having spent so short a time there, which I now regretted. When I had finished, I asked, "How's the telescope going?"

"Finished," replied Wiley, "and tested. What a marvelous thing. They've got a picture of a sunspot that will knock your eyes out! I never saw such clearness. You see when Dr. Forscher knew there was to be an astronomer shortly, he pushed the work to the limit, and they put it together in record time. It was tested out only a few days ago, and the old Doctor was so tickled with it he nearly smiled…"

This news set me all a-tingle. I would have set off at once for the observatory, but Wiley counseled otherwise.

"It's bed for you, young fellow," he said. "You're dog-tired, even if you don't know it. You look as if you hadn't slept for a month."

I agreed reluctantly, and we turned in; but sleep was long in coming, and filled with scrambled dreams of tiny worlds, sulfur meteors, huge telescopes, and diamonds from the Great Void.

After breakfast there was a conference. Forscher, Wiley and Quaile were there; I was invited as a courtesy. As usual, Forscher dominated the conversation. Addressing himself first to Quaile, he said:

"I have put forth every effort to produce the most perfect telescope humanly possible, as you have been informed. No doubt Mr. Marland has told you, as well, my principal motive in doing this. I have personally tested out the instrument, making photographs of the sun and other bodies, with very gratifying results; but I have deferred the work for which it was designed until your arrival. In our laboratories here on the moon we have worked out methods of photography that we believe excel those in use when I was actively engaged in astronomical work some years ago. However, there may have been developments in the technique on Earth of which I know nothing, and for this reason I shall turn over the major portion of the research to you, after giving you the benefit of our developments."

"I am greatly honored," said Quaile simply. "Of course I shall want to spend some time getting acquainted with the instrument so that I can interpret the results accurately."

"That's wise. You'll have ample opportunity to do so," said the Doctor. "The body upon which this research is to be conducted is the largest satellite of the planet Jupiter, euphoniously named Ganymede by its discoverer. Jupiter is not now visible from the observatory. It will rise in about two hundred hours and remain visible thereafter for about three hundred. I hope that in that space of time enough work can be done to give some indication of the condition of the satellite."

"I'll do my best," promised Quaile.

"Very well," said the doctor. "I'll leave you to your own devices, with the understanding that you may call on anyone here for whatever assistance you may wish."

The brief meeting broke up, the three of us leaving the doctor alone. Wiley had experiments in progress at the Physics Laboratory, but I was a man of leisure for the present, and at Quaile's invitation I accompanied him to the observatory. We had had a brief glimpse of the telescope shortly after his arrival, but had not yet had an opportunity to explore the observatory or look into the eyepiece. When we reached the dome we found one of the men who had been engaged in directing the construction and assembling of the instrument. He was clad in an air envelope, and before going further he motioned us to dress ourselves similarly. Then we proceeded through the nearby air lock and entered the telescope dome. Our conductor explained the operation of the instrument as we made a tour of the room.

It was obviously impossible to keep air in the dome of the observatory, but there was a small booth mounted near the base of the telescope that could be hermetically sealed so that the observer need not wear his envelope. Here he might look directly at the image from the big mirror, or guide the photographic plate by means of an auxiliary eyepiece.

The observatory was located exactly on the moon's equator. This served two important purposes. In mounting so enormous a telescope it would have been difficult in the extreme to tilt its axis at an angle, yet the mounting must enable the instrument to follow the path of any star across the heavens. At the equator the stars rose at right angles to the horizon, followed an arc of a circle across the sky, and set perpendicularly. In addition, every star in the firmament (except the Earth, for the observatory was on the side that never faces it) was visible at one time or another. The two pole stars lay always on the rim of the horizon, while all the rest circled about them, showing themselves for half of each twenty-eight-day revolution.

The polar axis of the telescope was connected to an enormous driving clock, timed to follow the slowly creeping stars across the heavens. Once set going, it required no further adjustment, pursuing the tiny lights as they wended their way in a body from east to west during their two weeks of visibility. The observatory dome also rotated, keeping its broad slit always between the great mirror and the stars on which it was trained.

Quaile examined every detail of the apparatus, uttering exclamations of delight and admiration. We climbed to the observer's booth and, removing our helmets, looked into the eyepiece. The telescope was trained on the star cluster known as the Pleiades, whose familiar "seven sisters" were now mingled with countless thousands of tiny points, dotting the field like raindrops on a pavement.

Quaile decided to tryout the telescope himself at once. He secured a number of plates already prepared and returned to the dome. I watched him as he swung the huge tube across the sky, training it upon Mars. He slipped a negative into the plate holder, made final adjustments of the direction and focus of the instrument, and climbed to the observer's station. I watched as he followed the progress of the planet. It was necessary for him to watch it constantly, shifting the photographic plate by a hair's breadth from time to time. The tremendous magnification of the planet's image also magnified imperceptible irregularities in the driving clock, so that the variation of a fraction of a millimeter would destroy surface details in the picture. In starting the exposure Quaile had centered his cross hairs on some minute spot of the planet's disc, and his trained eyes were best able to keep it there.

An Illusion Destroyed

AT length he climbed down from the booth and removed the plate.

"That should do it," he said. "Now let's see what we've got." We hastened off to the photographic laboratory, where the plate was carefully developed. A group of assistant astronomers and photographers surrounded us as we bent over the negative. It bore little resemblance to a visual image of the ruddy planet, for in addition to its colorless blackening, bright spots were marked by the deepest shadows, leaving blank patches in place of the darker areas. Nevertheless I realized that it was by far the best piece of work of its kind ever seen. The planet appeared 320 times larger than the full moon as seen with the unaided eye, so that only a part of its disc was shown on the plate. With a little imagination I could picture myself suspended a bare 750 miles from its surface, seeing it as it would look to the brave space pioneer who would first land there someday. I looked in vain for the famous "canals." There were irregular patches of dark color, the more prominent ones approximating straight lines, but that was all. The supposed irrigation system was an optical illusion, which disappeared on better examination.

Quaile went back to the observatory to make more photographs. He was immensely pleased with the success of his first effort, and now had the opportunity he had longed for to determine, once and for all, what was to be found in the Martian atmosphere.

During the next few days he told of his achievements along this line; and in doing so he blasted one of the most fascinating ideas that mankind has ever invented, namely, the existence of a race of super-beings who had engineered huge water channels to supply melting ice from the polar caps. He found that there was water, true enough, but only as a vapor and in very small amounts, while the total absence of carbon dioxide and oxygen showed conclusively that any such highly developed organism as the human body could never endure there. Without oxygen to breathe and carbon dioxide to retain heat, all animal life must have long since succumbed to the rigorous climate.

The results of this investigation only served to increase the impatience of the colony. Did this unpromising news mean that Ganymede, too, was a desert world, devoid of living beings, and that the Earth alone was capable of supporting an intelligent race? It was not encouraging, to say the least. Yet if this were true, how to explain the sulfur meteors? We must not jump to conclusions; the riddle would be solved in a short time, and all awaited eagerly the rising of Jupiter and its attendant moons.

Quaile and his assistants were in a bustle of preparation, while Dr. Forscher himself had taken charge of the construction of an extremely sensitive instrument to measure the temperature of Ganymede's surface. It was a refinement of an apparatus used for similar purposes by astronomers, and was based on the fact that when two wires of different metals are joined to form a closed circuit, an electric current is produced by warming one of the junctions. The current could be measured with a delicate galvanometer, and the temperature of a distant body thus computed.

As the hour of Jupiter's rising drew near, an audience gathered in the observatory. With eyes strained to the east they waited— scientist and laborer, standing shoulder to shoulder, waiting for the consummation of twelve years' efforts. Their voices, magnified by the radio speakers of their envelopes, bespoke the emotions that filled them. There were not a few who held watches in their hands, and by one or another the passing of each minute was announced. A heavy voice from somewhere near me roared a facetious admonition to the Prince of the Solar System not to keep his audience waiting, and there was a ripple of laughter. Then a shout broke through the tumult.

"There it is…Jupiter!"

An instant of awed admiration followed as the yellow dot of the planet's face balanced on the horizon, glowing steadily like a tiny diamond. Those on the outer edge of the group crowded forward to get a better view through the wide opening of the dome. The heavy-voiced joker called for a cheer, and it was given by the over-enthusiastic of those in attendance. Then someone set up a shout for Quaile that was taken up by the group.

"Where's the astronomer? Why isn't he on the job?"

I left the observatory and set off in search of Quaile. He was dozing in his apartment, stretched out in an easy chair. An open book lay heedlessly on the floor beside him; his burned pipe had slipped from his fingers, cascading ashes on the carpet. His face wore an expression of peaceful oblivion to the question that had fired the imagination of the entire colony.

"Quaile!" I exclaimed. "Jupiter's risen!"

He awoke with a start. "Take it easy, young fella. No rush—Ganymede's eclipsed right now, hiding behind Jupiter like a bashful kid. Maybe it knows we're looking through the keyhole. I was just catching forty winks before I get started. I'll be in for a long pull."

I apologized for my impetuousness. He waved it aside.

"Pull up a chair and chat a minute." I complied.

"This thing's got you all on edge, like the rest of them," he observed. "No doubt they think I'll have the answer in time for dinner, I wish I could, but, y'understand, there's a sight of work to do. I'm going to make dozens of plates; no one of them would tell the story. I'd be missing a bet if I didn't get all I could on the whole system—Jupiter and all the other satellites. Might turn up something from them that would tell us quite a lot. The doctor doesn't want guesses. He wants *proof.*"

I couldn't help admiring the man's quiet, common sense attitude. Why expect results in a day, after twelve years of pre-paration? And the doctor; he wasn't up there at the observatory yelling for action. No doubt, like Quaile, he was calmly awaiting the most propitious moment for his temperature measurements.

"Can't say as I blame these fellows for getting excited," said Quaile. "I suppose I must get along and start the show." He arose and stretched himself. "Want to come along and watch?"

"Thanks," I said, "but I think I'll do some reading and turn in. You'll have audience enough without me."

"I dare say," he agreed. "I hate to disappoint them, but they'll probably see little enough for awhile."

We set off, he to the observatory and I to my apartment, to kill time as best I could. As Quaile had said, there was no point in anticipating results so soon; Dr. Forscher had allowed the two weeks between the rising and setting of Jupiter as a minimum, and there was no doubt that the two of them would waste no time getting as much data as possible, leaving the examination of it until the planet was no longer visible. Forcing this thought into my mind I settled down to await the passing of the intervening time.

CHAPTER TEN
What the Telescope Revealed

THROUGHOUT the colony, the air of expectation and impatience continued. At mealtimes there was much speculation as to the progress being made, but no one connected with the observatory was present; they worked almost continuously, stopping now and then to eat or take a few hours' sleep at their posts. The workmen, who did not understand the scientific aspect of the task, could not understand the necessity of so much delay; not a few of them held the view that the inhabitants of Ganymede could be seen directly through the telescope, and that it was merely a matter of looking at them to discover their appearance, habits, and such. Having had some practical experience with a telescope in my college days, I undertook to explain the situation to a few who asked me about it, and presently I found myself conducting an informal class in elementary astronomy. I was glad of the opportunity that presented itself to discuss the subject, and lectured in such glowing style that Wiley, who happened in on one of the gatherings, dubbed me "Professor Marland" forthwith.

At length Jupiter disappeared below the horizon, and excitement reached fever pitch. Everyone was on edge, waiting for word of the results. But Quaile and Dr. Forscher had retired to their quarters for a well-earned sleep before doing anything further. And so forty-eight hours more passed and nothing was learned.

During the third day following Jupiter's disappearance, the word passed around that Dr. Forscher would meet those interested in the experiments at his office after dinner. "Those interested" turned out to be almost the entire colony, and the meeting adjourned to the dining hall, where a platform of tables was improvised and chairs gathered around. Dr. Forscher took the platform. Because of the size and heterogeneous character of his audience, he elected to begin his announcement with an explanation of the experimental procedure. The gathering thus assumed the nature of a popular lecture.

"As you are all aware," he began, "we have been testing a theory that I formulated fifty years ago, and which has been the greatest interest of my entire life. Because of the appearance of certain mysterious meteors, I was led to believe that the satellite Ganymede might be the abode of intelligent, civilized life. Scientists at the time were of the opinion that this was impossible because of its great distance from the sun. Ganymede revolves around the planet Jupiter once every seven days, three and three-quarters hours, at a mean distance from that planet of six hundred and sixty thousand miles. Its distance from the sun, therefore, is about four hundred and eighty million miles. The Earth is less than one-fifth that distance, so that Ganymede receives only about one twenty-seventh as much light and heat from the sun as does the Earth.

"This is obviously too slight an amount to support any animal life we know, for the temperature must fall many degrees below zero unless there are modifying factors.

"However, the appearance of the sulfur meteors seemed to indicate that there must be modifying factors. A few figures will suffice to show that too much must not be expected of even our great telescope. Jupiter is at present about four hundred and fifty million miles from us. The telescope magnifies it one hundred thousand times, reducing the apparent distance to forty five hundred miles. In other words, Ganymede appears to us about fifty-four times as large as the full moon. We have therefore been forced to adopt indirect methods in seeking the information we desire."

"Mr. Quaile and I have been working independently along different lines, and have had no opportunity to compare notes until a few hours ago. Our results are curious, but they are very satisfactory."

"We find that the four major satellites of Jupiter constitute a series much like the four inner planets of the solar system. They appear to show four stages of a progressive evolution from unendurable heat to freezing cold. Some of the phenomena of these stages have already been noted by terrestrial astronomers, notably their density and their albedo, or ability to reflect light. The amount of sunlight reflected from any planet depends on the nature of the surface we see. Thus Venus, the brightest of the planets, is covered with clouds, which turn back nearly three fourths of the sun's rays; while Mars, with its thin atmosphere and desert surface, can return only fifteen percent. It has been well known that Jupiter's satellites differed among themselves in this respect.

"Io, closest to the primary, reflects fully half the light that strikes it, indicating that it must be covered by an envelope of clouds, as is Venus. Europa is even brighter. The clouds are thinner, and perhaps broken in spots; certainly they are less dense over one part than elsewhere. As the satellite revolves about Jupiter we note that one part of its face always appears dimmer than the rest. Callisto, the outermost of the four, behaves similarly, its surface being the least, bright of all.

"It has also been previously noted that the density of the satellites grows progressively less from Io to Callisto. The latter would almost float in water, while the former is much like our moon in size and weight. A cubic foot of its soil, on the average, would weigh about three-fifths as much as the same amount taken from the Earth. Ganymede, in this respect is intermediate between Callisto and Europa.

"These facts are not new. But let us now consider the work we have just completed. The best measurements of temperature heretofore have shown that Jupiter never rises much above 140 degrees below zero (Centigrade) at the surface, and it has been supposed that the satellites are similarly cold. However, my figures indicate a different situation. The value for Jupiter is substantially correct, but the satellites are much warmer. Why this should be true I am not prepared to say at present, but nevertheless it is so. Io, revolving close to Jupiter, is around 200 degrees (Centigrade) above zero—twice as hot as boiling water. Europa shows a temperature of 96 degrees (Centigrade), which is just below the boiling point on Earth. It is worth remarking, however, that water boils at different temperatures, depending on the atmospheric pressure. By placing a dish of water in a vacuum it is perfectly possible to have it boiling and freezing at the same time. We cannot be sure, therefore, that there is liquid water on Europa; but with Ganymede such is very probably the case. The temperature is a few degrees above the freezing point. Part of the time, at least, there must be open water on its surface, and from the cloudiness of its atmosphere I venture to predict that streams, lakes and oceans may be found. Callisto is a frozen world, little warmer than Jupiter itself. It would seem that the satellites must receive some sort of energy from that planet, since the reduction of temperature corresponds to their increasing distance from it.

"Turning now to the photographs for which we have labored to build our magnificent telescope, the evidence of a progressive series continues. Mr. Quaile has made excellent photographs of the light of these satellites with the spectroscope, the greatest aid to astronomy since the invention of the telescope. There is a parody on a familiar jingle which runs:

'Twinkle, twinkle, little star;

Now we've found out what you are,

When unto the midnight sky

We the spec-tro-scope apply!'

"Mr. Quaile's photographs show that the four satellites we are studying have quite different atmospheres. Io is the hottest, we have found; hence we might reasonably expect active volcanoes covering its surface, which should have cooled only enough to be thinly crusted over with solid matter. Observations of the vapors from erupting craters have shown is what to expect in the air of such a world, and our spectroscope bears out the prediction. There is no oxygen whatsoever, but in its stead quantities of carbon dioxide, and choking poisonous gases such as chlorine and carbon monoxide. I hardly need point out that life in such an atmosphere would be impossible. Chlorine helped to make the World War the horror it was, and the frequent deaths from minute quantities of carbon monoxide in automobile exhausts indicate the unfriendliness of the latter to living creatures.

Life Discovered

"EUROPA is not much better off. The atmosphere is denser and better able to support clouds of water vapor. Volcanic gases predominate, though not to such an extent as on the sister satellite, as there is enough oxygen to reduce some of them to harmlessness.

"On Ganymede the volcanic activity is unimportant, if not entirely absent. Sunlight, heat, and growing plants have split up the carbon dioxide into carbon and oxygen. As on the Earth, nitrogen forms the rest of the atmosphere. This world has passed the destructive youth of its two smaller sisters, and has blossomed in motherhood.

"Callisto is the spinster of the quartet; she has passed into sterility without ever being capable of supporting life. Her frozen face is thinly covered with a layer of nitrogen, from which carbon dioxide, water, and oxygen have departed to unite with other elements or litter the ground with snow.

"To sum up, then: Ganymede is the largest and most massive of Jupiter's satellites. In its atmosphere we find all the conditions essential to life—water, oxygen and carbon dioxide, in the proper proportions. The temperature is mild, and there are bodies of open water. Volcanic activity is much reduced, and the poisonous gases are gone from the air. Plant life is indicated by the presence of free oxygen, which it helps to produce.

"To these facts add the appearance of meteors, which cannot be the work of nature, at intervals that correspond exactly to the length of Ganymede's day, and there can be little doubt that a race of intelligent beings lives here, building machines, investigating nature's ways as we do, and seeking to tell us of their existence and interest in us. Common courtesy requires that we make an attempt to acknowledge their message. It is to that end that I shall now turn the resources of this colony."

As the doctor finished speaking a hubbub broke out over the room. There were scattered cheers for the inhabitants of Ganymede, for the doctor, and for Quaile. But the scientific group was more interested in the last remark. Communication with an unknown race on another world hundreds of millions of miles distant! How was it to be accomplished? Did the doctor intend to fire sulfur meteors back to Ganymede, and thus let them know we recognized their interest in us? Possibly, though that seemed a rather unsatisfactory means of intercourse. Perhaps a better method would be to prepare a manuscript with a key to the language and shoot it at the satellite; but what were the chances of its ever falling into the right hands, even supposing it was not captured and engulfed by Jupiter?

As these thoughts ran through my mind, I discovered that the scientific staff was following Dr. Forscher out of the dining hall to his office. Wiley was among the group and motioned me to join them, so I fell into line, wondering what was in the wind. We entered the doctor's office and assembled about his desk.

"I have asked you here," he said, "to offer suggestions as to the best means of communicating with the inhabitants of Ganymede. I should like to see this accomplished before I am forced to retire, so let us waste as little time as possible in devising a method. Have you any suggestions?"

One of the group, whom I recognized as Alvin Dalton, a chemist of considerable ability, spoke.

"It would be quite possible to make a meteor that would behave like those you saw fifty years ago," he said.

"Undoubtedly," agreed the doctor, "but there would be too great a difficulty in aiming it properly. The attraction of the Earth is sufficient to capture a projectile that comes fairly close to it, but in shooting at Ganymede we should have to aim much more carefully, or Jupiter's tremendous gravitational field would pull it in. Then, too, I would prefer something that would lead to an interchange of messages."

"Such as radio?" asked a member of the staff of physicists.

"No good," put in Wiley. "We could never make a wave reach that far. The best that's been done yet is to send a message around the Earth. To reach Ganymede the waves would have to be sixty-four million times stronger."

"And even if they got there, how do we know the Ganymedians would have an apparatus to receive them?" The speaker was Dr. Ernst, a psychologist.

Quaile, seated at the back of the group, leaned forward through a cloud of tobacco smoke and observed.

"Y'know, that flying machine rather took my fancy. Couldn't you send it out there and talk to the fellows first-hand?"

"An intriguing idea," said the doctor, "but there are difficulties. None of the tractors could carry enough synthium to go out and back. Even if they could, it would take too long. They are built for a maximum velocity of fifteen thousand feet per second; not that they couldn't go much faster, for of course there is nothing to hinder them; but at that speed there is barely sufficient time to detect obstructions and avoid them. You had one encounter with a meteoric stone at high speed, Mr. Quaile. Yet at that pace it would require five years to make the trip in one direction."

It was Dr. Langley's turn to offer an idea.

"Suppose the machine were very long, and tapered uniformly. Any small bodies that chanced to meet it would hit a steeply slanted surface, and glance off. There would be no difficulty about building a telescope that could pick up the larger ones in time, and with a gravity screen—"

"Exactly," interposed Wiley. "That would have a great deal of power in getting away from the moon. Then, too, there would be no danger of falling onto Jupiter if we passed too close."

"We're getting on," said the doctor. "I suggest that we let Mr. Wiley and Dr. Langley work out the plans for the machine and show them to me. Perhaps that will be the solution."

Back to our apartment once more, Wiley and I fell to discussing the proposed space flyer. I had imagined it would resemble a torpedo, but Wiley's idea was different.

"The streamline form," he said, "is adapted to travelling in air or water, but it wouldn't suit the purpose of this machine. The idea is to present everywhere the least possible angle to its path, so that a meteorite would glance off readily no matter where it struck. If the machine had a snub nose and curving sides, the front end would be practically flat and there would be no chance for the obstruction to bounce off; it would go right through. What we want is a pointed end; and since the machine must be reversed to stop, both ends should be pointed, something like this."

CHAPTER ELEVEN
On To Ganymede

HE sketched the design rapidly. The machine resembled two narrow cones, base to base, coming to a sharp point at one end and cut off at the other to allow for the opening through which the driving gases would escape. The diameter at the middle was about fifteen feet, and the total length about one hundred and eighty.

"Must it be as narrow as that?" I asked. "You don't allow for much head room after you put in a level floor."

"Thinking of submarines?" he queried. "Consider a moment; which way will this thing travel?"

"Why—pointed end first, I suppose," I said.

"Right. And which way will the acceleration tend to push you?"

"Toward the rear," I said. "Of course!

The occupants will stand with their heads toward the point. So the floors will have to be crosswise, not the length of the machine."

"Exactly." Wiley continued to sketch the machine, placing the driving apparatus just back of the center, with the generators and cooling apparatus surrounding it, adding storage batteries and air tanks in the slender forward end, and finally the living quarters near the middle.

"That will serve as a preliminary design," he said. "I'll see Langley after a while and get his ideas. Now for some calculations."

He got out his slide rule and table of logarithms, and began filling sheets of paper with figures. Presently he emitted a whistle.

"Here's something to think about," he said. "I'm starting on the assumption that the trip is to be made in a month or less. In order to do that, it would only be necessary to increase the speed one and a quarter feet per second each second; yet halfway to Jupiter the machine would be going three hundred miles a second!"

It was my turn to whistle.

"But," I objected, "a velocity like that isn't safe. Suppose it was to meet a rock as large as ten feet in diameter? It wouldn't be visible in the telescope more than three hundred miles away. That would leave only one second to recognize it and change course."

"True," said Wiley. "We'll have to find some other way of avoiding them."

He dived into the logbook again, and presently came out with a new set of figures.

"If you were to use a larger acceleration—say twenty feet per second per second—you'd save a lot of energy, and get there nearly as soon. In the first two and one half million miles or so you'd reach a velocity of a hundred and fifty miles a second; then you could shut off the power and coast to within two-and-a-half million miles of Ganymede before slowing down. The work done in reaching that speed would be only about a fourth as much as in accelerating all the way."

"Still, a hundred and fifty miles a second!" I exclaimed. "Two seconds to get out of the way of obstructions three hundred miles off! That would be an awful strain on the pilot. He wouldn't dare bat an eye; a single slip, and it would be all over."

"Yes," admitted Wiley. "But you've got to get up a pretty good speed, or you'd take too long in getting there. I wonder if some sort of automatic device couldn't be arranged to steer the machine?"

He tilted back in his chair, felt around for a bit of moon-grown tobacco, and filled his pipe. Blowing a cloud of smoke, he gazed into it absently. His fingers drummed on the desk; now and then he seized his pencil, only to lay it down again. Finally he jumped up.

"I'll go see Langley," he said. "He may have some ideas. Two heads are usually better than one on a job like this."

HE departed, leaving me to while away the time. There was a copy of Edgar Allen Poe's "Prose Tales" on our bookshelf, and I thumbed through the leaves in search of something worth reading again. "The Unparalleled Adventure of Hans Pfaal" struck my eye, and I smiled in recollection of Poe's idea of inhabitants of the moon, particularly the little fellow without ears who had visited the Earth in a balloon. I wondered whether the Ganymedians would resemble human beings in any way. Dr. Forscher apparently thought not. But what other sort of creatures could possess a high order of intelligence?

I realized the futility of trying to imagine the inhabitants of another world. There was no foretelling the conditions under which they had evolved—their food, their enemies, their social life, and the many obstacles they must have surmounted in their upward march. We could not know until the trip to Ganymede was accomplished; and that waited on Wiley's ability to find a safe mode of travel at enormous velocities.

Wiley came in, his face wreathed in smiles.

"Excelsior!" he exclaimed. "Or is it 'Eureka?' We have it. On to Ganymede!"

"Explain yourself," I suggested.

"As I predicted, two heads are better than one. Langley suggested a photoelectric cell. You may have heard how sensitive they are. I recall an example. Some inventor built a machine for the purpose of sorting beans, which made use of the difference in color of the bad ones and good ones. There was a small lamp, which shot a beam of light on the beans as they passed along on a conveyer belt. The white ones reflected enough light to keep the cell working, but when a brown one came along the current through the cell stopped, letting a trap door fall open to drop out the undesirable bean. Unfortunately, however, the machine wasn't much good practically, at first, for it detected beans with fingerprints or specks of dust on them, and threw them out with the bad ones."

I laughed. "But what has a bean sorter got to do with Ganymede?"

"Suppose such an apparatus were placed at the eyepiece of a telescope, and connected to the controls of our space flyer so that it would change its course whenever there was a slight increase in the light ahead of us. The meteors would betray themselves by the sunlight falling on them, and our flyer would be headed off out of danger."

"Good enough!" I exclaimed. "That's the worst difficulty taken care of. Now we can go ahead."

"Wait a minute," cautioned Wiley. "You haven't heard it all yet. We can depend on the photoelectric detector to pick up objects an inch or so in diameter, but the smallest must hit the machine now and then. The telescope lens would present quite a large surface. Where are we to find an object-glass strong enough to withstand being hit by missiles as large as bullets at a hundred and fifty miles a second?"

"Then why do you say 'on to Ganymede'?"

"We have an idea," explained Wiley, "though it is only an idea at this point. Langley suggests that we make the photoelectric cell sensitive to waves that will go right through the hull of the flyer itself—high frequency waves. We could generate them aboard the tractor and project them ahead of us; then when they strike a meteor some of them would be reflected back to excite the cell. I think it can be done. If it is, we will make plans for an expedition to Ganymede."

The Comet

WILEY demonstrated once more the genius that had aroused Dr. Forscher's admiration. After nearly a month of experimenting he demonstrated the success of his cell. He had set it up on the moon's surface, trained it on the sky and connected to it a light, in such a way that a flash would announce the operation of the cell. We stood by and marveled as he tossed tiny pebbles, filings of steel, and such minute objects in the path of the rays, to be greeted each time by a flash of the light. Without a doubt the flyer would be safe from collisions, at least.

From that time forward all eyes looked to the day of departure of the expedition. The construction of the flyer was begun, and progressed rapidly. I assisted from time to time in various capacities as far as my abilities permitted.

Quaile had been given the task of mapping the best route from the moon to Ganymede, and I spent some time helping him. We photographed the section of the sky through which the machine would travel, seeking unknown asteroids whose presence might hinder our progress. There were a number of them, yet the danger they represented was surprisingly small. All of them were large enough to be picked up by the detector while thousands of miles away; and when one considers that if all the known and imagined minor planets were added together they would not equal the moon in volume, it is not difficult to realize that they are too widely scattered to offer much of an obstacle. Thus we decided on a straight-line course, after allowing for motion of the Earth and Jupiter in their orbits.

Meanwhile Jupiter and its satellites were approaching opposition, at which point they would reach a minimum distance of three hundred and ninety million miles. The construction of the machine was pushed to the utmost in order to have it ready in time for that favorable situation. Frequent reports to Dr. Forscher announced the completion of this or that component part, and the whole took shape as if by magic.

Superhuman feats were accomplished, and work that would have required months under ordinary circumstances, was done in weeks. At each of my frequent visits to the scene of the assembling I was amazed at the progress. At first there was only the framework, a long naked skeleton of steel; then the covering appeared, section by section, and was welded together in an unbroken, shining armor. Generators, gyroscopes, batteries, tanks, and piping took their places in the interior, while the outside acquired the dead-black gravity screen, diminutive wings and disappearing skids to be used in gliding through the atmosphere of Ganymede and landing on the ground.

In a time that seemed scarcely believable the flyer was assembled, inspected, and ready for a test. It was designed to carry only five men, and those who had been most instrumental in the building of it had the honor of proving its ability. They were Wiley, Dr. Langley, the chief chemist, the chief of transportation, and Dr. Forscher himself. Quaile and I, together with a large crowd of onlookers, stood by to watch. The machine rested horizontally on its skids, a tiny stream of luminous vapor issuing from the stern. The shining undersurface contrasted sharply with the nearly invisible black of the gravity screen covering the upper half.

The crew climbed aboard through an airlock below and disappeared. Shortly afterward the gravity screens slid into position, the skids were withdrawn, and the vapor-cloud grew in brightness, spurting out behind. The machine paralleled the surface for a short distance; then the rear end dropped slightly, and it headed upward in a long arc, pointing vertically upward and receding into the blackness until only the trailing streamer of gas was visible. High above our heads it circled about, dodged to right and left with the agility of a sparrow, and performed lightning-like maneuvers. After a time it shot off toward the horizon, dwindled to a tiny speck, and was lost to sight. In a moment we saw it returning. It flashed among the stars, turned end for end, and approached us stern first, retarding gradually. With marvelous expertness it dropped to the ground, shot out the landingskids, and came to rest a hundred yards away. The passengers appeared one by one from the airlock and approached the admiring group.

"WHAT do you think of it?" asked Wiley's voice from one of the air-envelopes.

"Wonderful," replied Quaile. "Most astounding! It looked like a comet gone balmy!" Wiley laughed.

"A graphic illustration," he said. "We might give it a name."

"The Comet!" I agreed. "What would be more appropriate than to name it for the wanderers of the Solar System?"

The suggestion was immediately popular, and forthwith the space-flyer received its christening.

There now remained only the question of who was to make the trip. The number who wanted to go far exceeded the capacity of the machine, and it appeared that Dr. Forscher would have a delicate problem in making the selection. He called an assembly immediately, and there was a large gathering on hand in the hope of hearing themselves named among the lucky five.

"I realize fully the interest that this journey to an unexplored world has aroused," began the doctor. "There are many unique experiences in store for those who undertake it. But I doubt if anyone here realizes the danger involved. Were it not for my own selfish haste to see it an accomplished fact I should never permit the *Comet* to leave the moon until it had been thoroughly tested. But I have confidence in the foresight and ability of its designers, and in view of the satisfactory performance on its trial journey, I believe that it may reasonably be expected to reach its destination.

"Much will depend on the resourcefulness of those who man it, however. They will meet situations that cannot be foreseen, and there is always the possibility that they will never return. In view of that fact, I cannot reasonably ask anyone to make the journey who does not sincerely wish to do so." He paused to give us an opportunity to think the matter over, then resumed: "I have selected five men as a crew. Anyone of them is at liberty to withdraw if he wishes, and I am sure he will not suffer in the esteem of the rest. There is a disappointment in store for some of you, but I hope you will see the matter as I do.

"There are three men present, all of whom want very much to go, whom I must ask to remain here. They are soon to assume the leadership of this colony, and I do not consider it wise to allow them to risk their lives in this expedition. I refer to Dr. Langley, Mr. Quaile and Mr. Wiley."

I looked around for the members of this trio to see how they took the announcement. Langley, who stood on the edge of the gathering, looked steadily at the Doctor, his face a mask. Quaile seemed surprised that he had been considered for the expedition at all. I reflected that the big telescope was still a novelty for him, and he could content himself with photographing the stars. Wiley, however, was hard hit, for he had counted heavily on making the trip. It seemed a shame that he should not reap the fruits of his efforts to make the trip possible, but the Doctor was right. He could not risk the loss of so valuable a man.

Dr. Forscher continued: "Those who make up the party must be able to take a hand in the operation of the machine, and must use their time to the best advantage in gathering facts about Ganymede and its inhabitants. The primary object of the expedition is to get into communication with these creatures—creatures that probably have nothing in common with us. The explorers will find on Ganymede strange surroundings, unfamiliar social customs—even habits of thought different from our own. They must draw on imagination and reason, rather than experience.

"With that in mind, I have chosen the five men of the party. Dr. Von Lichten, our medical adviser, is the first. His training will enable him to discover the constitution of the Ganymedians, the processes of their bodies, and their habits. The second member will be Dr. Ernst, whose ability as a psychologist should help him to an understanding of their minds. M. Lafourchette, the geologist and meteorologist, will examine the soil and climate of Ganymede. Mr. Dalton is well known as a capable organic chemist and has done notable work in zoology and botany in England. He will study the flora and fauna of the satellite. And to take charge of the party while en route and make a unified report of their adventures and discoveries, a man who, while not preeminently a scientist, has had no little training in astronomy and physics and much practical experience as a writer and explorer—Mr. George Marland..."

CHAPTER TWELVE
The Trip Begins!

THE last announcement overwhelmed me. The Doctor must surely have overrated my ability, to place me at the head of the expedition. But I was immediately surrounding by a group who seized my hands, congratulating me on the coveted opportunity. The other members of the party were similarly besieged by admirers who pounded their backs and wrung their hands. Dr. Forscher waited until the excitement had died down a bit before adding his concluding words.

"Jupiter is already three days past opposition; there is no time to lose. In forty-eight hours the moon will be in a favorable position for departure, and I ask these five men to be ready to leave at that time. The *Comet* will be stocked with provisions at once, and the members of the party will see that their personal equipment is aboard. That is all."

Forty-eight hours allowed little enough time to get ready for such an undertaking. The five of us scarcely had a minute's rest. Dr. Von Lichten pointed out a possibility that had been heretofore overlooked—that the atmosphere of Ganymede might contain bacteria to which the human body was not immune, in which case it would be dangerous to expose ourselves. He suggested that rubber suits be constructed that would enable us to move about easily and talk to the Ganymedians without exposing ourselves, but there was not time enough. Wiley succeeded in devising microphones that could be attached to the air-envelopes, enabling us to hear sounds directly and make ourselves heard, and these had to serve.

I had less baggage than the rest, taking only a table of the positions of the known bodies of the solar system and a large supply of writing materials. I searched the colony over for a typewriter, but there was none to be found, and while it would not have been difficult to make one, the time was too short. I contented myself with a three-inch pile of paper, a dozen pens and a quart of ink.

Meanwhile the moon pursued her course around the Earth, reaching the full phase on schedule. We were on the far side, and consequently the terrain was wrapped in darkness when our little party of five entered the airlock and shot to the surface. Quite a few had braved the blackness and penetrating cold of the lunar night to see us off; Dr. Forscher, Wiley, and Quaile stood at the airlock of the *Comet* to bid us farewell with a handshake and a word of encouragement. Wiley's voice was near breaking as he said:

"All the luck in the universe to you, old man." It wasn't necessary to him to say how terribly he wanted to go.

"I'll bring you a Ganymedian for a house-pet," I promised and climbed aboard.

The interior of the machine was divided off into compartments from end to end by heavy bulkheads. The various rooms were cylindrical, connected by a ladder along one wall, and were furnished with tables, chairs, and bunks securely bolted to the floor. The aspect was rather peculiar at present, for the machine lay on its side and the furniture appeared to hang from the rear partition. We deposited our last-minute impedimenta in the living quarters and assembled in the engine room.

The operation of the machine had been explained to each man present, but I took charge, having had experience with the tractors. Under my direction they checked over the readings of the various instruments, closed the gravity screen and sent the gas roaring behind us. We hung on desperately as the forward push of the acceleration turned us upright in the room; then a shift of the gyroscopes sent us curving upward away from the moon, gaining speed rapidly.

I took sight of the stars through a periscope at one side, heading the machine straight for Jupiter. Once on our course a non-magnetic compass indicated any deflection. Then we covered all the portholes against the onslaught of meteorites, withdrew the periscope and set the photoelectric detector working. This was connected to the gyroscopes so that whenever it picked up an obstruction in our path it shifted them, sending us off at an angle to our course; then after a few seconds it automatically righted our direction. At the same time a gong gave warning, so that we could hang on to one of the many holds provided, and save ourselves from a fall.

DESPITE the absence of gravity we stood firmly on the floor, for the push of the driving gas held us down just as a quickly accelerated auto throws its occupants backward. There was nothing more to do for awhile except to watch the instruments.

Our acceleration was plotted on a slowly turning sheet of paper—the sort of apparatus used to record changes of temperature by weather stations. It was actuated by a weight on a spring, so that the downward push of the acceleration moved a pen, and any relaxation allowed the spring to draw it back. In the first twenty-two hours we would have covered two and one-half million miles, and would then be traveling at about one hundred and fifty miles per second. From then on we would coast for nearly a month at a velocity unchanged except for dodging meteors, when the synthium would be called into service for a few seconds each time.

During the first twenty-two hours we kept a vigilant watch over the instrument board, seeking the slightest irregularity, but everything functioned perfectly and except for an occasional lurch sideways as we missed a passing meteor, there was nothing to break the monotony.

I had been introduced to the members of the party at the dinner table sometime before, but until now we had become little acquainted, and as I was in charge of the expedition I felt it was up to me to discover what sort of men were under my guidance. I took every opportunity to engage in conversation with each, and soon learned that Dalton and Lafourchette were not on the best of terms, having published controversial theories on Earth concerning the importance of rainfall in promoting the development of animals. Physically they were almost exact opposites; the Frenchman was short, dark, slender to the point of emaciation, and possessed of a nervous manner and a fiery temper, while Dalton stood nearly six feet, a corpulent red-faced man who took life casually.

As for the others, Dr. Von Lichten, who had revived me after the incident of Wiley's and my capture, was taciturn and inclined to keep to himself, while Dr. Ernst, the youngest of the lot, was the best mixer. He was German by birth, of Hebrew extraction, and possessed a remarkable insight into the human mind. I decided that I should prefer his company to the squabbles of Dalton and Lafourchette, or Dr. Von Lichten's perpetual silence.

"Help!"

MEANWHILE the *Comet* flashed on through the blackness with increasing speed, leaving the moon far behind. We arranged a schedule of watches in the engine room, and those off duty stowed their baggage and made themselves comfortable. There were provisions against the month of travel ahead of us, such as playing cards, chessmen, and works of fiction that had been borrowed for the trip. The journey promised to be tedious, for we must travel absolutely blind, not daring to risk leaving any of the portholes open. We would miss many interesting sights, but we consoled ourselves with the thought of those that awaited us.

The two-and-a-half million mile point was reached without incident; the power was shut off, and we were suddenly free of the pushing acceleration. Unavoidably we floated off the floor, bumping against whatever happened to be over our heads. We hastened to put on magnetic shoes like those Wiley and I had used. Some of the party were amused or disturbed over the weightless sensations at first, but quickly overcame their annoyance.

Dalton was due for the next watch, and presently looked at his timepiece and went into the engine room. The door remained open, and we heard his voice mingled with Lafourchette's voluble accents, I was about to investigate when the Frenchman came through the door, muttering.

"What's wrong?" I asked anxiously.

"Nothing," was the reply. "Monsieur Dalton is annoyed because I saw fit to take a nap at my post."

"But man, that's dangerous!" I protested. "Suppose something should go wrong while you were asleep. We might all be killed!"

"That would be very bad," yawned Lafourchette. "I am sorry; I shall be more cautious in the future." He rolled into bed and was fast asleep in a few seconds.

We had been on our way almost eleven days when the little Frenchman's second escapade aroused our excitement. I noted with mild curiosity that he had carried a mysterious bundle with him to the control room. I gave little heed at the time; but when, at the end of his watch, I went to relieve him, he beckoned to me in evident excitement. I closed the door and inquired what had happened.

"I have made a great discovery!" he said. "But we must keep it a secret between ourselves, and let no one else take the credit.

"What is it?" I asked.

"The Fitzgerald contraction theory. I have proved it false!"

"Then you've been making experiments on it?"

He nodded. "I have brought with me the most accurate micrometer in Dr. Forscher's laboratories. Before we left the moon I measured several steel bars with great precision. Now we are moving forward at the rate of a hundred and fifty miles a second; according to the contraction theory these bars should be much shorter when they are placed in the line of our motion, than when they are at right angles to it. Yet that is not the case. They are always the same length!"

I suppressed a desire to laugh.

"My friend," I said, "you overlook a simple fact. As you say, the Fitzgerald-contraction theory states that a moving body contracts in the direction of its motion; and it is true that your steel bars should be shorter when you point them along our course. But the theory does not exempt micrometers; yours must also be shorter, to the same extent, and of course you cannot measure the contraction when you're measuring instrument is moving at the same velocity."

Lafourchette's face fell.

"But then how can the contraction be discovered?" he asked.

"You must make your measurements on some body that is moving past us, or past which we move. In either case you would observe the contraction. The motion is only relative."

"Then I can still do the experiment," said Lafourchette joyfully. "I have a small telescope with me. I will set it up in the air lock, open the outside door, and look at the planets past which we are sweeping. Should they not appear distorted—contracted sidewise?"

"They should," I agreed. "We are entering the region of the asteroids, and will shortly pass close to one of the largest. The orbit of Pallas surrounds that of Mars, and the asteroid itself is only a few million miles from us."

Lafourchette rose. "I shall examine it at once," he declared, and disappeared in excitement.

I TURNED my attention to the controls. As we were among the asteroids it was important that our detector be kept in perfect order, to prevent hitting any of them. Pallas lay many miles off our course, but there was no telling how many fragments of some miscarried world lay ahead of us. Even at that moment the warning gong indicated the proximity of one of them, and the quick shift of the *Comet's* direction pitched me against the wall.

An hour or so later Ernst entered the control room.

"I'm worried about Lafourchette," he said. "He put on his envelope and went into the air lock with a telescope. He hasn't come back yet. Do you know what he's doing?"

"He wanted to make an experiment, which he pledged me to keep a secret. We'd best not interrupt him."

"Nevertheless," said Ernst, "I'm worried."

"We can talk to him with the radio of one of the envelopes," I suggested. "Just ask him if he's all right."

Ernst put on one of the helmets and called Lafourchette's name. I caught the frenzied response:

"Help!"

"What's the matter?"

"Come quick! *Mon Dieu,* I cannot get back!"

"Take the controls," I said. "I'll go see what the trouble is." I climbed into my envelope, closed the outer door of the airlock and entered. Lafourchette was nowhere to be seen! Exhausting the air, I reopened the outer port on an amazing spectacle. Floating parallel to the *Comet,* a hundred feet away, Lafourchette was struggling and kicking frantically in a vain effort to pitch himself toward the air lock.

"I'll throw you a rope!" I called, and hanging the port shut I heaved mightily on the inner door. It would not give until I had equalized the pressures, and I was forced to wait until enough air had hissed in through the valves. Inside, I set about a frenzied search for a coil of rope, finally unearthing a stretch of stout metal cord. I fastened one end about my waist and returned to the air lock. Lafourchette had calmed his struggles somewhat.

"Catch this!" I shouted, heaving the coil into the blackness. But I had unconsciously thrown high to allow for gravity, as on Earth. The cord missed him by twenty feet, remained stretched snakily and refusing to come closer. I hauled it in and tried again, this time with better success. Lafourchette seized the free end and I pulled him aboard. He was on the verge of collapsing, whether from fright or exposure to the intense cold I could not tell. I carried him inside, where we stripped off his envelope. He gasped violently several times.

"What happened?" we demanded in chorus.

"I went out to look at the asteroid," he said, struggling for breath. "Suddenly the bell sounded, and the *Comet* swung sidewise. I had no chance to catch something for a hold; the machine just floated from under me, and I was left in space. A little later the *Comet* straightened out and sailed right along beside me. I tried to kick myself back, to swim, anything at all, but it was in vain. Ah, my friends, the aggravation of it! There I was, a hundred feet away, yet unable to come any closer. Then, to make matters worse, the air pressure in my envelope began to fall. I was nearly suffocated when you threw the rope. The fabric must have burst somewhere."

I looked over his flexible covering carefully, but could find no break. Dr. Von Lichten picked up the helmet, and emitted a whistle.

"Look at this!" he exclaimed. "A hole clear through both front and back. You hit a tiny stone, my friend, which would have drilled you more neatly than a bullet had it touched your body. You may indeed thank your lucky stars that you are still with us."

"That is what I do not understand," said Lafourchette. "With the machine speeding along at one hundred and fifty miles per second, why was I not left behind?"

"When you fell overboard," I said, "you, too, were going a hundred and fifty miles per second. There was nothing to stop you—no air, no gravity; you just kept on going. You could have floated beside us indefinitely, unless the *Comet* swung away again."

"Then my telescope is still beside us?" he asked.

"Unless it was hit by the meteor that caused the *Comet* to dodge. Shall I try to get it for you?"

"No," said Lafourchette. "Let us take no more risks outside the machine. Besides, I have seen all I wanted to."

"Did you find the contraction?"

"No…that accursed asteroid was perfectly round!"

"Perhaps we can estimate how much of a contraction there should have been," I said, figuring on the back of an envelope. "At our velocity, Pallas' disc should have appeared out of shape by about three parts in ten million."

"Then I could not have seen it, after all," said Lafourchette sadly.

"True. In order for the contraction to become appreciable, our velocity would have to be comparable to the speed of light. That is why it is so hard to believe the Fitzgerald equation. If we see a railroad train rush past without appearing a bit shorter, we are apt to say to ourselves: 'This contraction business is the bunk!' "

Lafourchette had regained his normal composure. "At any event," he said, "I have learned a lesson. I shall stick to my own science, and refrain from questioning theories that have been developed by competent physicists until I am sure of the ground I stand on—scientifically and personally."

The days went on, marked only by the revolutions of our clock. Each passing hour reeled off half a million miles, eating up the distance to our destination. My calculations showed that we had only a few million more to go. I decided it would be safer to begin slowing down a little ahead of time, to allow a margin of safety. Our terrific speed made it unsafe to use the periscope, for a grain of dust such as had pierced Lafourchette's helmet would wreck it, and interplanetary space was more or less filled with such particles. After figuring our position as accurately as possible by dead reckoning, I allowed a million miles to spare. None of the satellites would bar our path, but Jupiter lay dead ahead, and we had no desire to plunge into its atmosphere. After slowing down to a safe speed we could take observation and alter our course so as to meet Ganymede at the proper time.

Nearing Jupiter

THE hour of starting up the driver would come during Lafourchette's watch. I offered to stand it as well as my own, but he insisted on taking his turn. Dalton had referred to him as "sleepyhead" since his first offense and his pride was hurt. Accordingly I set about writing up the log of our journey. Dr. Von Lichten was asleep in his bunk, and Dalton and Ernst were at one of their innumerable chess games, having "loaded" the board and the chessmen with magnetized iron so that they would remain in place, despite the lack of gravity.

This last circumstance made my writing difficult, for I had to lean against the wall, and my ink showed a great disinclination to stay in the bottle. To add to my discomfiture I found myself unable to collect my thoughts. I wrote a word, crossed it out, and re-wrote it, unable to make up my mind, I became increasingly drowsy, and finally fell into a doze.

I awakened with a hazy realization that the gong connected to the detector had rung. My head must have knocked sharply against the wall, though the throb of the blow seemed far off and unimportant. My glance fell idly on Ernst and Dalton, standing at grotesque angles sound asleep beside their chessboard. The spectacle was amusing, but slowly I realized that something must be done. With painful slowness I dragged my feet into the engine-room, and found Lafourchette blissfully unconscious. I peered drunkenly at the instrument board, my befogged brain unable to fathom the meaning of the many indicators. Slowly I grasped the fact that the air was horribly foul. I struggled toward the emergency oxygen tank and wrestled with the valve until it gave, pouring the life-giving gas into the room. Standing near the tank I inhaled deeply, and soon recovered my strength. Then I grabbed Lafourchette by the shoulders and dragged him to the valve. It was a minute or so before he recovered consciousness, protesting that he had been asleep only a moment. I looked at the clock. We should have begun slowing up two hours ago!

Yelling directions at Lafourchette, I set the gyroscopes turning and reversed the *Comet*. In another second the gas was shrieking through the discharge tube, the sudden acceleration sending me to my knees. We rushed into the living room, to find Ernst and Dalton sprawled on the partition and Dr. Von Lichten half out of his bunk with his feet tangled in the covers. We disentangled them and hauled them into the engine room. There, lying by the wide open oxygen valve, they quickly recovered consciousness, asking in great bewilderment what had happened. I explained briefly that the oxygen apparatus had gotten out of order, and that bad air had rendered us all unconscious. Dalton raised up and pointed an accusing finger at Lafourchette.

"Sleepyhead!" he shouted. "Dreaming on the job again. No thanks to you that we're all not dead now!"

"From those unmentionable cigars of yours," retorted the Frenchman, "it is a wonder we have not been asphyxiated before!"

I intervened, to stop further argument.

"We are going too fast for safety," I said, "with Jupiter less than two and a half million miles away. I've had to reverse the *Comet* by dead reckoning. The detector isn't turned around yet, so we are unprotected from collisions. I'll have to take a chance on using the periscope to get our bearings."

This was a risky proceeding, though the streamer of gas rushing out ahead of us offered some protection against small dust fragments floating in space. I uncovered the tube and extended it enough to get a view of the path ahead of us.

For a few seconds the flaming streamer of gas from the disintegrating synthium blinded me. Then, through the brilliant blue-yellow haze, I caught a glimpse of something that froze my stomach—a shining circle!

In one bound I reached the gyroscope controls and swung the *Comet* off at a tangent. The others had sensed my panic and stood motionless. Five—ten—fifteen seconds passed; nothing happened. I returned to the periscope just in time to see the pitted surface of one of Jupiter's tiny outer satellites sweep past, seemingly only a stone's throw away. In reality we had missed it by a mile or more; yet our terrific speed reduced that distance to a hundredth of a second in time. By so small a margin had we missed ending our journey prematurely, a tangled mass of heated metal, against a pigmy member of the Jovian system, so small as to be visible from Earth only in the very largest telescopes.

Incongruously enough, I roared in half-hysterical laughter. The wave of relief that swept over me reduced me to uselessness for the moment, but Dr. Von Lichten retained the presence of mind to swing the beam of high-frequency waves that actuated the detector ahead of us, thereby preventing the possibility of another such encounter. Then I looked out again, to straighten out our course.

Jupiter layoff to the right, with Ganymede beyond, moving majestically along in its orbit. Now that we had our bearings once more, we could change our course so as to meet it at the far side of its path, heading close to Jupiter on the way. I explained the situation and told the others of my decision. Then we made sure that the gravity screens were in position and the portholes all tight, for it would not do to expose ourselves to Jupiter's attraction at the short distance we would pass it. We agreed that for the rest of the trip two of us would always be present in the engine room, and Dalton and I volunteered for the first shift.

It was not necessary for both of us to watch the instrument board constantly, so I took the first turn. Between us we were to stand an eight-hour watch, during which time we would reach our minimum distance from Jupiter. The realization of that fact kept me constantly alert for the slightest variation in the instruments, but there was none. We continued our rapidly slackening flight, rushing toward our destination, nearing the belted planet around which Ganymede revolves. At the end of four hours Dalton relieved me and I set about recording the latest incidents.

CHAPTER THIRTEEN
Signs of Danger

WE must have been about half a million miles from Jupiter's surface when Dalton remarked:

"The acceleration indicator's a little high."

I walked over to the instrument board for a look. We were slowing down a little too much; the needle had risen two-tenths of a foot per second on the scale.

"No harm in a little deviation like that," I remarked, as I slipped the controlling rheostat into the next notch and resumed my place. In a half-hour more our angling course carried us a hundred and fifty thousand miles closer.

"Acceleration's up again," said Dalton. This time the indicator had risen three tenths of a foot. I again corrected the discrepancy, wondering at the steady increase.

Dalton spoke again. "It's getting hot. The thermometer's up three degrees."

"Probably from the extra heat of the driver," I suggested.

In the next few minutes all the instruments began to misbehave slightly. The gyroscope compass indicated that we were a fraction of a degree off our course, toward Jupiter; the temperature continued to rise; the photo-electric detector went into action with remarkable persistence, shifting our direction about continuously and at random, and the acceleration crept up again.

These disorders were not serious but they were unexpected and disturbing. Furthermore, when I again cut down the acceleration I realized that the sound of the gas had unquestionably diminished from its usual note. The synthium was not overworking; some other force was holding us back! The temperature of the interior rose until we had to shut off the electric heaters; the detector sent us skipping about with alarming frequency, and our course tended more and more toward Jupiter. Could it be that its atmosphere extended as far out as this and that we were encountering its outer limits? That would account for the heat of the *Comet* and the increased retarding.

As we approached our nearest point to Jupiter it became apparent that this was not the explanation. The detector misbehaved so badly that we were forced to shut it off at the risk of a collision, while all the electrical apparatus acted queerly. There were strange noises from the headgear of the air-envelopes, due to the static disturbances broadcast by their receivers. Even without the electric heaters the temperature inside the machine rose steadily; the acceleration continued to increase, and our course had to be constantly corrected to prevent our heading straight for Jupiter.

The simple explanation of these phenomena dawned on me in a burst of comprehension. We were in a strong magnetic field! Nor was I too long in discovering its source. The Earth, three hundred times less massive than Jupiter, has an easily recognized field that has been used for centuries to guide mankind by its effect on the compass needle. In view of Jupiter's great size, was it surprising that it should have a field many times stronger? Given that, the electrical and other phenomena followed as a natural consequence.

"This is about as close as we'll get," announced Dalton from the instrument board. We were just outside the orbit of Io; the magnetic disturbance had reached its height. In a flash of inspiration I saw the answer to the puzzling heat of the satellites. They too experienced Jupiter's strong field; they were doubtless able to conduct electricity as well as the Earth; the vast eddy-currents in their interiors must give rise to high temperatures that could not have otherwise existed.

Ernst and Von Lichten, who presently relieved us, had noted the behavior of the *Comet*, and were considerably upset. But my explanation set their fears at rest and they accepted my prediction that the annoying situation would disappear as we drew past Jupiter.

When my next turn in the pilothouse came, we were moving slowly enough to permit use of the periscope without danger. Ganymede lay to our right, a brilliant, dazzling moon. Beyond and somewhat above was Callisto, smaller and paler. I turned the glass about. The tremendous shadow of Jupiter's dark side hid a generous circle of the sky, bounded on the left by a gigantic crescent. The sun, as always, shone among the countless stars, but it was a shrunken, discouraged orb of day whose face lighted these far-off worlds.

In the distance I could see another celestial body. It was a planet...a planet that men like to think of as the most important spot in the universe...Earth!

I continued to watch through the periscope for the remainder of my turn, between looks at the instrument board. The difficulties from the magnetic field were decreasing rapidly, and we were now nearly half a million miles from Jupiter. There remained about three hundred thousand to cover, which would take the next eighteen hours. Dalton was as delighted as I with the view of the heavens and remarked on the appearance of this or that body from time to time. During his watch, the fifth of Jupiter's moons (in order of discovery) came into view. It was a little globe that revolved close to the surface at an amazingly rapid rate, its tiny disc peeping around the crescent of the giant planet's illuminated surface.

When at length we turned over the engine room to Von Lichten and Ernst and climbed to the living quarters we found Lafourchette cleaning and loading a huge automatic.

"What is that for?" demanded Dalton.

"I am prepared," said Lafourchette, waving the gun dramatically. "I alone had the foresight to bring means of protection. If we are attacked by the Ganymedians it is I who will save you." Dalton snorted.

"A fine attitude for an interplanetary ambassador!" he exclaimed. "What if they should attack us? They must be as big as elephants; they could carry cannons around with them."

"As big as elephants, indeed!" retorted Lafourchette. "Is not their world smaller than the Earth? And will they not be smaller than ourselves in proportion?"

"Not at all, not at all," ejaculated Dalton. "I weighed one hundred and eighty pounds on Earth; here I will weigh only thirty-six pounds. If they are to weigh one hundred and eighty they must be five times as large as I."

"And who says they are to weigh one hundred and eighty pounds?" exclaimed Lafourchette. "They do not fatten themselves like hogs!"

"Certainly they are too intelligent to starve themselves down to your weight," returned Dalton. I felt that the discussion was becoming too personal, so I took a hand.

"What is the use of idle speculation," I asked, "when in a few hours we can see for ourselves what they are like? We must not be surprised if they resemble nothing we have ever seen, I would advise, too, that we be as peaceable as possible with them; for we are here to understand them, not to conquer them."

"Nevertheless I shall have my pistol handy," said Lafourchette.

To prevent further bickering I suggested that we inspect the air-envelopes and have them ready when we wished to leave the machine. We charged the oxygen-producing apparatus of each, tested them for airtightness, adjusted the microphones that were to bring us the sounds from outside, washed the glass of the helmets, and hung them on the well near the airlock. This occupied most of the next eight hours, at the end of which it was time for Lafourchette to take his post at the instruments.

Dalton had stood the last watch with him, so it was my turn; for with only five of us in the crew someone must stand an extra trick occasionally. We took frequent looks through the periscope at Ganymede, now only a few thousand miles away. An unbroken stretch of clouds covered the surface, hiding the configuration of the ground from view. There was no way of knowing what we would find below them; we could not pick a landing-point, so we headed for the center of the disc, hoping to learn something of the terrain after we had passed through the atmosphere.

At the end of the watch our speed was reduced to about three miles per second; we were so close that I decided to remain on duty, for we would soon enter the atmosphere and I preferred to guide the *Comet* to its landing place.

I shut off the driver entirely and let the machine coast along under its own momentum. The cloudbank drew nearer minute by minute; the horizon spread away to right and left and in all directions. An hour passed, and we were less than a thousand miles away. I swung into position the diminutive wings that would serve to steer us like a dirigible through the atmosphere.

As the seconds passed I watched the acceleration indicator for the first sign of any drag. Several times I felt sure that we were slowing down, but the indicator was unmoved. Then at last it crept up, curving into a more rapid rise. I turned the forward wings at a slight angle. The *Comet* swung horizontal with a sharp thrust as they caught the rush of wind, while in the periscope's field the cloudbank wheeled dizzily. I leveled off and headed downward slightly, letting the friction of the air retard us.

Even at this height, which I estimated at a hundred miles, our barometer indicated six millimeters' pressure of atmosphere. On this world, because of the slight pull of gravity, a given volume of air weighed only one-fifth as much as on Earth; consequently the density would increase only one-fifth as fast, as we descended, and we might expect to find an atmosphere about half as dense as the Earth's at the surface.

First Experiences

WE DRIFTED, approaching the cloudbank beneath us and losing headway rapidly. The machine warmed up a little at first, but I kept it high enough so that the thin air would not heat it dangerously. We drew near the clouds, then dipped into their upper limits and were engulfed in a sea of gray-white vapor. It grew darker as the layer above us cut off more and more of the pale sunlight. I wondered whether the mist extended clear to the ground. If so we might suddenly crash into a mountain. I had about decided to head up again until we stopped, when we burst through the under side of the clouds and Ganymede's surface lay in a vast panorama below us. On all sides, as far as I could see in the gathering darkness, lay a body of water—a dark forbidding sea. There was no guessing at its depth or extent, but at least it offered a perfect landing place. I nosed down more steeply, opening the gravity screen a crack to counteract the buoyancy of our weightless spaceship.

We fell at a steep angle toward the water. It became increasingly difficult to see and I wondered at the darkness. We were well below the clouds; the light should be as strong here as at their level. I recalled my view of the heavens several hours before; the thin crescent of Jupiter, the sun close by, Ganymede almost opposite—of course! An eclipse! The satellite passed into Jupiter's great shadow for a few hours once in each revolution with the unvarying regularity of all celestial things, and this fact had helped navigators to determine the time and locate their position for years. We had chosen the hour of eclipse to arrive; the face of the sun was being rapidly obscured by Jupiter, and unless we landed soon we would find ourselves in total darkness.

I hastened our descent as much as possible. When we were within a few yards of the water, I leveled out, opened the gravity screens wider, and we settled like a seaplane on the waves, skipping over their crests as we lost speed, then coming to rest on the long smooth swell just as the satellite was shrouded in darkness.

Despite the fact that for a few hours there would be nothing to see, we donned our air-envelopes with one accord and hastened outside the ship, lighting our way with pocket flash lamps. The *Comet* rested easily on the surface of the water, rising and falling with the long lazy swell. All about us was the intense blackness of a cloudy night, lighted by neither moon nor stars. The waves were unruffled by the slightest breeze. We walked from end to end of the slippery hull, glad for even this liberty.

Lafourchette, eager to begin gathering data on Ganymede's weather conditions, had brought a thermometer , which he fastened to a string and dropped into the forbidding water. Dr. Von Lichten took samples of it for analysis and to determine whether it was fit to drink. Of course, under no circumstances would we touch it until it had been boiled, but we would be glad of the opportunity to recharge our tanks and insure an ample supply for the return journey.

A shout of laughter from Dalton attracted our attention. Lafourchette was staring in dismay at the end of his string, from which the thermometer had been neatly bitten.

"Our friend has taken to fishing!" roared Dalton.

"The monster!" stormed Lafourchette. "The unspeakable pig, to swallow my best thermometer! I hope he gets indigestion!"

Our merriment at his expense was tinged with other reflections, however. This positive indication that the little world harbored living creatures was gratifying; but what sort of fearless denizens dwelt beneath the surface of this murky sea? And what untamed terrors might inhabit the land, beside the people we had come to seek? The same vague doubts lingered in the minds of all of us, instinctively drawing us together as though for protection. The inky darkness was not conducive to high spirits, and presently we retired below to await the termination of the eclipse. Before permitting us to enter, Dr. Von Lichten insisted on spraying the air-envelopes with disinfectant in order to kill any germs that might have settled on them. This was a tedious procedure, but wise, for we had no knowledge of the bacteria of Ganymede.

WHEN the first streak of gray appeared overhead we got the *Comet* under way skimming above the water in search of the shoreline. Since we had no idea which way to turn, we arbitrarily chose the north, and held our course for upwards of an hour before I spied a hazy line on the horizon, which quickly resolved itself into a small island. We steered close to it, flying low, but a few minutes' scrutiny sufficed to show that it was a barren stump of rock, a volcanic peak upthrust from the ocean bed. As we continued our way we sighted another, larger, and still another. Presently we were skimming over a maze of islets of increasing size, some covered with dark mossy vegetation. Excited comments burst from the scientists peering through the forward portholes.

Suddenly Lafourchette uttered a shout, pointing ahead of us.

"Another thermometer-eater?" asked Dalton.

"No!" cried Lafourchette. "A huge bird! A flying monster! It's coming toward us. It's going to attack us!"

I turned my periscope and saw an immense, ungainly creature in the act of alighting on our prow. It suggested somewhat a monoplane come to life and endowed with savage ferocity. There was a long gray-black body, torpedo-shaped and scaly, beginning in a prodigious mouth armed with double rows of dagger-like teeth and extending without any semblance of neck to a four-vaned tail, like that of an airplane. Underneath were four stubby legs with which the creature tried vainly to gain a foothold on the surface of our machine, thrashing its twenty-foot wings madly. Spying the periscope, it made a rush for the projecting tube, jaws agape. I cringed from the spectacle of that huge maw seemingly bent on swallowing me alive. The *Comet* quivered at the impact of the gigantic body as it tried to wrench the periscope loose. Then, angered at its inability to dent the shining surface, it circled about us, above and below, keeping pace with our swift flight. I put on more speed and the creature dropped behind, plunging into the blazing gas-discharge. We saw no more of it. Without a doubt it had been incinerated alive by the terrific heat.

"Whew!" exclaimed Dalton. "I hope that wasn't the reception committee of the Ganymedians!" For my part, however, his jest fell on unreceptive ears; the spectacle of that horrible mouth was too fresh in my memory.

We flew on in silence for another fifteen minutes. The islands became larger and more frequent, while in the distance ahead of us appeared a dim line of unbroken shore extending to the horizon. I slowed the machine down, watching for signs of civilized life. Presently I sighted a break in the dark vegetation on one of the large islands near the shore, a patch of lighter color. Steering closer it resolved itself into rows of dwellings of some sort, nearly circular as seen from above and apparently built of stone. Without question it was a village, designed by intelligent, reasoning minds. I headed for it, shutting off the power and dropping into the water close to the nearest of the stone buildings. The tractor drifted toward land, grounding gently on a shelving muddy beach.

No one made the first move to go outside. We remained at our vantagepoints, I looking through the periscope and the others out the windows. There was apparently no doorway to the building before us; it presented a regular stone wall, roughly circular and pierced here and there by narrow openings suggesting the windows of medieval castles. The inhabitants, if there were any, were either unaware of our arrival or suspicious of us. We waited some time for them to put in an appearance, but saw nothing.

"Shall we go outside?" asked Ernst at length. "It may be that the creatures take the *Comet* for some sort of animal."

His suggestion appeared logical. We put on our envelopes and went out, looking warily around for signs of other flying creatures, I led the way, stepping gingerly onto the oozing beach, and we approached the stone building. We were within ten yards of it when we saw an unmistakable movement behind one of the window-like apertures. The next instant there was a hair-raising shriek, followed by a bedlam of indescribable sounds, suggesting the cries of a multitude of beasts in awful torment.

"Stand still," directed Ernst. "We'll only alarm them by moving. Perhaps if we wait they'll come out."

The noises died down gradually, giving place to low rumbles now and then, interspersed with another note—inarticulate, yet with a rising inflection, as if in question.

"They're talking it over," said Ernst in a stage whisper. We continued to stand motionless while the rumbling went on. Suddenly we saw the ground apparently rising up in front of one of the buildings. A trap door leading underground was being pushed open from beneath. It rose to a vertical position, and from behind it stepped a Ganymedian!

CHAPTER FOURTEEN
A Reception Committee

THERE could be no doubt that the creature standing before us was a rational being despite its fantastic appearance. A walking carrot—a fish on stilts—but no simile can describe the apparition that met our astonished gaze. On the large end of the body, which faced toward us, a broad, wicked mouth and two enormous eyes represented a face that, nevertheless, lacked any suggestion of a nose. The head joined directly to a tapering body, slanted downward toward the rear. Two pairs of legs as poorly matched as those of a giraffe raised the creature on skinny supports to a height of five feet at its forward end. Behind the head, where there should have been a neck and shoulders, projected something like a pair of arms, jointed at the center and again near the ends. Here they divided into tentacle-like fingers several inches in length. The arms must have measured fully four feet from body to tip. Save for a belt about its midsection the creature was unprotected by clothing or fur, exposing a shiny slate-gray skin to the weather. In its left "hand" it carried a weapon, which I judged to be a sort of rifle. It consisted of a bright metal tube, a couple of feet long, fastened to a cylindrical chamber several inches in diameter. The creature grasped the weapon in its skinny tentacles, half-raising it as though in doubt whether to turn it on us.

Ernst slowly raised his hands over his head in a gesture of peace, but the Ganymedian evidently did not understand, for it leveled the weapon. Lafourchette reached for his pistol, but he was too slow; the barrel was trained on him in the twinkling of an eye, there was a slight *pop,* and a missile struck his envelope squarely at his chest. He was uninjured, though startled, and fired his automatic wildly into the air. At the noise the Ganymedian disappeared behind his trap door, slamming it shut, while a chorus of shrieks filled the air.

"Now you've done it!" stormed Dalton. "They'll never come out after that."

But we had not seen the last of the Ganymedians. On all sides of us trap doors opened, pouring forth creatures armed with weapons like that of the first. They formed a semicircle, and at a signal from one, fired a volley of shots. Missiles struck our envelopes, our helmets and the ground about us in a perfect hail. They were unable to penetrate our thick covering, though a number of them stuck in the fabric until we fairly bristled. Then abruptly the fusillade ceased and the Ganymedians fled to their stone dwellings.

"What's to be done?" I asked.

"I suggest we return to the *Comet* and talk it over," said Ernst.

Accordingly we left the hooting Ganymedians and returned to our ship. Dr. Von Lichten picked the darts off our envelopes before permitting us to remove them, saving a few for examination.

"Poisoned, perhaps," he said by way of explanation. We later discovered this to be true. The guns were glorified blowguns, fired by compressed air stored in the cylinders attached to them.

Gathered once more in our living quarters, we considered how to make our peaceable intentions known. Dalton immediately took Lafourchette to task for firing his gun and the two had little to offer in the way of constructive suggestions. It was Ernst who first saw through the attitude of the Ganymedians.

"Let us reason from their point of view," he said. "Suppose it was they who had come to Earth. Knowing nothing of its geography, where would they land? In the most conspicuous place— the largest body of water, or the greatest plain. Now suppose that, having landed there, they went to the nearest settlement. What would they find? A fishing village, or a country town—certainly not the home of our scientists. That is exactly what we have done; we have met with a group of uneducated, suspicious beings to whom we are outlandish and frightful. What more natural than that they should fear us? It is not here that we shall find those who have tried to communicate with us; we must seek a larger settlement, a civilized settlement perhaps."

Without further ado we left the settlement by the water and turned inland. As before, I steered while the others stationed themselves at the windows armed with binoculars. We swept back and forth in a zigzag course covering a strip of land a hundred miles wide. The vegetation gradually lost its dark color; acquiring the green shade of that on Earth, and there were taller plants, sometimes reaching a height of a hundred feet. There were many small creatures in the air. They might have been birds, though they did not come close enough to be seen clearly.

Presently Ernst, who was stationed on the left side, called out:

"Here's another of those flying animals."

"Steer away from it!" exclaimed Lafourchette. "I have seen enough of them to satisfy me."

"No, steer closer," said Ernst. "This one is different. Perhaps—yes it is! It's a flying machine."

"A flying machine!" repeated Dalton and Lafourchette in chorus. They rushed to Ernst's window and quickly verified his statement. "Yes, it is!"

I picked up the machine in the periscope and swung after it, keeping pace. The pilot must have sighted us, for he increased his speed, but I was easily able to follow him. I remained several miles behind, not wishing to alarm him, but he seemed determined to shake us off. He executed a number of maneuvers, diving as though to land, then climbing to a height of several miles, I followed him with ease, however, and he presently gave up the attempt, heading off in a different direction and keeping steadily on this new course.

As I swung in behind him the radio sets of our air envelopes began to speak—high pitched jerky sounds, resembling somewhat the signals of our International code. I surmised that the plane ahead was reporting our appearance by some kind of wireless. Then the pilot slowed down to barely fifty miles per hour and traveled along at an altitude of a few thousand feet.

Fifteen minutes or so later, Dalton reported the appearance of a second machine on our right. It had crept up behind us and was now keeping pace a thousand feet or so away. Presently another appeared, and another. Looking back I saw a huge fleet overhauling us, spreading out around us, until we were surrounded on all sides, above and below, ahead and behind. Whichever way we looked, there was a vast throng of planes—hundreds of them, following us in a silent convoy. There was no sign from them; they kept their distance in perfect formation. We could not guess their intentions. There was not a hostile move from any of them. The members of our party fell to discussing them.

"Perhaps it's a reception committee," suggested Dalton. "They're escorting us to a landing place."

"But then why are there so many of them?" inquired Lafourchette.

"An accomplishment as great as ours deserves a big reception," returned Dalton.

However, our wondering was cut short. In the distance a pall of smoke appeared, surrounded by circular buildings like those in the waterside village. We were approaching a Ganymedian city. Our convoy drew in closer, descending slowly. It was obviously their wish that we should land. As we drew closer to the city our speed was further reduced; the planes below us withdrew, those above came closer, and those on our flank formed a circle about us, wheeling about as though to cut off our escape in any direction. We were being forced toward a large field, about which were more planes, and large buildings resembling hangars.

We descended, perforce. Half the machines followed suit, surrounding us in a close circle, while the others remained aloft, forming a moving dome over our heads. From one of those on the ground appeared several four-legged Ganymedians who approached the *Comet* boldly and peered into the windows, waving their tentacle-like arms.

"They want us to come out," said Ernst. We donned our envelopes and left the machine through the airlock, Lafourchette carrying his gun despite Dalton's admonitions. The Ganymedians stepped back, forming, a semicircle about the airlock, obviously inviting us to descend to the ground. We closed the air lock and jumped down—not without some misgivings. But the creatures seemed friendly enough, waving their arms and giving voice to questioning hoots. One of their number advanced and extended his arms in a reassuring gesture. Ernst stepped forward to meet him, and endeavored by pantomimic gestures to show our peaceable intentions. I was intent on watching him, and did not notice for a moment that the passengers of the other planes had come out and were slowly advancing toward us. Then Von Lichten uttered a shout:

"Look out behind!"

Trapped!

BUT he was too late. A dozen of the skinny creatures had climbed over the *Comet* and as we turned they jumped upon us, pinning us to the ground. Before we realized what had happened we were overwhelmed by the crowd; strong metal cords were fastened about our aims and legs, and we were bound, helpless prisoners. Amid shrieks of anger we were picked up bodily and carried to the nearest plane, thrown roughly into a dark compartment and locked in. The plane took off with a rush, bound we knew not where.

I strained at my bonds, but it was useless. The darkness was pitchy; I could not tell where the rest were, or whether they were all in the same plane. I called softly:

"Ernst!"

"Here," came the whispered response.

"Are we all here?" I asked. Four whispers assented. At least we were not divided.

"What does all this mean?" I asked.

"They seem to take us for enemies," said Ernst.

"What shall we do?" asked Dalton.

"Nothing now," said Ernst. "Wait until we can see."

As we spoke the plane landed with a light jar, the compartment was opened, and we were carried out one at a time onto a flat room. We appeared to be in the midst of the large city, on top of one of the buildings; but I had time for only a fleeting glance before I was bundled with the others onto a platform, which descended swiftly into the depths of the building. We must have been carried down a hundred feet or more when the platform came to a stop and we were carried into a small room with stone walls.

It was devoid of furniture and had only one window, a tiny slit near the ceiling. Beyond a doubt we were in a prison cell.

Our captors removed the metal cords from our hands and feet, and departed, closing a massive stone door behind them.

"Well," said Dalton explosively, "what do you make of this?"

"We are prisoners," said Lafourchette dejectedly. "We have come four hundred million miles to make friends with them, and they treat us like invaders."

"That's not the point," said Ernst. "We have aroused their anger in some way. We must explain the situation to them and gain their confidence."

"What do you suggest?" I asked.

"I believe they will presently return to feed us and examine us," said Ernst. "I shall try to communicate with them, tell them who we are and where we are from. Perhaps we resemble some other race that inhabits this globe, with whom they are at war. But when they know that we come from the Earth they cannot fail to realize their mistake, and welcome us accordingly."

"And if they do not—" said Lafourchette, producing his gun.

"No!" exclaimed Ernst. "We must not antagonize them in any way. That will only confirm their suspicions of us."

"I should prefer to return to the *Comet* and leave this inhospitable race," said Lafourchette.

"Don't be discouraged," said Ernst. "We have come a long way for the opportunity to meet these creatures. Dr. Forscher would be disappointed in us if we failed to reach an understanding with them."

I admired the man's levelheaded courage. In spite of the alarming turn of affairs he had not lost sight of the purpose of the expedition. His attitude buoyed our spirits greatly, and we looked forward eagerly to the return of our captors.

To pass the time, we examined the walls of our cell. They were built of heavy blocks of a kind of granite and there was not a flaw anywhere. It was obvious that escape from the cell was out of the question. I hoisted Lafourchette to my shoulders and he examined the window. It was about two feet high and a little over a foot wide. The blocks were joined together by a tongue and groove in each, neatly polished to a perfect fit. Several heavy bars of metal ran crosswise, blocking the opening effectively. Lafourchette reported that he could see a large circular park outside, surrounded by tall buildings of similar shape. Evidently this circular form was the predominant note of their architecture, just as man-made buildings are almost universally rectangular.

We heard footsteps beyond the door, and presently it swung open, admitting a number of Ganymedians. They were without clothing as usual, and each was armed with a mechanical blowgun shooting poisoned darts. One of them advanced and, singling out Ernst, took him to the opposite corner of the cell, where they began a close examination of him. They peered through his helmet and tried to remove it, but without success. Apparently they were puzzled, for they uttered hoots of amazement and stopped from time to time to raise their arms and move their fingers rapidly. I perceived that this was their method of conversation; their language consisted of finger-signs, like those of deaf mutes. They searched Ernst closely for weapons, turned him about, plucked at the heavy envelope, and subjected him to an intense scrutiny. When they had finished they led him back to the rest of us, and took Dalton next. Perceiving that each of us was to be similarly searched, I whispered to Lafourchette:

"Hide your gun; they'll seize it if they find it."

He withdrew behind the rest of us and concealed the gun in the corner of the room. The movement attracted the attention of our examiners, and they stared at us searchingly for a moment, but seeing nothing wrong they finished their scrutiny of Dalton. Lafourchette came next, and to our relief they had not noticed that he carried the gun when we were captured. However, they realized that the heavy envelope was not his skin, and motioned him to remove it. He refused, and one of them produced a sharp knife-like instrument. Dr. Von Lichten cried out in protest and started forward, but he was immediately seized and held. We were forced to watch while the Ganymedians slashed open Lafourchette's envelope and clothing. He winced as the knife-blade scratched his skin, and the Ganymedians emitted howls of amusement.

"This has gone far enough," growled Dalton, and with a swift movement he picked up the gun, uttering a yell that attracted the attention of the Ganymedians. The wielder of the knife drew back his arm to throw, and Dalton pulled the trigger. The gun roared; the smoke cleared, and the knife-thrower lay dead on the floor. The others fled in terror, slamming the door behind them. We heard the bolt snap into place and we were alone once more.

"Are you hurt?" demanded Von Lichten of Lafourchette.

"Not at all," replied the latter. "A mere scratch; but the devils have ripped my envelope."

Dr. Von Lichten examined his cut, from which blood trickled.

"If only I had my medicine case," he exclaimed. "An open wound, in this strange atmosphere—there is danger of infection."

"Do not worry," said Lafourchette. "I shall be all right, I am only sorry that it was necessary to shoot. They will never forgive us."

"I fear you are right," said Ernst. "However, let us learn what we can from this dead creature."

We dragged the Ganymedian to the light beneath the window, and Dr. Von Lichten set about examining the body. I possessed myself of the creature's blowgun and knife and stood back. Corpses, human or otherwise, have never had much attraction for me.

The doctor brought to light several interesting features of the physical nature of the Ganymedians. Each hand had six fingers of nearly equal size, about eight inches long. There were five joints in each, which were capable of bending in both directions, enabling the hand to close either forward or backward. There were likewise six toes (if they may be called such) on each foot, but with only one joint in each, and entirely covered with a scaly substance, instead of the nail at the tip of the corresponding human members. The skin of the creatures was likewise scaly and glistened like that of a fish.

Prying open the mouth, the doctor discovered that there was no tongue, explaining the lack of an articulate language among the creatures. Between the head and shoulders were tiny openings that evidently served as ears, though their form suggested that they might be remnants of what had been gills in prehistoric times. The striking resemblance of many physical characteristics to those of water creatures of the Earth pointed to the possibility that they were akin to that family, having perhaps emerged from their abode in the ocean to evolve into intelligent creatures on land.

CHAPTER FIFTEEN
A Race with Death

AFTER a time our attention was attracted by a commotion outside our window, as of the gathering of a throng of people. I hoisted Lafourchette to my shoulders again, and he reported that this was indeed the "They are gathering from all sides," he reported. "They shout; they gesticulate; they point toward this building, toward our cell. They seem exceedingly angry. Some are bringing tree-trunks, or logs; they pile them in the center of the great circle. Now they are setting fire to them. They are building a bonfire. They dance about it, shouting with rage; still they point to our cell. Can it be that the bonfire is for us—that they intend to burn us alive?"

"Let them try!" exclaimed Dalton. "As long as we have this gun they'll have a fine time getting us out."

However, our defense was not to be as easy as that. Presently Lafourchette reported:

"They are setting fire to something on the end of a stick. It burns with a blue flame. Now they are approaching our window with the stick. There is a lump of something yellow on the end of the stick; it burns dully, with heavy fumes. It's sulfur! They are going to asphyxiate us with burning sulfur! Then they will carry us to the bonfire…"

"Give me the gun!" exclaimed Dalton. "Let me up there. I'll stop them!" He climbed to the window and leveled the automatic at the approaching throng. The gun barked, and there was a shout of dismay from outside.

"They're running away," said Dalton. "That'll teach them not to monkey with us…"

But they were not through yet. The crowd withdrew to a respectful distance, taking with them the sulfur torch. Presently some of them carried it out of our view, and we wondered apprehensively what they were up to. We heard, faintly, the tramp of feet above us, and shortly there was a choking whiff of sulfur dioxide from the window. Dalton pressed his face against the bars, and reported:

"They are hanging the torch from a rope, just above the window. The fumes are heavier than air, and some of them drift into the cell. It'll take longer that way, but they'll get us eventually!"

He climbed down, and we faced one another in despair.

"I'm afraid this is the end," said Ernst. "If only—"

The door grated open, its lock twisted and cherry red with heat. Beyond it stood a Ganymedian—a strange Ganymedian. His attitude bespoke friendliness, not ferocity. As we surveyed him we noted that the bestiality that stamped the features of our captors was lacking; his massive head and kindly eyes indicated a superior order of intelligence. Somehow, we felt this creature was our ally.

He carried a peculiar looking instrument, whose lingering glow indicated that it had been used to melt the bolt of our cell door. At its tip was a tiny glowing point that was raised to a white heat, in some manner, electrically or chemically. Back of this was a parabolic mirror, which caught the emitted energy and focused it at a point a few feet beyond the instrument. The focus could be shifted forward or back by sliding the mirror along the handle. It served the purpose of a blowtorch, and from the neatness with which it had severed the steel lock, an efficient one.

THE Ganymedian motioned us to come out of the cell. The sulfurous fumes left us no choice but to obey, so we followed him into the corridor. We were led through a series of passages to the far side of the building, where a barred window blocked our path. Our guide neatly clipped off the bars with his torch and we dropped to the ground outside. A row of circular buildings confronted us, beyond which was another open park. We quickly made our way there and saw before us a machine as unlike those we had encountered as our guide was unlike the hostile crowd that had imprisoned us. It gave every evidence of being tremendously speedy, yet withal it was large and roomy.

We ran for it at a signal from the Ganymedian. We had covered half the distance when a shout announced the discovery of our escape. The crowd rushed in hot pursuit, firing darts. Dalton whirled and emptied the magazine of the automatic, accounting for four, while I stretched another on the ground with the dead

Ganymedian's airgun. Then we reached the machine and climbed aboard through a lowered door, which clanged shut behind us. The plane shot into the air with a silent rush, while the enraged crowd below us fired futile missiles and waved their arms in the air.

From external appearances the machine bore little resemblance to man-made machines. To be sure there were similarities here and there; the ship had wings and was shaped in general like the familiar type of monoplane. But inside, things were bewilderingly different. There were no seats; the four-legged Ganymedians squatted on their hind legs in the fashion of earthly quadrupeds. The controls were likewise unfamiliar—a dial here, a lever there, and nothing commensurate with the size and power of the machine. I judged it to be controlled by compressed air or electricity. Strangest of all was the motor. It aroused my interest, and lacking the ability to question the crew I determined to discover as much of its mechanism as I could.

To begin with, there were no cylinders, and this set me to wondering about its source of power. I quickly discovered an odor and identified it as some member of the hydrocarbon group, from which gasoline springs. Yet instead of being fed into a cylinder, compressed by the upstroke of a piston and fired by an electric spark, it apparently burned continuously in a small chamber, where the gas was maintained under pressure and fed into a set of rotating vanes. It was a gasoline turbine—the dream of internal combustion engineers!

The plane was heading away from the ocean, toward the area of the satellite that is never lighted by Jupiter. The clouds thinned rapidly, and below them we could see the ground, bare for the most part—with clumps of desert vegetation here and there. These grew more and more sparse, finally disappearing altogether, and we flew over a vast waste of sand. Overhead the stars shone weakly, pushing their faint rays through the pale sunlight. Jupiter's great body, its darkened side turned toward us, sank lower and lower, finally disappearing below the horizon. The sun followed him a few moments later as, we crossed to the backside of the satellite.

In the darkened heavens Callisto and the four tiny outer satellites threw a ghostly moonlight on the swift panorama of the desert. We were flying low now, yet the brilliance of the starlit sky showed that the air about us was thin and dry. The great pull of Jupiter—four thousand times stronger than that of the moon, even at this distance—had raised a permanent tide in both the air and water, leaving the outer side of the satellite with little atmospheric covering and no moisture to speak of. Dr. Forscher had predicted a cloudless region on Ganymede; we saw now the reason for its existence.

The plane suddenly slackened its pace and began to descend. Looking ahead we saw the lights of a tremendous city, extending for miles in all directions. Tall cylindrical buildings marked a magnificent skyline above which many small planes scurried in a bustle of busy traffic. As we approached, the air was cleared to make a pathway for us; and we settled gracefully to the top of one of the nearby buildings. An elevator waited to carry us to one of the lower floors, where we were escorted to a large circular room.

It contained little furniture—a strange looking table, a carpet, and a few bizarre cushions in lieu of chairs. The windows were without glass, for the temperature on this world varied but little and there was no need for protection against the weather. A number of large globes filled the room with a soft heatless glow resembling intensified moonlight, in which the blue shades of the room were brought out distinctly.

The Story of a Destiny

OUR guides left, save one, who turned to us and pointed to his mouth with a questioning hoot, I surmised he was asking whether we were hungry, and responded to his gesture vigorously. He disappeared, and Dr. Von Lichten observed: "There's no telling what sort of food he'll bring us. We'd best be careful."

"I'm so hungry I could eat a tree," said Dalton.

"In order to do so you'll have to take off your helmet, my friend," said the Doctor. "It's risky; remember that."

"Going without food and water is more than risky, it's certain death," retorted Dalton. "Our oxygen won't hold out much longer, and we can't recharge the apparatus. I'm for taking the envelopes off…" Suiting his action to the word, he removed his helmet and stripped off the flexible covering. The rest of us followed suit with some hesitation. Dr. Von Lichten last of all. However, there was no use trying to refute the logic of Dalton's statements, and we felt rather secure, since Lafourchette's ripped envelope had apparently caused him no discomfort.

Presently our rescuer reappeared with several metal platters bearing food. It was entirely unfamiliar, but appeared to consist for the most part of raw vegetables and fruits of some kind. If any food on this world would be safe for us, edible planets probably had the best chance, so we decided to take a chance. After a cautious nibble or two we consumed the whole meal with great relish. A container of water accompanied it, and was emptied in short order. It had a queer fishy taste but we didn't mind it. Then we stretched out on the rug for a nap. The Ganymedian climate was quite cold, and we found it necessary to wrap the carpet around ourselves, but otherwise we slept comfortably for several hours.

We were awakened by the reappearance of the friendly Ganymedian, who seemed much taken aback at the spectacle of the five of us unconscious on the floor. He seemed quite relieved, however, when we sat up and waved to him, but he was obviously puzzled. It occurred to me that perhaps sleep was unknown to him. Even some terrestrial creatures are known to spend their entire lives awake.

He brought with him several sheets of greenish, parchment-like paper, and a pencil that deserved the name of "lead-pencil" more literally than ours, for it consisted of a stick of lead sharpened to a point. With these writing materials he seated himself at the table and motioned us to do likewise. We gathered around, sitting on the cushions, and watched. He handed the pencil and paper to Ernst, pointed to him, and hooted in evident interrogation. Ernst wrote, "Man," and pointed to each of us in turn. Then the Ganymedian pointed to Ernst again, and hooted once more. Ernst wrote his name, then that of each of us, indicating to whom the names belonged.

From names he progressed to parts of the body, objects in the room, and other things on Ganymede, sketching them at times to make himself clear. The Ganymedian exhibited a remarkable aptitude for understanding the sketches and the words, and it took but a short time for him to learn to write brief sentences in English. For the sake of simplicity Ernst spelled words phonetically and gave all the verbs regular endings, writing "hed" for head, "fut" for foot, "runed" for ran, and so forth. The language thus evolved was clumsy, but it served the purpose of a means of communication, which was all that was required.

Then they took up some simple arithmetic, writing out the Arabic numerals. A curious yet nevertheless natural circumstance arose in connection with this. Our number 10 represented 12 to the Ganymedian. The explanation of this was easily seen when we remembered that there were twelve fingers on their hands. When mankind first learned to count, he used his fingers as the base of his system of numbers.

When Ernst had counted up to ten he started over again, counting "ten and one, ten and two," and so on, indicating the ten by a digit in the second column. When a hundred was reached, being ten times ten, he added a third column. The Ganymedians counted right up to twelve in the first column, and the figure 10 represented twelve; 11, twelve and one. 100 means twelve times twelve, or one hundred and forty-four in our system.

Another difference between our physical makeup and that of the Ganymedians appeared when we tried to name the colors of the spectrum. The four-legged scientist wanted to assign the adjective "black" to things that appeared red or orange to us, while he could distinguish differences above violet that were invisible to our eyes. This meant simply that the range of wavelengths that affect the human retina was slightly lower than the corresponding limits of visibility to the Ganymedian eye,

We spent several weeks in building up a vocabulary that the Ganymedian could understand. We made no attempt to develop a spoken language, since the Ganymedians could not speak, and we could not learn their finger-language readily; but with the use of the table of words we had recorded we were able to write intelligible messages at the end of this time.

At length we were in a position to exchange ideas with considerable facility. Then the Ganymedian began to ask us questions about ourselves, where we had come from, how we had happened to land in the city near the ocean, and the details of our capture. When we had satisfied his curiosity, he explained the situation on his planet to us in some detail. For or the sake of clarity I will summarize his statements in plain English. What he told us was essentially as follows:

"ON GANYMEDE, as on Earth, life began in the sea. The land at that time was barren and the air unbreathable for lack of oxygen. Certain forms of fish developed the knack of gliding above the surface on their enlarged lateral fins, much as the flying fish of the Earth; and when plant life appeared on the land to provide food and oxygen in the air, they became amphibious, living both on land and in the water. Certain of these flying amphibians eventually came to live on the ground entirely, and gradually lost the ability to fly; while others soared in the air and preyed on weaker creatures. You met one of these amphibians shortly after you arrived here; there are many like them, some still wild, some, however, we managed to tame to the use of our race.

"My own people are the descendants of that species that lived on the ground, surviving by its superior cunning rather than relying on brute strength. They became civilized, learned to cooperate with one another, and established a democratic government. As our knowledge advanced, we developed industries; a class of laborers appeared to work for wages under the control of the capitalists. Unfortunately complications developed from this situation. The laborers were dissatisfied with their lot. There was unemployment now and then, and the industries were run with a philosophy of producing goods cheaply and selling at high prices, with no regard to the quality of products.

"This finally led to the seizure of the government by the workers, but in their poorly educated state they were unable to manage it, and chaos resulted. Finally a brilliant student of economics gathered around him a following of intelligent people. They ousted the laborers from their control, and set up a dictatorship. Under his regime, those that followed our civilization advanced by leaps and bounds. Institutions of learning were established, and the study of science assumed an important place in our order of things. More and more of the laws of nature were discovered; the scientists published their discoveries for the benefit of the world, and the race grew prosperous.

"However, it seems that the nature of our people is to scoff at that which they do not understand. Scientists were well paid for their work in those days, but the working class and middle class could not see the practical value of theorizing about chemistry, physics, astronomy, and the like. They became dissatisfied, and threatened to confiscate the pay of the scientific class and force them into exile if they did not turn their efforts to tasks that would result in the immediate enriching of the world. The scientists gave little heed to the mutterings of the multitudes, until one day they rose in open revolt. The rebellion was quelled, but it became apparent that the rule of the intelligent students of science, economics, and politics was threatened.

"The final crisis was brought about by an experiment with which you are doubtless familiar. I refer to the firing of projectiles at the planets of the solar system in an effort to elicit a response and so determine whether or not they were inhabited. This experiment was misunderstood by the lay populace, and a rumor circulated that the rulers were trying to bring people from other planets to keep the masses in subjugation. A bloody war resulted, in which the ruling class was driven from the land into this desert that covers almost the entire half of Ganymede that turns away from Jupiter.

"Many of them died of thirst and starvation, but a number escaped to the spot on which this city now stands, and succeeded in recovering from the air enough hydrogen, oxygen, and nitrogen to irrigate a patch of the desert, fertilize it, and raise food. With the aid of their scientific knowledge they built this city, supplied it with water and plant-food, and now a race of a million people flourishes, advancing their civilization and adding to their knowledge.

"MEANWHILE the remaining classes of the population around the ocean have carried on their former form of democratic government, and have reverted to their old form of cutthroat competition. The government is run by the workers and manufacturers, aiming as always at selfish profiteering. They lay waste the forests; mine coal and burn it without regard to the available supply; release mineral oils and gases with reckless abandon. In a few generations there will be no more natural fuel on the planet unless they are stopped. They make use of the inventions our scientists had developed before they drove us out, but there is no progress among them at present. Every student, research worker, and inventor has been exiled.

"Realizing that they will destroy the planet in their greed if we do not intervene. We have tried several times to conquer them and reestablish ourselves as their rulers, but without success. They have defeated us—in spite of our scientific knowledge—through sheer force of numbers. For this reason we are now seeking means of raising a large army equipped with the most deadly instruments of warfare we can devise. Fully a third of our number is trained to military service, only the aged, the very young, and the scientific geniuses being excepted.

"Now that you are acquainted with the state of affairs on Ganymede, you will realize our need for help. When the news of your arrival and capture was reported by one of our spies, the machine in which you were brought to our city was immediately dispatched and we rescued you, hoping that you might consent to send men from the Earth to assist us in capturing the land about the ocean and regaining our rightful place as its owners."

THE five of us read the message of the Ganymedian in silence. When we had finished, we looked at one another in amazement.

"The proposal is ridiculous!" exclaimed Lafourchette. "The outrageous presumption of the creature, to suppose that we will supply him with men and arms from Earth, to interfere in a war that does not concern us or the people of Earth in the least!"

"Softly," cautioned Ernst. "I would suggest that we consider the proposal, without committing ourselves definitely. Remember, we must have the help of these people in the desert to get the *Comet* back."

He took the pencil and a sheet of paper and wrote:

"We appreciate your situation and sympathize deeply with you. We ourselves will be willing to help you to the utmost, but we must of course return to Earth, obtain permission of its governments, and enlist the necessary men, to say nothing of building the machines to transport them. The first thing to be done, therefore, is to recapture our space-flyer, the *Comet*, which still rests in the city where we were captured."

"I understand that," replied the Ganymedian. "Your acceptance of my proposal is most gratifying. Let us now consider means of recapturing your flyer."

He explained to us that there were many difficulties involved. To begin with, no airplane was permitted to land on any flying field on Ganymede unless it bore a license number issued by the government. Furthermore, each field had a particular password, which was changed from day to day. These measures, he told us, had been adopted to prevent the landing of enemy planes. In short, a landing could only be effected by force, and in view of our escape, the *Comet* would doubtless be heavily guarded. A surprise attack would be necessary.

"I noticed," he said further, "that one of your number made effective use of a weapon that is strange to us. I mean that blunt instrument carried in the hand, which literally exploded with violence and dropped our pursuers in their tracks. If we had a number of those, it would be comparatively easy to drive off the guards and reach the *Comet.*"

"You mean the gun," wrote Ernst. "They are not hard to make if you have the necessary tools and materials."

"We have excellent machinists," replied the Ganymedian. "You need only give us the principle by which it kills. We will attend to the rest."

CHAPTER SIXTEEN
A Mutual Discovery

WITH Dalton's help, Ernst explained the construction of the gun. The formula for black powder presented difficulties, for it was necessary to first explain something of our system of chemical notation. The first two ingredients, sulfur and carbon, were easily named, but the third and most important, nitre (potassium nitrate), was not easy to describe. However, by naming its characteristics Dalton learned that the substance was well known and used by the

Ganymedians, who had found deposits of it in the desert. The scientist wished to take Lafourchette's automatic as a model, but we demurred, as we felt safer with it in our possession.

It was a queer anomaly that although the Ganymedians were able to shoot projectiles hundreds of millions of miles into space, they had missed altogether the application of explosives to firearms. The reason we never discovered.

"It will take until the next rising of the sun to make the guns," the Ganymedian wrote. "At that time we will be prepared to attempt the capture of the *Comet.*"

It now lacked some thirty hours of sunrise, during which we had nothing to do. We obtained the permission of the Ganymedian to explore the city, and he gave us a map so that we might find our way around. We took with us the list of words we had compiled so that we might ask questions from time to time, and we were given letters of introduction explaining whom we were.

Armed with these documents we set out. The city presented many interesting sights and not a few surprises. The first thing that struck our attention was the fact that there was no vehicular traffic on the streets. Overhead the air was full of flying machines of all sizes and types that served the purposes of transportation. These landed on and departed from the roofs of the buildings, never descending to the level of the streets. Pedestrians hurried about, intent on their own business, scarcely giving us a glance. I thought ruefully of the mad stampede for souvenirs that would have followed the appearance of a party of these creatures in the streets of an American city, and could not help admiring their dignified self-control.

We entered what appeared to be the shopping district and gazed into the stores. The lack of gaudy display and high-pressure advertising aroused our wonder, and we inquired of one of the shopkeepers why this was so. He explained, using our improvised dictionary, that each store enjoyed a monopoly in its line, the prices being fixed by governmental regulation. This did away with the waste of time and money spent in trying to influence the buyer to decide among a number of essentially similar articles.

Later we found our way to the University at which this nation of scholars received its education. We inquired our way to the department of astronomy, and found it located on the roof of one of the immense circular buildings. There were a number of telescopes there, the largest of which was a reflector somewhat similar to those on the Earth. Its mirror was about fifteen feet in diameter, not quite as large as the Earth's 200-inch—but it was remarkably well built, especially in view of the fact that Optical glass was unknown to the Ganymedians. Throughout the instrument metal mirrors took the places of lenses.

I asked for a chance to look through it, and the astronomer in charge agreed willingly. I would have chosen to take a look at the Earth from this distance, but that was impossible at present. The sun had set, and here the Earth, like Venus, was a morning and evening star, close to the sun. I chose Pluto; whose great distance has prevented the Earth from learning much of its physical nature.

"Pluto?" repeated the astronomer, "which of the planets do you call by that name?"

"I beg your pardon," I wrote. "Pluto is the name we give to the outermost planet of the solar system."

The telescope was trained on the heavens arid I peered into the eyepiece. A tiny disc of pale yellow, so faint as to border on invisibility, occupied the center of the field of view. I was puzzled; the power of this instrument should have shown Pluto much brighter and larger.

"This is the outermost planet?" I asked. The astronomer nodded confirmation.

"The ninth?" I inquired.

"To be sure," he replied.

"But surely this magnificent instrument should show it better," I persisted. The astronomer was displeased.

"Perhaps you expect too much," he said. "At fifteen times our distance from the sun it receives very little light."

I saw that something was amiss. Pluto is less than nine times as far from the sun as Jupiter. Could it be that this was the trans-Plutonian planet, the discovery of which had been made by younger astronomers one Earth after my departure to the moon? Yet the Ganymedian astronomer called it the ninth planet.

I made a rapid sketch of the solar system as I knew it, showing the orbits of the nine planets with their distances from to sun, and presented it to the Ganymedian astronomer. Comprehension dawned on his features, and he seized the pencil in excitement.

"We revolve around the *fifth* planet from the sun?" he demanded. I agreed.

"Then there are ten planets in all! We have never seen the innermost—it is too close to the sun. You have never seen the last. What I would not give for your vantage point and the knowledge you must have of the inner planets!"

"I would be equally glad of your opportunity to study the outer ones," I returned. "Are you sure there are none beyond this tenth?"

"We cannot tell," he replied. "If another exists, it is much too faint to be found by accident. Some of us think there are irregularities in the behavior of the tenth that may indicate another, but it has been known too short a time to say definitely. Our calculations show that this tenth planet takes hundreds of years to circle the sun just once. Until we have determined its path accurately and eliminated the effects of all the others upon it, it is useless to consider the question of still another world."

I spent some time conversing with the astronomer, telling him what I knew of Mercury. In return I learned that my theory of the manner in which Jupiter's satellites received their heat was correct; electric currents induced by its magnetic field were responsible. The scientist also satisfied my curiosity regarding the shooting of sulfur meteors to the Earth. He explained that they had built an enormous cannon, three feet in diameter and over two thousand feet long, buried in the Earth in the manner of the *Columbiad,* around which Jules Verne wrote his entertaining story "From the Earth to the Moon." This cannon, he told us, had been located very near the building that housed the observatory, for the desert city was located at the point farthest from Jupiter, where the sun, and the inner planets passed directly overhead once every seven Earth-days. He also explained how the projectiles had been constructed so that their brilliant blue light would attract our attention

This trip of exploration served to pass the time while the guns were being made. Finally the hour of departure arrived with the rising of the sun, and we set out to re-capture the *Comet*. In addition to us, a crew of twenty Ganymedians climbed aboard, each armed with an automatic pistol and a hundred rounds of ammunition. We took off with a rush amid shouts and hoots from the onlookers, and headed for the cloudy land surrounding the ocean. We five had worn our air-envelopes, for they gave protection from the poisoned darts of the hostile Ganymedians and provided an easy means of conversation at a distance, through the radio equipment. As the miles flew away below us a tension grew on the entire crew. We realized more keenly now our desperate situation. At all costs we must regain the *Comet;* yet we would have a battle on our hands, with the ever-present possibility of capture and death.

The Decoy

THE plane began to descend, and with tightening about the heart I realized the moment was at hand. Below us lay the landing field, and with a tingle of joy I recognized the slender body of the *Comet,* apparently unharmed. But as we drew closer I saw a swarm of Ganymedians surrounding it, armed with blowguns and knives. Planes patrolled the air above the field, cruising slowly about. I realized that poorly armed as were the guards, our five men would stand no show against them in a direct attack; we must resort to strategy.

The commander of the plane evidently thought likewise, for he headed up toward the clouds. A council of war was hastily called, and I made a suggestion.

"I think it best," I offered, "that you land on the outskirts of the city, and let the five of us go to the field on foot. Meanwhile you can return in the plane and draw the attention of the guards. While you engage them in battle and lead them away from the *Comet,* we will dash out and take possession of it."

"Your plan is good," replied the Ganymedians. "However, we will send a few of our number with you to guide you and assist you in case you are attacked."

Accordingly, the plane turned about and soared across the city, landing in an open field near the outlying buildings. The five of us, together with an equal number of Ganymedians, disembarked and stole into the city. The streets were shrouded in semidarkness, for while the sun had recently set on this side of the world, Jupiter was always above the horizon and its huge crescent sent a diffused light from the overcast sky. We wound our way through the narrow streets, keeping in the shadows wherever possible. The Ganymedians formed a circle around us so that our unfamiliar forms would be less likely to attract the attention of a casual observer.

At length we saw the lights of the landing field ahead of us. The plane of our rescuers was nowhere in sight as we approached, but it shortly made its appearance, diving through the clouds and heading straight for the field as if to land. The planes of the guarding party rose to meet it. Swinging into formation, they soared in a body above the attacker, while from one plane and then another appeared fiery torches, which they had hurled downward in an attempt to set fire to it. The scientists' machine dodged cleverly and turned away from the field, leading the defenders away as we had planned. A large share of the ground force followed at a run, to meet and destroy the scientists should they succeed in effecting a landing, but we noted with dismay that half a hundred remained at their posts in a circle about the *Comet*.

My plan of decoying the guards away had worked once, however, and I decided to try it again. I turned to the group.

"Ernst," I said, "we must get those guards away from the machine somehow. You and Dalton take three of the Ganymedians with you; make your way around to the other side of the field and stir up some excitement. Shoot—yell—anything to attract attention. Make them think there's a large party attacking. Then retreat and hide. Meanwhile we'll sneak up from behind and board the *Comet* and then pick you up." Ernst nodded his agreement, and picking out three of the Ganymedians, set off through the streets to circle the field, Dalton with him.

Dr. Von Lichten, Lafourchette and I, together with the two remaining Ganymedians, kept our posts. For perhaps fifteen minutes the silence was broken only by the faint sounds of the distant commotion, indicating that the bulk of the Ganymedians were still pursuing the decoy plane. Then from my radio receiver came the sound of Ernst's voice, yelling like a Comanche, while the microphone brought the rapid reports of five pistols. The fifty

Ganymedians about the *Comet* turned to face the noise, some advancing at a run, a few lingering. I signaled to my companions and we dashed for the center of the field. Ernst had done his work well; we were within ten paces before we were discovered. Our guns spoke in unison; four Ganymedians tumbled to the ground, while the others rushed about in confusion. We vaulted to the top of the *Comet* and snatched open the door to the airlock. One of our Ganymedians caught a poisoned dart in his shoulder, a flying knife cracked against my helmet, and then we were out of danger, the door closed behind us.

In my radio receivers I heard faintly the shouting voices of Ernst and Dalton, retreating. I sprang to the control room closed the gravity screens and set the *Comet* in motion. Ernst's voice came again: "Marland! Have you got it?"

"Yes!" I shouted.

"Come quick!" I heard. "We're surrounded! They've got us!"

"Where are you?" I yelled.

"North side of the field, first street!" was the answer. "Hurry!"

I swung northward, flying low. A roar from the sky announced the return of the enemy planes as I reached the first street beyond the limits of the field. Looking down I saw a tremendous crowd milling excitedly into the street, but I could not make out Ernst and Dalton in the semi-darkness, I dropped the *Comet* down between the buildings in the hope of scaring off the Ganymedians, but they stood their ground. I did not dare try to crush them with the machine for fear of killing my comrades at the same time. I peered vainly about, trying to locate them.

"Marland!" Dalton's voice.

"Where are you?" I shouted again.

"On the field! They've knocked Ernst out and tied me up, and they're putting us aboard a plane!"

"Coming!" I yelled, and turned the *Comet's* nose up, noting with satisfaction that the gas discharge enveloped a number of Ganymedians.

The flying field was covered with planes, some in the act of landing, others just taking off.

"Marland!" came Dalton's voice again. "We're going up!"

"Which plane?" I asked.

"I don't know how to describe it! I can't see out—it's dark in here! Fully a dozen planes were leaving the ground at that moment. I rushed for the nearest, shouting Dalton's name. His answer came, fainter. Not that one! I tried another, but with no better luck. The planes were scattering in all directions. The Ganymedians saw what I was up to and knew how slim were my chances of finding the right plane before Dalton's radio would be out of range. Desperately I tried to circle the field and round up the planes, but five of them escaped, with Dalton aboard one. His cries grew fainter, and finally faded out; I could not keep track of the speeding planes in the dim twilight.

Von Lichten and Lafourchette were at my side in the control room. I turned to them.

"We must do something quick!" I said. "We must find them and rescue them!"

"What can we do?" asked Lafourchette hopelessly. "They are lost; we cannot hope to find them. They are miles away by now, and there's no telling how far they will be carried."

"But we cannot leave them to the mercy of the Ganymedians!" I protested. "They will probably be taken to some city; let us fly over every city on the planet and try to bring our radios within hearing range."

"It would be useless," said Lafourchette. "The radios are good for half a mile—three quarters at the outside. It would take days, perhaps weeks. They will be killed before we can reach them."

"True," put in Von Lichten. "And further, the Ganymedians may foresee that we will search their cities and hide them in some forsaken spot. If we passed within half a mile of every point in the inhabited strip between the ocean and the desert, it would mean traveling a path thirty million miles long." He shook his head. "If only the radios were more powerful—"

"Can we not make them so?" demanded Lafourchette suddenly. "The desert people are excellent workmen; perhaps they could make us a powerful set."

"No," I said. "It would take them several days at the least." Then I recalled the code-messages of the Ganymedians that had spoken from our receivers on our first encounter with their planes.

"We can do better!" I exclaimed. "They have radios already made! We can borrow one of their planes and fly along, calling to Dalton and Ernst." I swung the *Comet* about and rose above the clouds, seeking the plane of the scientists. After a moment I spotted it some miles away and made for it with a rush. The commander recognized us and flew to meet us; then as we drew close, he headed for the desert to return to his city. This did not suit my plans at all; it was a six hours' trip in his machine, and I must talk to him at once. I headed in front of him, trying to indicate that I wished him to land, but he evidently did not understand, for he only put on more speed. At length, in desperation, I decided to climb out on the *Comet* and attract his attention. I turned over the controls to Von Lichten and entered the airlock.

CHAPTER SEVENTEEN
We Search Through Ganymede

I was still clad in my envelope, and the magnetic shoes served to give me some extra foothold in spite of the slight gravity. We were traveling at a good five hundred miles an hour; it was a desperate chance, but the lives of two men hung in the balance. Fastening a rope to the airlock door, I tied it about my waist and climbed out.

We were traveling at an altitude of many miles, and the rush of air, though terrific, was not as great as it would have been nearer the ground, for which I was thankful. I lay flat on the top of the *Comet,* clinging to my rope and waving an arm above my head. The Ganymedians finally saw me and drew near. A daring plan entered my head; the circular door opened, and the face of a Ganymedian appeared. I motioned him to come nearer. The plane settled slowly until it was a bare ten feet above, then dropped back slightly. Ten feet! On Earth it would be impossible, but with the weak gravity—could I make it?

I crouched, and jumped with every ounce of strength, arms outstretched. Somehow my hands encountered the rim of the door. I drew myself up against the drag of the whistling wind, and was safe aboard the Ganymedian plane.

In the reaction from the awful chance I had taken, I was speechless for a moment, as were the Ganymedians. The commander was waving madly. In his excitement at my jump he was trying to question me in his language! I motioned for pencil and paper, and quickly related the capture of Ernst and Dalton, the necessity of their immediate rescue, and our plan to use their radio. The scientist shook his head, and wrote:

"The instrument you call a radio passed out of favor with us some years ago. As you know, we are unable to converse directly through sounds alone, so we have devised an apparatus for projecting moving images by means of electromagnetic waves. That is the only equipment for communication aboard this plane."

A television machine! Interesting, but useless to us. I thought for a moment.

"Are not the planes of your enemies equipped with radios?" I asked.

"Yes," he replied. "They send messages by means of intermittent signals, using their code. Their instruments will not reproduce actual sounds, however."

"Nevertheless," I decided, "we may be able to use them. We must capture one of their planes at once."

"We will help as well as we can," replied the commander.

"Then let me return at once to the *Comet,*" I wrote. "Give me a rope and I will drop onto it."

A metal cord was procured, and after a few breath-taking moments I was back aboard the *Comet.* I explained the situation to the others as I turned it about and headed back for the flying field.

Most of the planes had landed, but there were a few still in the air. They saw us coming and rushed out to meet us. I singled out one and cut it off from the others, threatening it with the blazing gas discharge as I circled quickly around it. The pilot recognized his helplessness, and allowed himself to be shepherded away to the edge of the city. Here I forced him to land, and armed with our automatics we approached it cautiously. The scientists landed their plane on the other side, and seeing that resistance was hopeless the enemy aviator surrendered. We tied him securely and boarded his plane.

The radio apparatus was mounted back of the controls. At first glance it appeared hopelessly unfamiliar, but on examining the details of its construction we saw that the essential principles were all there. To be sure, the various parts were strange and bewildering, but we recognized the vital functions of each piece of apparatus. In its present form it would not serve to transmit our voices, but with the attachment of our microphones and receivers, and perhaps a variation here and there, it could be made to serve. We decided to transplant the apparatus intact to the *Comet,* and set to work at once.

The Ganymedians, being familiar with the construction, did the work, while I showed them how to connect it to our generators. With what tools we possessed we set it up in the *Comet* control room and tested it out. Finding that it was in working order, we took off once more and headed up above the city. Dr. Von Lichten took his place at the microphone while I steered a course around the city, then off to the west. He kept up a continuous fire of talk:

"Dalton! Ernst! Can you hear me? Von Lichten speaking, aboard the *Comet.* Answer if you can hear me." A few seconds wait. "Dalton! Can you hear me—?" I sent the flyer hurtling along at a terrific pace above the inhabited strip, zigzagging so as to come within a hundred miles or so of every part.

AT the end of half an hour we had heard no response. We had covered nearly four hundred miles in the direction I thought the planes might have taken. They had two hours' start on us, but could not have covered more than that distance, judging from their speed. Evidently they had not gone this way. I circled about and headed back, passing to the north of the city, toward the desert. Now and again we flashed over a small settlement, or crossed a river or lake, but the country was for the most part bare. Lafourchette replaced Dr. Von Lichten at the microphone and took up the endless monologue. Still we rushed on, heading east now, zigzagging again. We seemed to be entering a range of low mountains; here and there signs of long-past volcanic activity appeared. Lafourchette was waxing eloquent: "Dalton...Ernst! Where are you? Answer—it's Lafourchette! Fear not, *mes amis,* we will rescue you! Speak only a word and we shall come on swift wings! Ah, *mes enfants,* can you not hear?"

Half an hour more. If we did not reach them quickly the Ganymedians would have time to land. With their cold-blooded contempt for life and their devilish ingenuity—I shuddered to think of the fate of my comrades.

Lafourchette stopped short in the midst of his impassioned entreaties, then uttered a joyous shout.

"I hear him! Dalton has answered!"

"Ask him where he is?" I exclaimed.

"He doesn't know!" replied Lafourchette after a moment. "They have been taken out of the plane and are imprisoned in a stone building on the side of a mountain. He says a cloud of smoke is visible through the window to the southwest of him; he thinks they may be on the northeast slope of a volcano..."

"Northeast slope of a volcano," I repeated. "That should be visible for quite a distance. Keep in touch with him, Lafourchette, and tell me whether his voice grows louder or fainter. Dr. Von Lichten, look out for the smoke cloud."

Lafourchette kept up his conversation with Dalton.

"Ernst has recovered consciousness," he reported, "but is too weak to talk. He isn't seriously injured, however." There was then a slight pause. "Dalton's voice is now louder," he finally added.

I looked out through the periscope, but could see no smoke. We were definitely over a mountain range now, the peaks of some extending a mile or two above the ground. I noted a mighty snow-capped patriarch to the north of us, reaching almost to the clouds. I pulled the *Comet's* nose up a bit in order to get a better view of the landscape. Still no smoke was visible.

"Wait!" cried Lafourchette. "Dalton's voice is growing fainter!"

"We must have passed to one side of him," I said, swinging about. We dashed back over our course, coming abreast of the high peak I had noted.

"It is loudest here," said Lafourchette.

"He is north or south of here then," I said. "We shall see which. Listen closely." I swung south, toward the ocean, but Lafourchette quickly called. "Not this way!" I swung about once more, and headed for the snow-capped mountain. It could not be long, now. I put on an extra burst of speed, and Lafourchette reported, "Louder." Still no smoke was visible. I wondered what range our radio outfit had.

We could see easily fifty miles ahead.

At the Volcano's Edge!

THE *Comet* sped over the big mountain's snowy tip, a few hundred feet below the lowest clouds. A vast panorama lay ahead: wild, rugged, and uninhabited. We were nearing the northernmost point on the globe, yet there was no trace of ice and snow such as we might expect. The internal heat of Ganymede kept its surface at a nearly even warmth throughout, and the polar region was much like the rest of it.

Far ahead, on the dim horizon, lay a murky patch of haze— rising, falling, wavering. Even as I realized what it was, Von Lichten shouted:

"The volcano! Dead ahead!"

The *Comet* quivered as I speeded up another notch. The terrific wind-pressure made it hard to handle, and we skipped about through little air pockets. A tiny flying creature tried to cross our path and was impaled on the ship's pointed nose. The volcano drew closer, its murky umbrella of smoke stretching out toward us. I slackened speed now. "Northeast slope," I muttered, dropping down.

"Hurry!" exclaimed Lafourchette suddenly. "The Ganymedians are coming for Dalton and Ernst!"

The *Comet* was close to the ground now, I spied the planes of the Ganymedians near a small stone building, halfway up the slope, and drew up to it, letting the landing skids plow the ground without bothering to reverse and stop. Automatics in hand, we jumped out as a crowd of Ganymedians left the building, starting up the slope, with our comrades in their midst. Seeing that they were pursued they broke into a run, dragging Ernst and Dalton with them. I tried to take aim for a shot, but they were a good hundred yards ahead, and at that distance there was grave danger of hitting one of our party. I sprinted madly, Lafourchette and Von Lichten at my heels, bounding in long steps up the slope. I saw only too clearly their diabolical intent—to push the Earthmen into the smoking crater!

We were gaining slowly, due to their difficulty in dragging our captive fellows. As the distance lessened I decided to risk a shot, when suddenly two dozen or more detached themselves from the rest and turned to meet us. I pulled up and fired into their midst as did the Doctor and Lafourchette. They divided, flanking us, and closed in. I fired carefully, dropping a Ganymedian with each shot, but there were too many. We were suddenly surrounded, pinned to the ground, deprived of our guns, tied, and carried to the others. It all happened so quickly we hadn't had time to think. We had stepped from the frying pan into the fire!

This promised to be literally true—too true. The five of us were dragged up the volcano slope despite our struggles. I watched with fascination the heavy pall that hung over the mountaintop like a vast death-shroud, shifting, swirling, as though beckoning us to our doom. The earth trembled beneath our feet; a streak of fire shot up from the crater's rim. A fine hail of volcanic stone rained about us, covering the ground, blackening the surroundings.

A shout of terror came from the foremost Ganymedians. I looked to see what had alarmed them, and beheld a tiny, trickling stream of lava spilling over the edge of the crater, snaking down toward us. With one accord the Ganymedians fell to their knees, extending their arms in supplication toward the mountaintop. As if in answer, a great crack appeared in the rocky rim above us and a torrent of red-hot molten lava gushed out. The Ganymedians turned and fled, leaving us, bound, on the slope. I strained at the metal cords that fettered my arms, trying to free myself, but to no avail. The blazing stream came closer, writhing and twisting like a living tongue of fire. Desperately I struggled to rise.

"Come over here," called Ernst weakly. "They didn't tie my hands; I can get you free!" I rolled over to where he lay, too weak to rise. He pulled at the knots of my bonds, and after an eternity I felt my hands come free. I loosened the cord about my feet, then I dragged Ernst to the others, and between us we managed to free them before the smoking lava reached us. I picked up Ernst like a sack of flour, light as he was, and fled down the hill bounding like a mountain goat. I have no doubt that we five broke all existing records for rapid travel afoot in the quarter-mile between us and the *Comet*. We scrambled aboard as the stream of lava licked against the stone house, and shot into the air a few seconds later.

Up above the clouds we rose, blessing Mother Nature for our second escape from death by fire. We climbed into the high, thin air where no Ganymedian plane could penetrate, and set off northward toward the city in the desert. I say north, yet that is incorrect; there was no north from that spot. Looking behind us we could see Jupiter's half-illuminated face, bisected by the horizon. Ahead and directly opposite, the sun's pale rays divided on the skyline. The plane of the ecliptic, dotted here and there with the tiny lights of the outer planets, lay about us, its whole circle visible on the horizon. We were over Ganymede's north pole, marked almost exactly by the erupting volcano.

Dr. Von Lichten assumed a professional attitude as soon as we were above the ground. He examined the lump on the back of Ernst's neck, where the butt of a Ganymedian gun had struck him just below his helmet. His envelope had lessened the stroke somewhat, and beyond some slight dizziness, he felt no ill effects. A dose of stimulant put him on his feet in short order and he quickly regained his usual cheery disposition. Lafourchette's knife scratch showed signs of infection, causing the Doctor some concern. The diminutive Frenchman grudgingly submitted to treatment, calling Von Lichten's liberal application of antiseptic "war paint" and making light of the whole affair.

We made good time to the city in the desert and found the scientists' plane waiting for us. They congratulated us on our success in recapturing the *Comet* and planned a banquet for the morrow in honor of our safe return. Meanwhile we gratefully retired to rooms prepared for us and reveled in the blissful relaxation of sleep.

On arising we were visited by a delegation that wished to hear the details of our raid. They listened with interest to the story of Dalton and Ernst's capture and our efforts to locate them. When we mentioned the evident awe of our captors for the erupting volcano, they showed considerable amusement.

"That is but one of the superstitions of those people," they explained. "Our race has long known that the heat of our planet came from within. The ignorant ones believe that the interior of Ganymede is the home of a fiery demon, Pyros, who rules their destinies. They make sacrifices to him from time to time, a custom that we condemned during our rule. The periodic eruption of the several volcanoes on this planet they interpret as manifestations of Pyros' displeasure. Of late the north polar volcano has been unusually active, and their two attempts to incinerate you alive indicate that they took your arrival to be the cause of its eruption."

The hour of the banquet drew near, and our visitors excused themselves, saying they would return shortly to escort us to the celebration. On our departure from the moon we had made no preparations for formal entertainment, and had to be satisfied with a hasty shave and change of clothes. Lafourchette exhibited a flare for gaudy raiment and blossomed out in a well-saved suit of pre-war cut, a two-inch standup collar and a brilliant necktie of many colors. A sickly green boutonniere, picked from a Ganymedian garden, added the finishing touch to a makeup that would have taken first prize at any masquerade ball.

We were escorted to the banquet hall where the leading scientists of the city were gathered. Someone with courteous fore-sight had prepared stools for us, while the Ganymedians, as usual, seated themselves dog-fashion in a great circle on cushions. Food was served on little individual stands placed before the diners by servants from the uneducated race, captured during battles. On our left sat the Ganymedian with whom we had conversed frequently, and next to him a venerable old fellow who presided over the affair. He had recently celebrated his thousandth sunset (about thirty-four Earth years) and held in his domed cranium the wisdom of the ages. During the progress of the dinner he made a long speech in which, according to the interpretation of our friend, he discoursed at length of our daring accomplishments in traversing four hundred million miles of interplanetary space and defeating unaided a host of their enemies. At each pause in his finger gymnastics, the listeners threw their arms in the air in silent applause and turned admiring glances in our direction. When at length some sort of reply was evidently expected of us, I requested our interpreter to announce that the possibility of the trip and the credit for it belonged to the men who had remained behind: Dr.

Forscher, Wiley, Langley and Quaile. In reply the orator declared that credit would be given them for their theories, but to those who had taken the risks belonged the glory.

CHAPTER EIGHTEEN
The Return!

AFTER the meal we were informed that for our special benefit there would be a moving picture of life and happenings on Ganymede. At one end of the hall a curtain was withdrawn, exposing a translucent screen. It seemed that the apparatus for projecting pictures was an elaboration of their television machines. There was the usual receiving apparatus, except that instead of being connected to an antenna that picked electromagnetic waves out of the ether, the impulses were recorded on a fine tape and reproduced by a needle that followed its markings.

The scenes that flashed on the screen dealt for the most part were industrial operations in and around the great city. There were views of the great plants where nitrogen was removed from the air and "fixed" for use in fertilizing the sterile desert. Others showed the water works, where hydrogen was recovered from decaying plants, from the air, and every other conceivable source, burned in oxygen, and the resulting steam condensed and doled out through pipes to the houses of the city, the farms, and other places where it was required. It was one of the most expensive substances in the economics of this city of scientists, which accounted in large measure for their desire to return to the oceanfront. In another view we saw the government's great nursery, where the eggs of Ganymedians were hatched and the young reared, given elementary training, and fitted for life upon maturity.

Their period of growth was about ten years, at which age they were considered adults and expected to take part in the maintenance of their civilization. Considering the short span of their life we were amazed to realize how thorough was their education and how rapid their progress. The facts and principles that require eight years of elementary schooling in America were absorbed by these youngsters in two or three. From that point each individual specialized in some line for which he was considered suitable, and his intensive training enabled him to reach the mental caliber of our average technical school graduate before his three hundred and fiftieth sunset—about seven Earth years.

Finally the banquet adjourned, and in company with our interpreter and a few others we returned to our quarters. The scientists were anxious to discuss the subject that had been broached when they rescued us and brought us there, namely, the enlistment of aid from mankind in their war to regain possession of the lands held by their enemies. As usual, the interview was carried on in the simplified English we had taught them. The interpreter came to the point without formalities.

"You have seen pictures of the way in which we struggle for existence," he wrote. "Our supply of water is expensive and inadequate, and the food is not much better. Our race is badly nourished, and in the few generations we have existed in the desert there are signs of physical deterioration. We ask help—armies and equipment. You five Earthmen are strong, intelligent, and resourceful. You have given us the secret of one powerful weapon, and you tell us there are others. With a few thousand beings like you, armed as you are, it would be a simple matter to put the enemy to rout. Give us this aid—enlist a force of men and arm them; teach us to build ships like that in which you came, and we will be forever indebted to you. In return we can show you the construction of our television apparatus, our high-powered airplanes, and many other devices of which we know. Our two races can exchange ambassadors and maintain communication. We can pool our scientific knowledge, and together rule the universe!"

Acting as spokesman for the party, I replied: "We realize your situation fully, and so far as it is within our power we will help you. However, you must understand that we came to Ganymede, not as the accredited representatives of a planet, but as five scientists exploring the solar system. We are backed, at best, by a colony of researchers numbering but a few hundred members, under the direction of the man who has the sole right to say who shall copy our machine. The implements of war known to us we will describe to you willingly, and we will promise to inform the people of Earth of your request for assistance; but we must confer with Dr. Forscher, our superior, before giving you the secret of *the Comet.*"

After a short discussion of my message by our interviewers, the interpreter wrote:

"We receive your promise with pleasure, and will respect your wishes. We ask, further, only that you make haste to send us what aid you can. Meanwhile, during the remainder of your stay, this city is yours to inspect, and our people at your command." After this announcement the scientists rose and took their leave.

MY first thought was to inspect the *Comet*. I went over it from stem to stern, testing the apparatus and checking up on our supplies. I found to my chagrin that we had unwittingly left the machinery for renewing the air running during our stay on the satellite, with the result that it now held barely enough chemicals for our return trip. On making inquiries, I discovered that the mineral salts necessary for the manufacture of potassium chlorate, from which our oxygen was derived, lay close to the ocean, and we were unable to obtain them. It was therefore imperative that we start back as soon as possible.

We had spent altogether about eight terrestrial weeks among this strange race. The satellite was past its nearest approach to the Earth, and would not reach that point again for another five days, but the additional distance would mean only a few hours' more travel. Furthermore, the Earth and moon had reached their least distance from Jupiter before our start, and each day's delay increased the intervening space. Accordingly, we bade the Ganymedian scientists a hasty farewell, climbed aboard, and turned our nose skyward. I picked up the Earth in the periscope and turned on the full force of acceleration. This time our course angled away from Jupiter, and we did not experience the annoying disturbance of its magnetic field. Soon the giant planet with its system of moons was dropping away behind us as we flashed along through the ether in our little shell, cut off from the entire universe.

Five days ticked by on our clocks. The monotony of the trip held its sway over the group, causing us to cast about for diversion. Dalton suggested that we draw up a map of Ganymede from the data we had procured, indicating our route on it. The idea was adopted at once. I was elected to do the drafting, the others contributing suggestions as the work went along. The final result was sketchy, due to our meager knowledge of the country around the ocean, but it would serve to give Dr. Forscher and his staff an idea of the physical characteristics of the little world. We discussed plans for equipping an expedition to take part in the wars of Ganymede, and daydreamed over the future relations of the two worlds, some of us imagining ourselves as diplomatic representatives to their government in future years.

On the twelfth day a shadow crept over our high spirits. Lafourchette, corning off duty in the pilot hours, complained that he felt poorly. Dr. Von Lichten's examination disclosed the fact that his knife scratch was badly infected. The doctor ordered him to bed at once and treated the reddened sore.

At the next meal he felt no better, refusing food. Dr. Von Lichten seemed worried, and at his suggestion we withdrew to the engine room, leaving Lafourchette to sleep quietly. The doctor made no response to our questions, busying himself with his medicine case and presently joining Lafourchette. His elaborate precautions against unknown bacteria in the atmosphere of Ganymede came to my mind. Could it be that the little Frenchman had contracted a strange malady, peculiar to that world? The idea was not comforting. We had faced death at the hands of our captors, incineration in the crater of the volcano, and even the risk of annihilation by a wandering meteoric rock, without a qualm. These were tangible things, to be foreseen and understood. But the torturing anguish of an unknown disease was enough to sicken the strongest heart.

Presently Von Lichten appeared in the doorway, his face grave.

"What is it?" was asked in chorus.

"I don't know," replied the doctor with a gesture of helplessness. "The infection's spread through his whole system, inflaming muscles, which cramp his whole body. In spite of my efforts he grows rapidly worse. So far his heart has not been touched. If it should be—"

"Can't we do something?" I demanded. "The disease must be known to the Ganymedians; why not head about and take him back?"

"It would be useless," returned the doctor. "We have been on our way nearly two weeks. His malady is progressing very rapidly.

If he is to be saved through medical aid, it must be at once. In forty-eight hours it will be too late."

"Is it as serious as that?" asked Dalton in a whisper.

"I fear so. He is very weak; his breathing is shallow and rapid. With a strong man it might be different. We can only hope for the best. Meanwhile," he said significantly, "no one save myself must go near him. You will be safer in the control room."

"But what of your own risk?" demanded Ernst.

"That is the physician's lot," said the doctor shortly. "I shall take every precaution."

He reentered the living quarters, leaving us to face one another in despair. From his conservative habits of speech I knew he had not exaggerated the seriousness of Lafourchette's condition.

A Tragedy in Space

THE door reopened. Dr. Von Lichten was a haggard ghost of his usual self. His face was drawn and gray; his bloodshot eyes stared from hollowed pits surmounting blotchy circles that bespoke the ordeal he had passed through. He spread his hands in a gesture of finality.

"Gone?" whispered Ernst. The doctor nodded.

"Fifteen minutes ago. It was hopeless."

"May we see him?" asked Dalton.

"I think not. He is—unrecognizable."

There was a moment of ghastly silence, while the clock ticks jarred on our ears like pistol shots. Von Lichten pulled himself together with a visible effort.

"We must get the body out," he said.

"Overboard?" protested Dalton. "Surely he deserves a decent burial on Earth!"

"The risk of contagion is far too great," said Von Lichten. "Lafourchette himself understood this."

We stood in the airlock, with its outer door opened to the emptiness beyond, our envelopes hiding the emotions that filled the four of us. As we watched a shapeless bundle drift slowly out of sight, the marvelous courage of the dead man commanded our utmost respect. Lying there in the darkness of the *Comet's* close quarters, he had known that the life he loved and enjoyed had but a few minutes to run; that he stood on the brink of a precipice that was crumbling, even as he spoke, to plunge him into the silent, blank, timeless eternity of non-existence. Yet he had faced the thought of his body being tumbled into nothingness, to wander through the solar system, drifting on and on—

Back in the engine room Dr. Von Lichten examined each of us for the slightest sign of infection but found none. To keep busy, we set about a general overhauling of the *Comet*. We checked over the apparatus carefully and cleaned and polished the machine throughout. Working like beavers, we asked only to be busy.

At the end of thirty-four days we were within three million miles of the Earth and its satellite. As the hour approached when we would turn on the power for our final stop, I fancied the colony on the moon preparing for our return. In all probability Quaile would be sweeping the skies in the direction of Jupiter with the hundred-foot telescope, seeking the tiny blue-yellow streak in his eyepiece that would herald our return.

The four of us awaited our arrival no less anxiously than the members of the colony. Our supplies were nearly gone, and the oxygen would not last over forty-eight hours. We should reach the moon in twenty-two, and be safe in the colony in two more. So it would be twenty-four hours at the outside before we were to see the faces of our colleagues.

We stood alternate watches in pairs as we neared our destination. The moon was not yet full, but it was past a line from our vessel to the Earth, since the latter was two months advanced beyond conjunction with Jupiter. The direction of our flight carried us toward the center of the moon's disc, a tiny circle of blackness among the stars.

Half a million miles out, about ten hours before our landing, Ernst and I sat before the instrument board. I noted with a start that one of the generators was running hot, and hurried to investigate. The insulation of the armature was giving way under the strain of many hours' running at full load. I recalled the sight of the tractor that had burnt out—its generators and flashed away into the sky, a mass of white-hot steel. I must cool off the driver at once; but to do so the electrical apparatus must carry an extra load for a moment.

Would they stand it? Obviously better now than later. I stepped up the rheostat a notch. Their whine rose half a tone, then fell in slow diminuendo. I pushed the controller another notch. The roaring gas grew quieter, like the baffled voice of a dying tempest. In another second it would be under control. One more notch. The overheated generator resigned its task in a blinding flash. Automatically the others took up its load, groaning under the increased flow of current. But they carried it; the driver cooled, easing the strain on the electrical apparatus. I drew a breath of relief.

The burned-out generator had filled the *Comet* with smoke, bringing the others of the party at a run. In answer to their excited questions, I explained our situation. We had three generators left to do the work of four; our deceleration must be cut to three-fourths of normal. After covering the remaining half-million miles to the moon we would still be speeding along at a pace sufficient to outstrip the fastest bullet. It was out of the question to land here; we must steer past and continue slowly down until we could return.

But was there time? The vital supplies of oxygen were perilously low; our margin of safety was too small. I peered out of the periscope toward our fast approaching satellite, noticeably larger now. A quarter of a million miles further on, gleaming cheerfully in the sunlight, lay the only way out of our difficulties— the Earth. We could dive into the welcoming blanket of its at-mosphere, let it check our fall, and coast to the ground where we chose, safe and among friends. At the City College our burned-out generator could be repaired and our oxygen tanks recharged. Then we could return to the moon at our leisure. The *Comet's* flaming tail would announce our safety to Dr. Forscher's colony, and from our velocity and direction, an astronomer of Quaile's caliber could easily compute our destination. They would know that we had sufficient reason for not landing on the moon, and would expect our return in good time.

Meanwhile, a question remains. What of our promise to interest the Earth in sending aid to the Ganymedian scientists? I cannot visualize the governments of Europe and America lending ear to such a proposal, nor would I advocate detailing their armies. The majority of mankind is opposed to interfering in affairs that do not concern us; and to send troops against their will hundreds of millions of miles from their homes would be a colossal injustice.

Nevertheless, I am giving this message to the world in the hope that it will be read by some in whom the spirit of the pioneers many linger. I have spared no details of our trip and the discoveries that made it possible, so that my readers may understand the situation fully. If they wish to see the scientists of Ganymede restored to control of their planet, they may lend a hand in putting them there.

The prospect is at once alluring and terrifying. They will find new and exhilarating sensations in striding as though in Seven League Boots, across hills and valleys covered with plants and animals, which might have materialized from the smoke of an opium pipe. They will behold wonders of the starry heavens such as are never seen from Earth. But they will meet with the hatred of four-legged foes possessed of human intelligence and inhuman fiendishness, and they must beware of the attacks of microscopic enemies.

But I do not wish to act as a recruiting officer. Let those whose love of adventure surpasses their fear of the unknown decide the matter, each for himself. They may find me among them—I cannot tell as yet. Perhaps Dr. Forscher has other plans for me.

As I write these concluding lines, the *Comet* hovers above the City College. When you read them, Dalton, Ernst, Dr. Von Lichten and I will be on our way back to the outpost on the moon.

THE END

If you've enjoyed this book, you will not want to miss these terrific titles…

ARMCHAIR SCI-FI & HORROR DOUBLE NOVELS, $12.95 each

D-111 **THE MOON ERA** by Jack Williamson
REVENGE OF THE ROBOTS by Howard Browne

D-112 **SON OF THE BLACK CHALICE** by Milton Lesser
SENTRY OF THE SKY by Evelyn E. Smith

D-113 **OUTPOST ON THE MOON** by Joslyn Maxwell
POTENTIAL ZERO by S. J. Byrne

D-114 **OUTPOST INFINITY** by Raymond F. Jones
THE WHITE INVADERS by Ray Cummings

D-115 **TIME TRAP** by Rog Phillips
THE COSMIC DESTROYER by Alexander Blade

D-116 **THE OTHER SIDE OF THE MOON** by Edmond Hamilton
SECRET INVASION by Walter Kubilius

D-117 **DANGER MOON** by Frederik Pohl
THE HIDDEN UNIVERSE by Ralph Milne Farley

D-118 **THE WAILING ASTEROID** by Murray Leinster
THE WORLD THAT COULDN'T BE by Clifford D. Simak

D-119 **THE WHISPERING GORILLA** by Don Wilcox
RETURN OF THE WHISPERING GORILLA by David V. Reed

D-120 **SPECIAL EFFECT** by J. F. Bone
WARLORD OF KOR by Terry Carr

ARMCHAIR SCIENCE FICTION CLASSICS, $12.95 each

C-37 **THE GREEN MAN RETURNS**
by Harold M. Sherman

C-38 **THE SHAVER MYSTERY, Book Five**
by Richard S, Shaver

C-39 **MARS CHILD**
by Cyril Judd

ARMCHAIR MASTERS OF SCIENCE FICTION SERIES, $16.95 each

MS-9 **MASTERS OF SCIENCE FICTION AND FANTASY, Vol. Nine**
Poul Anderson, "The Star Beast" and other tales

MS-10 **MASTERS OF SCIENCE FICTION, Vol. Ten**
Robert Moore Williams, "Time Tolls for Toro" and other tales

WERE THE ALIENS FRIEND OR FOE?

It had been an amazing event. The Vanyans had journeyed across space and landed their flying saucers right in the middle of Washington, D. C. Their ships had been surrounded by every conceivable piece of weaponry the military had in its possession. But the Vanyans had come bearing generous gifts and knowledge for all of humanity. And the people of Earth, at first, received these interplanetary visitors—and their gifts—with open arms. But as it is with human nature, such a show of unadulterated kindness prompted many toward fear…and distrust…and eventually hatred. Soon men were asking questions: What was behind the Vanyans seemingly unselfish good will? And what would they ask from Earth in return?

But the biggest question of all was how would mankind treat their newfound friends from space?

CAST OF CHARACTERS

RAY SANDERS
This brilliant linguist never imagined he'd fall head over heels in love with a naked female alien.

KRIA
She held a secret of vital importance to the Earthmen. Unfortunately, they had to figure out her secret themselves.

MR. MOTTER
He was a well-respected Vice U.N. Consul—but appearances can sometimes be deceiving.

SANAL
He welcomed the Earthling into his home and blessed him with his daughter in matrimony—but had his faith been misplaced?

RALSYAN
A revered Master teacher of the first order, he confirmed that the Vanyans would put up no resistance to their destruction.

SECRETARY HENRY
This politician not only insisted that Sanders tell his whole story, but that he release it to the public as well.

THE PRESIDENT
Would the annihilation of an alien race become his greatest transgression or the best prevent-defense ever?

POTENTIAL ZERO

By
JOHN BLOODSTONE

ARMCHAIR FICTION
PO Box 4369, Medford, Oregon 97504

CHAPTER ONE

You rise up to accuse me of being traitor to my kind—I, who merely sought to save the life of one immortal creature. I, who lived in the Vanyan city and knew those golden benevolent god people, knew the untranslatable intricacies and stimulating ideation patterns of their language and understood the inimitable design of their architecture, the purpose of their way of life and the vital magnitude and scope of their philosophy. It is I who stand before the world accused of treason, to be judged by you who used the gift of gods to turn upon your benefactors and destroy them without warning, like so many superstitious savages, like raving witch-burners and blood-thirsty assassins—murderers of Angels, destroyers of Utopia, desecrators of Justice, enemies of Mercy, traitors to Gratitude!

The court-martial that will decide my guilt or innocence in this matter is insignificant here in the light of eternal values—a dried leaf that must fall from the tree of Time and be lost in the dust under the feet of those myriad generations, which must recover from the far greater crime that YOU have committed against them and the tarnished name of Man.

You ask me for my story. You condescend to give me the privilege of speaking my piece. And I say it is your guilt complex that bends you to this decision, an awareness of a basic meanness in the nature of Man with which you will have to live. Nor do I pity you for it. It is the law of retribution...

"Ye gods," ejaculated the President, looking up from the manuscript. "This fellow should have written my campaign speeches."

"You can see why it would be inadvisable to release his story to the Press," commented his secretary.

"But what am I to do? The people want his story before he is court-martialed. And there's the big problem. One man—the only man who really learned the Vanyan's language and understood them—could turn the tables on us and the United Nations. If we allow his story to come out before the trial—and if he managed to throw world sympathy toward himself and the Vanyans—we could not convict him of treason and carry out the execution without becoming guilty of the crime he's screaming about."

"And yet on the other hand, sir, if you court-martial him without letting him tell his story publicly you know what that will mean..."

The President supported his forehead in his hand, shook his head.

"Sir, do you think you have committed an historical blunder?"

The Chief Executive looked up, startled, suddenly on the defensive. "You mean—in having destroyed the Vanyans? Not a bit of it." He looked beyond the secretary to make sure the door was closed. Then he smiled a secret and confidential smile. "Come on, Henry—where's your political think-cap? They arrived in an election year. What they pretended to stand for would have ruined the whole Party platform. Why—if we had played along with them the people would have been ready for World Federation in another year."

The secretary sighed. "I suppose you're right. But you're getting a terrific reaction to this Ray Sanders situation." He indicated a mountain of telegrams and urgent memos from congressmen and senators. "Something has to be done."

One of the President's phones rang and the secretary picked up the receiver. He said, "Yes, that's right." Then he listened, and suddenly his haggard face lighted with enthusiasm. "That's marvelous," he exclaimed into the phone. "Keep this under a lid till it's okayed for release."

"What is it, Henry?" asked the President, hopefully curious.

"It's about Ray Sanders' lady love...you know who..."

"Oh, you mean the Vanyan woman. I wonder if Sanders is bitter about what we did to the Vanyans or what we did to *her*—what is that beauty's name?"

"Kria, sir."

"Kria—that's it. She's the only Vanyan left alive. What's the news? Is she finally going to die?"

"Not even the doctors are sure of that. Her blood looks like blood, but it isn't. Her pulse is not a pulse, merely a pressure. With all those bullets in her—"

"Well good God. Haven't they taken an X-ray *yet?* Ever since the Vanyans arrived it has been the major objective of our Secret Service to obtain an X-ray of a Vanyan. Now here we have this woman at our disposal—"

"That's just it, sir. They have taken a complete set of X-rays…"

The President tensed, impaling his secretary with a glare. "And?"

"She is strictly *not* human."

"Not human? A gorgeous woman like that? But—if she's not human, what *is* she?"

The secretary smiled, shaking his head. "You might not believe me if I told you. Don't take my word for it. Call Rear Admiral Herndon in Navy Medicine and Surgery. But here's the point, sir—" The secretary interrupted the President as he was about to reach for the phone. "I think I've found my political think-cap, after all. This is the break you've been looking for. Don't tell Ray Sanders the truth about his extra-terrestrial wife. Release his story. Then bring the real truth up at the court-martial. She's inhuman. Let the Press take up the monster angle from there—and then see where world sympathy goes. It's basic human nature to distrust and fear the unknown."

The President compressed his lips in an expression of sudden decision. "Henry," he said, picking up the phone, "if what you say is true—"

The secretary shrugged, indicating the phone, and the President put in a personal call to the Navy hospital. His conversation with the rear admiral in charge of the Department of Medicine and Surgery consisted mostly of exclamations punctuating long periods of wide-eyed listening.

"But—" he almost spluttered, "that's more incredible than the Vanyan visitation, itself." He stared, aghast, as he listened to the admiral. "If you told me she was a robot, it couldn't be more— What? Well of course that's a form of life, in a way. I danced with her at the first reception ball, I've shaken hands with many a Vanyan. I'd say they're vibrantly alive—or *were*—but I didn't think of *that kind* of being alive... How could a species like that ever evolve? In fact, how does that Vanyan woman— She *doesn't*. But I mean, how would she— She *wouldn't*. Well then how the hell—"

When he finally put down the receiver, he looked up at his secretary in open-mouthed amazement. "Where in ten thousand hells did such a race come from?" he asked. "And they looked exactly like humans—even more so."

"Is that important now, sir? They've been destroyed."

"Do you suppose that Ray Sanders knows the truth—about his Vanyan wife—what she really is?"

Despite himself, the secretary colored slightly about his ears. "Well—I understand she was a flawless facsimile—or still is. And she's no robot. She's a form of sentient life, with more personality than human women. How could any man tell? I know Sanders doesn't realize what she is. Would he have married her if he knew the truth? This is going to be news for him..."

"I wonder what purpose she had in deceiving him. After all, there could be no procreation—"

"Again, sir, what does that matter? This is an ace up your sleeve."

The Chief Executive's sleepless eyes and tired mouth crinkled into a brittle smile of triumph. He pointed at the thin manuscript before him. "This is just Ray Sanders' preamble," he said. "You tell the Secretary of Defense I am authorizing a full release of Sanders' story—and confidentially, tell him why. We want Sanders to blab his heart out."

The two men looked at each other and laughed. It was another political triumph for their side.

CHAPTER TWO

RAY SANDERS heard the distant clamor in the streets outside his prison before he knew what had happened. He thought he heard newsboys shouting. Then he heard streetcars jangling their bells and a persistent bedlam of automobile horns. He could not know at that moment that there were traffic jams all over the country caused by people stopping to buy extras and to read the papers right in the middle of the street. Or that business had come to a standstill to discuss him.

He merely sat on the edge of his bunk and looked through some of the letters that people had sent him. He had bundles of such letters beside him, unopened—and he did not intend to open them. The warden had mail sacks full of correspondence for him that he would never see.

Most of the letters started out like the one he had just read:

Dear Mr. Sanders:
Our organization represents a worldwide affiliation of civic groups who are vitally interested in the Vanyan form of government. We must apologize for approaching you at this time, but we feel that now is the only time to hope to hear from you regarding your personal views and opinions on the subject…

Then there were the letters and telegrams from publishers and news syndicates:

UNIVERSAL PRESS WILL PAY YOU TWENTY-FIVE THOUSAND DOLLARS FOR EXCLUSIVE SYNDICATE RIGHTS—

Or from the people who really considered him to be a traitor:

Sir:

The Patriotic League of Delbrook, Arkansas, wishes to go on record as being in full accord with the Government of the United States and the United Nations in relation to your indictment for treason against humanity—

And then there was that other kind he was reading now, which disgusted him the most:

Derest lover boy
Plese dont worry ul get out and wen you do I hope ul come and see me—

Sanders got up and began to pace the floor of his cell. He noticed that he had an unlighted cigarette in his mouth and he threw it violently into a corner. Then he paused, listening to a sudden commotion in the corridor.

"Hey Sanders!" yelled a scrubby-bearded prisoner across from him. "Here comes your public."

Sanders went to the bars, grasped the cold steel in his big hands, and glared at the crowd of people bearing down on him. There was Warden Baker, trying to keep ahead of them, his eyes bloodshot from lack of sleep. Next to him was some sort of government official, and on the other side two men in Army brass. Behind came eager men and women waving notebooks and cameras. This, ostensibly, was the Press.

He tensed, angered. *Now* they were all so friendly and interested. He was a shining new martyr, the only ghost to represent those thousands of benevolent Vanyans who lay dead and dismembered in the rubble of their wonder city. These were the gibbering idiots who had permitted the United Nations to destroy the benefactors of Mankind. These people were behind the cold-blooded shooting of Kria.

They could all go straight to Hell.

"Sanders," cried one reporter. "You can tell your story now—not just to the authorities. You can tell it to the world."

"You people will have to be quiet," interrupted Warden Baker. "Sanders, this is Mister George Hackman. He represents the President of the United States. This gentleman is the Provost Marshal, and this is Colonel Bigsby, representing the Secretary of Defense—Public Relations. They want to talk to you."

"I guess I'll have to listen," retorted Sanders. "I haven't any other place to go."

The President's special agent looked the prisoner over. He saw a tall, gaunt man with reddish brown hair and bushy, forward jutting brows, underneath which was a pair of dark brown eyes that had become shadowed, somehow, by the things they had seen far beyond the skies of Earth. He also discerned a curious admixture of opposing types—a compromise between the rugged adventurer and the sensitive dreamer and scholar. Beneath a not too aquiline nose was a wide mouth that had tightened into an expression of contempt, bitterness, disillusionment, torment and hate.

"Sanders," he said, "the President of the United States has authorized you to tell your story to the Press, as you see fit, before you are court-martialed. Do you wish to take advantage of this privilege?"

Sanders sneered. "It's a great privilege, to be able to talk *after* the damage has been done. You can take your privilege and—"

"Just a minute," interrupted another reporter. "If you tell your story they'll let you see Kria again."

Warden Baker roared, *"I said you folks would have to be quiet and wait your turn."*

They were quiet then, because they were watching their victim's face. They had him, emotionally, where they wanted him. Two flashbulbs popped. And they all waited.

"This *is* quite officially authorized," said Colonel Bigsby.

Sanders glared at him and saw an elderly war-horse with Lord Calvert gray at the temples and a highball tan.

"We are here to corroborate the statement made by the President's agent."

Sanders clutched at the bars and glared out at all of them. He looked the colonel up and down, his lips tightening. The crowd could see the tension mounting in him like an earthquake.

"What would be the use?" he finally blurted out. More flash-bulbs went off. "Even if my story got me acquitted? What would be the use? Do you think I give a damn about living in a world inhabited by idiots? You had Utopia handed to you on a golden platter and you sliced the throats of your benefactors. Why? Did they threaten you with invasion?"

"Look," said the colonel. "We can understand, in part, how you feel about what happened. But what you do not seem to be able to grasp is that we could take no chances. And living next door to a superman civilization like that was taking too big a chance…"

"So you used the very technology they gave you and massacred them," yelled Sanders. More flashbulbs.

"Another thing you seem to forget," put in the Provost Marshal, who looked more like a shore-bound admiral, "is that you were a citizen of the United States of America when you warned the Vanyans about our attack. You endangered your own world. That makes you a traitor, Sanders, I'd get down off that martyr's pedestal if I were you."

"May I speak a moment, Warden?"

A distinguished looking, elderly reporter from the *New York Times* stepped forward wearing a powder blue suit, a pink boutonniere and a pocketful of slim, expensive cigars. When the warden looked at the government men and received a triple nod of approval he passed the nod along and the *Times* representative continued, addressing Sanders. "Whether you become acquitted or not," he said, "your story will be important to the world, especially in times to come. We cannot say here whether you are really right or wrong. The court-martial will have to decide that for the present. But let future generations judge you—and let them judge us. That is what will really count."

Sanders left the bars and paced his cell, brushing a hand through his hair. He thought of Kria, struggling against death in a hospital. And he thought of the times they had spent together on her own world. He had to see her again.

"All right," he said, suddenly. "I'll give you the story, but I'll write it myself. I'll give it all to you, in every detail. But don't come back and say I opened your eyes. Just remember one thing." He came back to the bars and glared at them. "When you realize the cataclysmic mistake you have made, you will have to live with the knowledge that now there is no remedy. You have obliterated the Vanyans. One golden chance in eternity, one ray of light out of space and time, never to return."

No flashbulbs now. Only silence, while they stared at him and he glared at them, his forehead beaded with cold perspiration. Prisoners along the cellblock stood behind their bars and waited, watching and listening.

"It's too late for conscience," he continued. "You can't take back a barrage of atomic bombs and magnetic disintegration. I've seen the Vanyan city. I lived in it. I learned the language of the people you killed. I know what they stood for. There is only one conclusion you will be able to draw from my story. It is that *you* are the traitors, not against your country alone, but against humanity."

Three days later, the world read Raymond Sanders' story.

CHAPTER THREE

YOU all know when they landed—August 17, 1956—on the lawn of the Capitol Building, in Washington, D. C., shortly after eleven P.M., Eastern Standard Time. Three traditional flying saucers, complete with peripheral observation panels and the shallow dome on top.

They came smiling before the tanks and artillery and machine guns lined up to greet them, and they offered gifts. Their greatest gift was one of vital knowledge. Within one month, by means of sign language and mathematics, they proved that we were poisoning ourselves with mere practice blasts of atomic energy. Even the Russians agreed to universal control of atomic energy after that.

The Vanyan mission was one of peace. How could the world ever come to fear such a people when they offered Utopia and asked for nothing but good neighbors?

But you did come to fear and suspect, didn't you? And I know why now. It was instinctive egotism. Since we had all become accustomed to benevolence in the form of a false front behind which somebody was always paid off, it was perhaps a natural reaction in the beginning. Nobody could be *that* benevolent, you told yourselves. They wanted something. The whole thing was a trap.

But when time went on and the deception never revealed itself, you still could not accept pure benevolence at face value. You had to reduce the Vanyans to the level of your own understanding. The only way you could understand them was as a threat to your own existence. And so, you destroyed them. But perhaps this was to be expected. Christ was crucified.

By the end of that first day, many more discs had arrived, all over the world, and by the second day you all knew in general what the situation was. They had come from Mars but they were not Martians, Mars was the poor little oxygen-depleted world that astronomers always said it was. But the Vanyans had come to the solar system from interstellar space, searching for a new home, because their scientists had predicted that their own sun would soon become a nova. They had searched for centuries to find a suitable world, and at last they had found Earth—and Mars. Venus was still too hot and stormy. Earth was green and fair, but heavily populated. Mars possessed oxygen locked in a chemical state with its soil. Being benevolent and believing in fair play, the Vanyans did not come to Earth and tell us to make room for them, which they certainly could have done. Instead, they had set up machinery on Mars, developing a heavier gravitational field, building plants to release the oxygen again into the atmosphere and placing artificial sun satellites in orbits around the planet to give them the proper temperatures to support life as we and they knew it.

They had worked with Mars for fifteen years and established their own form of civilization there before they decided to establish contact with us. At first they investigated us without contact, in order to learn more about us, so the flying saucer reports of previous years turned out to have an actual basis in fact. When they became aware of our advances in the field of nuclear energy and finally saw us teetering on the brink of atomic war they knew they could wait no longer. So they landed and started negotiations.

After they had succeeded in freeing us from the fear of atomic warfare, tensions began to be relieved among the nations of the world regarding themselves—but a new tension was arising—a fear of the Vanyans. What was their real purpose and intent? What did they really want? You watched them and discussed them daily, and as time passed without their giving any basis for your fears this fact only served to heighten your suspicions more. The Vanyans were fiendishly clever.

They were small in number and great in science. They offered us technological knowledge in exchange for various useful materials and products we could give them. They readily instructed us how to overcome gravitation and build spaceships exactly equivalent to theirs. They even gave us their own weapons.

At first this latter move on their part was considered to be incredibly naive, but then the doubters came forth again and said that such naivete was wholly incompatible with such advanced mentalities. The Vanyans were accused of allowing us to build our own booby trap.

Yet they opened Mars to us and allowed us to come and go at will. They hid nothing from us and answered every question. Except one thing. They would not permit themselves to be X-rayed or carefully examined, physiologically. Since they were obviously flesh and blood humans, we wondered what they were hiding.

Just that one mystery fanned universal doubt and fear to overwhelming proportions. The Vanyans came to us offering a new era, but they reserved one little right to privacy—and for that they were sinister monsters masquerading in human form. Imagination ran riot. Superstitious dread mounted to the point of insanity. If a Vanyan smiled and held out a precious gift of knowledge to us, we would tremble inwardly, instinctively fearing to accept and thus contribute another choking strand to the imaginary web they were supposed to be weaving about us, inexorably, day by day and month by month.

In regard to my own reactions during those first weeks of wonder, I was more or less neutral, willing to give them the benefit of a doubt, searching through their deeds and their way of life for some wisdom lying beyond our comprehension, which would in the final analysis explain the things they did that seemed irreconcilable with our own realities.

Then, in early September of that year just prior to the opening of the public schools, a group of Vanyans visited Los Angeles...

THEY came in one of their saucers, as they had come to Washington and New York and Chicago, or to London, Paris and Moscow. They came happily, cheerfully, trustingly and without subterfuge—simply to learn what they could about us and enable us to get acquainted with them.

At first it was impossible to get a close look at them except on television, because it was worse than the Rose Parade or the Rose Bowl by far. I wanted to see them in the flesh, but milling crowds were anathema to me. I waited—and finally my opportunity came.

It came because of one outstanding difficulty, which was, of course, the vital matter of communication. In that one respect their arrival on Earth differed from wishful thinking. They were not telepathic, nor did they have any of those convenient machines that you fit on your head in order to get your languages translated automatically. Their language was extremely difficult and involved. Up to this time they had been indulging in a very rapidly developed and publicized system of sign language, in addition to mathematical symbology for expressing scientific concepts. But communication was slow, and they were vitally interested in solving this problem, as were we.

So it was that by the natural process of groping their way and making their wants understood they gravitated toward the institutes of learning and especially toward the teachers. For some reason, which we were to understand at a later date, they treated teachers with an unusual amount of respect—even deference. Second only in popularity with them were the linguists, the first being of course the teachers of the physical sciences. And in a way this still had a lot to do with language. They could understand the language of science most readily, although art and music were also highly favored media for expression. But they recognized the fact that if they were to expand their concepts and understanding of us they would have to get down to the business of actual word ideation. And so, at last, the Vanyans and the local linguists got together—and I was included, as a fairly well recognized comparative philologist.

It was at the banquet given by the Alpha Phi Gamma, a national teachers' honorary society for philologists, that I first met Kria. Not all the visiting Vanyans were present, but we had three of them, which was enough to put us in the television spotlights during the whole evening—or at least up to that point when the evening was violently interrupted.

There was a bright young male Vanyan named Drganu who turned out to be Kria's brother, and there was an apparently young man of much graver bearing, named Sanal. We were not quite sure at the time what the Vanyan lifespan was, but I later found out that Sanal was over fifty Earth years old. He was the father of Kria and Drganu.

I wish that I were telling this story to someone who had not experienced the visitation of the Vanyans, because a description of their well-known peculiarities would be of particular interest.

I mean such things as, of course, their clothing, or lack of it, those hundred and one little differences in the sense of value, or etiquette, or morality, which were the result of a much different social system, and which more often than not resulted in considerable embarrassment on our part before we could make an adjustment to their ways.

For example an uninformed reader might be shocked to know that our three guests sat almost in the nude at our banquet, nor did any amount of sign language appear to influence them. They were not stubborn about it. They merely laughed the whole thing off and continued brightly with the intellectual pursuits at hand.

Not that their semi-nudity was repulsive to any of us. On the contrary. Like all Vanyans, our three guests were almost breathtakingly beautiful. Indeed, if we learned academicians had possessed one-half the physical attributes of our guests we might have considered relieving the tension by at least removing our shirts. These were a golden people, both inside and out. It was a tonic to associate with them. On their faces and in their eyes one could detect a great intelligence coupled with the enviable insouciance of a child.

To me a most satisfactory arrangement was the fact that I was seated at the table within only two places of where Kria was sitting. Before I became involved directly in the sign language and other meager forms of communication, I was perfectly content to study her, wearing an expression of purely academic interest but not feeling it in the least.

I do not wish to appear facetious, but I must say that I stopped thinking like a bachelor the moment I laid eyes on her. To say she was beautiful would be as vacuous an expression as to say that the sun shines. Her bluish hair was parted in back and done up in those thick braids that they slip under the double ringlets on their arms—a very practical method of getting it out of the way and yet very decorative. She wore a tiara of precious metal and sparkling jewels, which had been fashioned into the likeness of living flowers. Her eyes were slightly more lavender than blue. Her brows were black and perfectly formed, and her lashes were thick and long, without mascara. I've seen women play with men with their eyes in an effort to express their sophistication and feminine prowess in general, but Kria played a breathtaking game with her eyes that was just exactly that. A happy, innocent game. But deep behind the game you could see what seemed to be mirrored vistas of interstellar space—something vast, terrifying and unutterably beautiful, like a fleeting sense of Nirvana grasped only for a moment and leaving you dedicated thenceforth to the single purpose of finding out the meaning of it.

Her lips were full, above and below, like those of the Grecian gods, and there was a mystically pagan tilt to them and her smiles were as comprehensive as a Thesaurus. Those lips were enviable, too, to Earthwomen, because they possessed a natural hue of deep rose, and an apparently velvety texture that would have been spoiled by lipstick.

I could go on and on. You have seen her. You know of the golden texture of her skin, her supple grace, the single, veil-like garment all Vanyan women wear that is only half a sarong and much more transparent. To complete the picture, there were her perfect breasts, only partially covered by the veil. In fact, one was and one wasn't. Her bearing and her sparkling personality made you somehow accept her as she was, but you could never take those beautiful young breasts for granted.

You all know why I am dwelling upon the fact of her near nudity here. It has an important bearing on what I was to discover later in relation to their whole attitude on the subject of sex—which is one of the greatest differences between Vanyans and Earthmen.

Then on the other hand their concept of love was another story. In that regard we could meet on a common ground. More or less...

CHAPTER FOUR

I HAVE mentioned that a wave of superstitious dread was developing throughout the world in regard to the Vanyans. Whether or not certain economic or political factions helped to augment that wave of fear and distrust and resentment is a subject that need not be elaborated on at present, but the fact remains that the adherents to this ideology of alienation were already taking matters into their own hands—a fact, which actually brought Kria and myself together. In fact, our banquet that night at the Town House turned out to be one of the focal points of attack for the now historical anti-Vanyan uprising.

I believe we had just finished the shrimp cocktails and the bouillon was just being served when I made my first direct communication with Kria. By means of sign language I was indicating a curiosity in her reaction to our kind of food and trying to get her to describe to some extent what they ate on Mars. My two colleagues on my right were doing their best to help me out.

Kria beamed at me in a way that positively embarrassed me. Furthermore, she seemed to be oblivious of my would-be assistants. In a few moments, so was I. I was wallowing in her eyes and gamboling with her through pristine glades of thought engendered by her smile, her facial expressions, her manual gesticulations, and her whole personality. We did not seem to require a language of word symbology. Nothing crude enough to create sound waves and tickle our eardrums would have served to convey the consciously indefinable yet subconsciously delectable impressions she passed on to me. It was not telepathy, I insist, but rather a form of communication achieved through sheer personal magnetism.

I was thinking: *My God but you're beautiful. Who cares what you eat?*

And with her eyes and lips and her radiant personality she laughed soundlessly. Yet I heard that laughter echoing through the thought-glades of the extra-dimensional sort of little world that was a-building between us. I saw myself running with her, hand in hand, through dreams more vivid than reality.

I came to, with a start, to find Anderson, my colleague who sat next to me, pulling at my arm. He was on his feet. Others were on their feet, too, and there was shouting. On Kria's face I saw a look of alarm as she stared at the main entrance to the banquet room.

"What is the meaning of this?" I heard our master of ceremonies shout.

"There they are," shouted someone else.

"Down with the Vanyans!"

A mob of men moved into the banquet room, brandishing guns. Drganu and Sanal rose slowly to face their attackers. They were unarmed, I heard them say something in their own tongue to Kria and she, too, got up.

It appeared immediately that there was going to be no opportunity of arguing with the intruders. They were after the Vanyans. The television camera next to the master of ceremonies turned just in time to give the outside world a glimpse of violence as one of the invaders struck the master of ceremonies over the head with the butt end of his pistol. This precipitated swift action on the part of the other members of Alpha Phi Gamma, but just as the free-for-all started someone conveniently turned out the lights.

In that exact instant I ran around the end of the table and grasped Kria's arm. It was the first time I had touched a female of the species, so I was unprepared for the delightful shock of vibrant warmth and personal electricity that shot to my brain. I knew a few words of the Vanyan tongue, so I was able to say, "Kria—friend—follow…"

She must have recognized my voice, because she followed me instantly.

I had officiated at several functions held previously at the Town House and happened to know where the doors were, which led both to the kitchen and to the service sections of the building. We were knocking over chairs and banging into tables in the kitchen before anyone knew she had left the banquet room.

Fortunately, I made a mistake and opened a door that I thought would lead out the back way. Instead, I found myself groping about in a service closet. But the first thing I laid my hands on was someone's raincoat, which turned out to be equipped with a plastic hood. I immediately threw this around Kria and tucked her hair well in under the hood. Then I actually found the exit I sought and we went out. Behind us we could hear shouts, fighting, and the sound of furniture being thrown about.

Inasmuch as bold, swift action had accomplished this much so far, I reasoned that it was our only recourse until we reached ultimate safety. So I led her out onto the side street where I had parked my car.

We were just emerging from the narrow passage between buildings when three news reporters sprang out of a car and dashed toward us. They were about to pass us in an attempt to reach the scene of the turmoil through the rear entrance, but in the same moment one of them caught a good view of Kria's bare leg, then her Vanyan style sandals.

He gave a shout to his companions, and in the next instant the three of them blocked us as efficiently as an All American team.

"Here's a Vanyan dame!" yelled the first one.

"Luck," responded one of his companions.

But they made the mistake of laying hands on her and myself to detain us. I took hold of two of them and shoved them off violently. I think I must have struck the third one in the chest, because he staggered back and came at me belligerently.

"All right, fella," he shouted. "You're in the way. We want stories and pics and we're gonna get 'em. Don't let's get rough."

Already one of them had his camera ready and a flashbulb went off. People who had been running toward the entrance to the Town House now began to converge on us.

"See what you've done?" I argued. "This girl's life is in danger. Now we've *got* to make a run for it."

As the reporter still blocked my way, I called upon an old reserve of strength and muscular coordination left over from my athletic days and threw my two hundred pounds at them. I made a path for Kria and took her hand. Silently, she followed me on the run.

But it was exactly like a foxhunt. The hounds had scouted out their prey and the howling and the chase began.

"Hey! There's a Vanyan trying to get away!" I heard someone shout.

"Who's the guy with her?"

"Probably a copper. Get her, quick!"

Flashbulbs popped behind us. The sound of many running feet grew loud in our ears. Some men tried to intercept us and I straight-armed them rather neatly. Hands reached out and tore at Kria's raincoat, which soon came off.

Suddenly, we were piling into my Ford convertible and I was starting the engine. Bodies crowded around us, hands reached in. There was a bedlam of shouting.

"Get out of the way," I yelled, as the engine started.

The Ford pulled away sluggishly as the crowd actually tried to hold it back. In the next instant, I was racing toward Sixth Street, intent upon reaching Virgil Avenue so that I could head for the Hollywoodland hills, Cahuenga Pass and the San Fernando Valley. I crossed Sixth and went on up to Third. Just as I turned into Virgil I discerned three sets of headlights in my rear vision mirror. When you are traveling as fast as the road will allow, you know when you're being followed.

At Beverly the lights were against me. I couldn't wait, so I went through. As luck would have it, there were no police cars or motor cycles on hand to intercept me—as yet. But I knew I couldn't race across town at this pace and keep ahead of my pursuers without attracting the police, and then the whole thing would be at an end. I reasoned that even the police might not be able to do anything against the mob, and before order could be restored Kria might actually get hurt.

For the moment, the situation all seemed to boil down to one thing. Outracing my pursuers was a bad choice. Outsmarting them would be better. It all depended on who knew the city best. I needed a temporary hiding place.

I darted into a side street and began a laborious threading of residential mazes in the general direction of Vermont Avenue. The Los Angeles City College was not far away, and I had keys to some of the buildings. Several times I still discerned headlights in the rear vision mirror, but now there were only two sets.

All this time I was only vaguely aware of Kria sitting next to me. She had been fumbling in the glove compartment for something, and finally I knew she was looking at a city map.

Suddenly, just as we hit the bright lights of Vermont Avenue, I did a double take at her and almost wrecked the car.

She was completely naked. Even the veil had been torn from her in the mad rush.

"Kria," I shouted, inanely, as I barely missed colliding with a streetcar.

She looked up at me sweetly, just as though nothing were wrong. She murmured something at me in the Vanyan tongue, and I caught the word, "Where?" She was indicating the map.

I signaled to her to get down out of sight. As she failed to comprehend, I put my hand on her back and gently pressed her down beside me. Suddenly, she understood, and in the next moment she was curled up on the seat beside me like a contented kitten. It was all I could do to concentrate on my driving, and there was no time to remove my coat to cover her with it.

But why should she want to know *where* I was going? Furthermore, she did not seem to be overly concerned about her father and her brother, back there at the Town House. Then the thought struck me that the Vanyans, after all, might have taken certain precautions prior to coming to the city. Did they have an emergency plan of action in case of danger? Why should Kria be so interested in a city map?

Vague apprehensions assailed me. Were the witch-baiters right, then? Were these beings from the stars truly supermen who merely presented a gentle face to conceal their real proportions and abilities? Would this attack upon them cause them to reveal their true natures, their hidden weapons and powers, making us seem suddenly like so much captured livestock?

"That's for the comic books," I muttered, angrily, and pressed the accelerator to the floorboards.

And now, at last, I discerned a red light in my rear vision mirror and heard the blood-chilling sound of a police siren. Sooner or later, it had to happen.

But Melrose was close, which meant that the City College was within reach. I took a chance, intending to explain later to the authorities. There were racing headlights following that police car, and I knew what that meant. Reporters, mobs, violence.

I swung around behind the college and skidded to a stop. In an instant, I was out of the car, leading Kria toward the darkened buildings. There was a trapdoor under the bushes nearby. It led into the tunnels that carried the steam and water pipes. I doubted that they'd think of looking there.

I found what I was looking for, and we climbed down into the dark passage. I lit a match and we duck-walked along next to the insulated steam pipes, putting a good distance between us and the trapdoor. When I came to three branch tunnels I relaxed, momentarily, and we caught our breaths. And I stopped lighting matches. Retinal fatigue came in handy to keep reminding me of Kria and how she looked, crouching there beside me like some idealized version of the primordial *she*.

Through it all she had remained as calm and unworried as a clam. I even began to wonder if her species were possessed of an instinct of self-preservation. It was at such times that I sensed the alienness of her, for all her obvious and natural attractions.

She put her hand on my arm, trustingly, waiting. I had a distinct feeling it was she who was waiting for certain foreseeable developments of her own imagining—not I. And I wondered who was leading whom. All I could do was wait for the dust to settle and then take her to a more suitable hiding place.

Suddenly, the small lights went on in the tunnel, and I knew what that meant. The police had found the watchman, and he had led them to the boiler room, which gave access to the tunnels. We could hear the pipes clanking. They were coming for us.

For one fleeting moment I considered what might happen to my reputation as a college professor, caught in a tunnel with a stark naked Vanyan woman—and just at the beginning of the school year. But then I thought of graver things. The primordial reasoning that was behind all of this confusion and turmoil. Apes chasing lost angels. A rotten egg splattered across an original Michelangelo. A bowling alley terminating at an altar.

It all made as much sense, this terrestrial reaction to the Vanyan visitation. There was an aspect to finality to my situation—like bridges burned behind one. Irretrievability.

Kria grasped my arm and spoke one of the few English words she had mastered. "Up," she exclaimed, urgently.

I looked into her eyes, or tried to. In the illumination offered by the lights of the tunnel I observed her more plainly than I had before. There was something of finality in that, too. Possessiveness. The threads of our years had come together, somehow. From here on out I had the feeling that those two threads would be woven together.

"Up," exclaimed Kria, tugging at me. "Out." Something in her eyes told me that she had reasons for getting out of the tunnel, which might surprise me.

I moved, leading her back toward the trapdoor we had entered. When we came out under the bushes we could see about fifty men running about the campus. Kria tugged at my arm, trying to lead me out into the open, right into the center of the campus, where everyone would see us.

"Follow," she commanded, in her own tongue.

"Are you crazy?" I blurted out, in English, and I held back.

But suddenly she pointed to the sky.

Even before I saw it, I knew what to look for, I might have known it. The Vanyans were prepared for an emergency, and their powers were beyond us. Kria had been *en rapport,* somehow, with her people. They knew exactly where she was.

The disc settled slowly, almost majestically, toward the campus. It showed no lights. It was merely a lesser darkness in the night sky, dully reflecting the city lights. If Kria had not pointed it out to me, I'd not have seen it until it landed. The men running about the college buildings looking for us did not see it.

We began to run, then, out into the open. Even before we reached the general area in which the disc was going to land, our pursuers spotted us. Somehow, a white, naked body shows up well in the night when it is running across green grass, with or without a bewildered college professor in tow.

"There she is," came an exultant shout.

"There they both are!"

"Get 'em, men!"

The mob began to close in. But suddenly they all came to a standstill as the disc lowered abruptly into view and then quietly landed. Its great port lights glared into sudden brilliance and a door opened. A Vanyan guard appeared with the familiar little birdcage and glowing bulb, which had been described as a paralysis weapon. I guess it was, because the crowd did not move or cry out.

Kria and I went up the ramp and into the Vanyan ship without molestation. The ramp folded inward, the door closed, and the floor almost buckled my knees as we rose into the sky.

CHAPTER FIVE

MY FIRST impressions of the flying disc were necessarily blurred because of the rapid maneuverings, which were forced upon the pilot in this tense situation. I had an impression that they were trying to rescue Drganu and Sanal, which they did, because I saw them later. Long afterward, I gathered the story that the two had simply surrendered to the crowd. The police had interfered and managed to place them in protective custody. Then the Vanyans had come with their paralysis weapons and rescued them.

But this was only the beginning of trouble. The anti-Vanyan revolt was worldwide. I soon perceived that we were being followed as we raced outward into space. And the only thing that could follow a flying disc was another flying disc. Ergo, my own kind had either succeeded in building facsimiles of them by now, or they had captured a few Vanyan vessels.

Their one weak point, I gathered, was a human limitation in regard to acceleration. As I struggled to keep my consciousness, I caught a blurred view of Drganu and Sanal bending over me. Beyond them I saw a weird, three-dimensional miniature of space behind us. There was the vast globe of Earth, pale lavender in the moonlight, and silhouetted against it were half a dozen pursuing discs. I knew what the problem was. To outdistance the pursuers would be to kill me with the pressure of acceleration, which only they seemed to be able to stand. The Vanyans *were* different, after all. They were superhuman.

I stared back at Drganu and Sanal, like an animal caught in a trap. The terrible pressure of acceleration was causing their facial contours to sag into grotesque caricatures of men, thus accentuating the impression in my wavering mind that they were monsters in human form. I think I screamed at them and told them to go away.

Then later I thought: They could destroy the others, but they don't wish to. They are benevolent. It was not they who started the trouble. They intelligently recognized this momentary uprising as something that would soon be quelled by established governmental agencies.

But delirium twisted my thoughts again, and I told myself that they were very, very clever—not wishing to spoil their camouflage of benevolence. It was not yet time for the blow they were preparing. With phlegmatic calm they were sidestepping the insult and fiendishly biding their time.

After that, I passed out. But I dreamed of Kria. I saw her smiling face. I saw her naked body, afar, running toward me across an infinite plain of black ebony, arms stretched out in yearning. She wanted me. I think the thought sustained my life's forces under the brutal pressure of acceleration that finally caused the pursuers to give up the chase. Or it might have been the injections they gave me. Or both.

But I was in love with Kria. It was a fact, which I accepted without questioning why.

The Vanyans brought me to Mars at her request, because she thought I would be in danger back on Earth. As it developed, the danger to myself was not great. I might have been arrested for questioning and then released.

But that is how I came to Mars and took up residence there—until certain governmental forces from Earth caught up with me...

THE rest of you came there later. I was the first to behold the new planet. And then I knew, with a certainty, that the Vanyans were truly benevolent. They were a god race, which could have destroyed us as a mere whim if it chose to do so. They were great enough in their science and intelligence to handle us without subterfuge. There was no necessity of laying groundwork for conquest. That could have been accomplished at any time.

They came to that starved out world and filled it with titanic stresses, awakening within its core the ancient fires and the sustaining forces of nature. Long before they landed, earthquakes were caused to rage through the ancient crust, raising whole new mountain chains, which were designed to catch the moisture that they intended to provide for the Martian skies, to catch it and pour it through rejuvenated soil into fresh new rivers, which led into lakes, which poured into embryonic seas, thus establishing the cycle of evaporation and return.

They bored swiftly into the planet's depths and installed their gravitation equipment, capturing the globe in a restrengthened spherical vortex of sub-electronic fields of force, which comprised mass attraction—and thus a stabilized atmosphere was assured. Their great engines of power operated electro-chemical plants designed to release oxygen from the soil. They established miniature suns in orbits between Deimos and Phobos, providing additional light and warmth.

All their stupendous technology was not dedicated to necessity alone, but to the aesthetic sense, as well. A harsh, soulless race might have been content to eke out an existence in barren deserts under skies that were unrelieved by the changing phenomena of nature, but not the Vanyans. Their eyes were not blind to the beauty of the rainbow and the splendor of cloud-framed sunsets. Their ears were not deaf to the patter of rain and the crash of thunder. They required the aesthetic setting of broken horizons, of verdure clad hills and the misted plumes of distant waterfalls, the cool presence of placid lakes, the crashing spray of an ocean's surf—and the song of birds. That was one of the first things they wanted of us. A shipment of live songbirds.

Those scaremongers who were behind the anti-Vanyan uprising should have thought of that. Their bogeyman from space asks not for unconditional surrender. He requests a shipment of songbirds. And later, sheep, cattle—and honeybees. A very sinister race, indeed.

There are only about fifty thousand Vanyans, or rather, there *were* about that many; yet their city covered almost one hundred square miles. It was a city that offered the ultimate in techno-logical efficiency and yet succeeded in not being a city at all.

The only stationary buildings were the Palace of the Council, the Central Research Laboratory, a few specialized factories and the oxygen plants. There were no shopping centers, no restaurants or amusement centers—not even colleges in the architectural sense. Each Vanyan household was a self-contained unit, which could fly when desired. According to individual tastes, each household "sky island" could land where its owners pleased—beside a lake, at the ocean's shore, on a mountain top, or in some secluded valley. If it became necessary for one member of the household to travel to another location, he could do so by means of teleportation, which to the Vanyans was as simple a matter as dialing the desired call frequency of one's destination. A Vanyan citizen could visit a spot a hundred miles distant and return home all within one minute if he chose to do so. To attend concerts or attend to business it was not necessary to come to "town." As we see events via television they indulged in the cultural life by means of tri-dimensional visi-sonic apparatus. By means of remote controlled robot extensions they could even sign papers at a distance.

Education was another matter. Every mature Vanyan was a third order teacher. A third order teacher conveyed knowledge. Leisure was such that every younger Vanyan could find a teacher of the third order and acquire knowledge at will. Motivation was such that the students learned on the basis of personal volition. There was no institute of third order learning, but knowledge was dispensed with an underlying pattern of prescribed order—on the unit system. Certain broad units of knowledge were delineated for mastery. When the student could demonstrate a satisfactory accumulation of knowledge, he sought out those second order teachers who actually made it a life's work to guide the minds of others. A second order teacher was on the social level of our most prominent medical specialists. He taught intelligence, or developed it. The application of knowledge, and the evaluation of it.

It was only the first order teacher who lived in a structure designed for mental instruction. There were many such "sky islands" dedicated to first order education. A first order Master dedicated his life to the awakening of wisdom in his advanced pupils. He could take them to a secluded spot on the planet and spend weeks there, if he chose, without interruption. Sometimes there were no lectures at all, nor any discussions. There was only an exemplary way of life—a grasping of concepts for which there was no word ideation possible. Wisdom could not be taught, actually. It was acquired through the method of exposure to higher wisdom.

Thus—new Mars, a Shangri La surpassing all others...

CHAPTER SIX

MY FIRST instruction was in language. And my charming third order teacher was none other than Kria, herself. Thanks to an extensive academic background in philology and a highly sensitive "Sprachgefühl," or language feeling, I was able to find my way gradually through the intricacies of a language that had no limitation on the number of its grammatical cases or its types of declensions. Once one mastered the key to the underlying basic language of inflections, original composition of the whole morphology was possible, and in each case the listener would be able to understand and appreciate the method of expression. Here was a place where the true poet was envied, indeed. As a philologist I could digress at great length on this subject, but that would lie beyond the scope of my objectives here.

The most eloquent commentary I can make in regard to the Vanyan language is that its poetry could *never* be translated. An attempt at translation would be like the crash of a tree in a forest where there were no ears to hear. I have read poems or heard songs written in three different ways, all with the same words, the same rhyme and meter, but with subtle changes in inflections or declensions, which brought about increasing intensities of meaning, or sometimes a different meaning entirely, often conveying a concept not attainable through words alone. Thus far can description go, but no farther.

Weeks passed, and months passed, while I lived and moved about in a world of dreams more poignantly vivid than any reality that my own world could have offered. News trickled through, from time to time, regarding events on Earth. I was even aware that Earthmen had come to Mars—that some of them were even residents there, on a temporary basis, for technical reasons. But I never saw them during the first few months of my sojourn. I succumbed to the overwhelming charm of this synthetic little world, to the point of irresponsibility. There was something there waiting for me to absorb—wordless, indescribable. I felt its slow development in me without being able to describe it other than to say that, perhaps, I was becoming, in fact, a Vanyan.

At the end of the fifth month, I was ready to really have a talk with Kria. My basic vocabulary and mastery of the inflection key enabled me to compose new meanings and thus get my point across. There were many things I wanted to know. There was much that I had to say—to her alone. By this time I was an established member of Sanal's household, and many mysteries had presented themselves to me, which demanded an explanation. For example, so far I had not seen one Vanyan child. Nor a very old man or woman.

At my request, they had moved their "sky island" into a picturesque valley, which was just over the hill from the plain of Tharsis, on which stood the permanent center of the Vanyan civilization. From the hilltops you could see the marble-hued towers of the Palace of the Council and the simpler lines of the Central Research Laboratory, in addition to dozens of the flying discs, which were always on hand. Beyond lay the shimmering expanse of the new Sea of Tharsis, and along its shores were atmosphere plants, releasing oxygen from the soil and augmenting the processes of evaporation from the sea.

We had taken a walk to see the sunset, and naturally we turned our steps toward my favorite spot, at the foot of a waterfall, by a beautiful pool, from which point of vantage we could look out upon the plain and the sea. There were young trees about us, but the chief item of vegetation was a vine that grew everywhere, rapidly sheltering the soil and conserving it against erosion from the frequent and sudden showers. One other type of vine bore large, white blossoms at this time of the Martian year. It grew up the cliffside on either side of the waterfall, making of the whole place an area of pristine beauty, a place for meditation and, I knew, lovemaking.

Kria wore the traditional Vanyan veil sarong, which hardly concealed her beautiful form, and a gentle wind from the sea pressed it enhancingly against her. As for my own apparel, I had adopted the dress of Vanyan men, which consisted of little more than a short, split skirt and the equivalent of a G-string, plus sandals. Drganu had presented me with a jeweled medallion, which I wore around my neck. It distinguished me as a guest of honor living under the protection of the house of Sanal. A simple series of exercises had helped me to put muscle tone back into my physique so that now I was not ashamed to match contours with any of the Vanyans. Even in outward appearance I was getting to be like them.

A description of this setting would not be complete without mention of the *sleth,* a three-foot, silvery globe that accompanied us, floating through the air and guided by a small box of controls and electronic gear attached to my waist. The Vanyans were addicted to moods as many Earthmen are to a graceful indulgence in alcoholics. They could not be happy for very long without music. The *sleth* was a floating portable radio, of sorts, but which filled the surrounding area with three-dimensional music. The symphonic notes seemed to emanate from everywhere, until you felt you were a part of them. After due adjustment to the effects of a *sleth,* you ceased hearing the music, and there was only the mood—like a subtle addition to one's personality. It was like feeling "high," but infinitely refined in its subtleties.

I did not know, as yet, that the *sleth* had other functions...
At which time, I suppose, it might be called a *sleeth,* or a *slith,*

depending on the shades of meaning, which were applicable in relation to its activities…

"Kria," I said, abruptly, after a considerable period of silence during which we had watched the distant natural sun sink out of sight and observed the rise of a synthetic, nearer sun, "why are there no children or old people here?"

She answered me with silence. I looked at her and found her eyes surveying me with an expression, which could only be interpreted as sorrow—or perhaps, wistfulness.

Finally, she said—and somewhat hesitantly, I thought— "Perhaps it is time to tell you more about my race. Sooner or later, you would have to know…"

Which remark left me waiting for her to continue. I waited.

"We are immortals."

"You—*what?*"

"There is no death unless it is willed. Of course—violent destruction—"

"But—to live forever—how is that possible? No, skip that. Tell me this. How old are you—*really?*"

"By Earth years, I am as young as you."

"Then—not long ago you were a child…"

Again, the wistfulness. "I was—" She hesitated, groping for words. "Yes. Yes, I was a child."

"Then why don't I see any children of a newer generation?"

"We are immortals. New—that is, an increase in the population is a serious thing. There is a very strict control on that."

"You mean birth control."

"Well, yes… You see, when someone chooses to die, another Vanyan can come into being. During this important period of our transference to a new world, there is no time for such considerations. Later, when things have become quite well established, the oldest philosophers will go and make way for the youngsters again."

"Oh. But you know the same relationship does not seem to exist here between man and woman as it does on Earth. You're all quite indifferent to each other's attractions, just like so many brothers and sisters. Don't any of you ever fall in love?"

The *sleth,* as though responding to our moods, rose to a crescendo with its music, then faded to a whispering lament that was barely audible above the roar of the waterfall.

Kria grasped my hand, tightly. "There is love," she said, quickly.

"So? In that case, what do lovers do?" I was being deliberately pointed in my remarks, I held on to her hand, not willing to let it go.

We were playing breathtaking games with our eyes. It was a sort of duel, and I must have broken through her guard.

"Oh, Ray," she suddenly cried out. And she was in my arms.

I crushed her to me and kissed her, and she responded with all the feverish thirst for love that had been pent up within myself.

"Kria," I whispered to her, when I could catch my breath, "didn't you know this was happening?"

"Yes, yes. I did," she exclaimed. And with that, she pushed away from me. There were no tears in her eyes, but there should have been, from the looks of her.

I have mentioned before that there was much to be seen in Kria's eyes that was a fascinating mystery—something vast, terrifying and unutterably beautiful, like an awareness of a pitiful cry that wants to reach you but can't, as though the gods were trapped in a bottle at the bottom of some lost ocean and were crying out, unheard. This is what I saw in her eyes now. It was a distant pleading that was forbidden expression.

"Kria, darling," I blurted out, taking her into my arms again. "What is it?"

She only sought my lips and clung to me in unutterable desperation. Then at last she said, "There are things I should tell you—yet I can't. But I love you."

Love was a sword that had cut many a Gordian knot cleanly through. The immortal opening lines of Oscar Wilde's Panthea came to me, accompanied by indescribable music from the *sleth:*

Nay, let us walk from fire unto fire,
From passionate pain to deadlier delight,
I am too young to live without desire,
Too young art thou to waste this summer night
Asking those idle questions which of old
Man sought of seer and oracle, and no reply was told.

I picked her up in my arms and carried her over to a large, flat rock next to the pool. She lay there silently until I lay her down on the rock and kneeled there looking down at her.

Then she said, "Something I should tell you cannot be told, but someday—"

I kissed her. "Someday you mean everything will be straightened out?"

"Yes. Oh Ray, I swear it." She reached out for me…

For sweet, to feel is better than to know,
And wisdom is a childless heritage,
One pulse of passion—youths first fiery glow,
Are worth the hoarded proverbs of the sage:
Vex not thy soul with dead philosophy,
Have we not lips to kiss with, hearts to love, and eyes to see!

These lines were but a mild reflection of what the ingenious *sleth* was singing to us on high, as pale Deimos rose to face the diminutive Vanyan sun across the Sea of Tharsis and I lay beside my love.

SUDDENLY, the *sleth* became silent, and Kria suddenly tensed, staring up at it. She sat up quickly, pushing herself away from me, straightening her hair.

"Kria," came the voice of Sanal, her father.

When I looked up at the *sleth* I saw there his face looking down upon us. He was not angered, nor was he smiling his blessing upon us. He was sad.

"Come home, you two…"

Before we could argue about it, his face disappeared. And the *sleth* was silent. It hovered, waiting for us to leave.

I looked at Kria, embarrassed and a trifle piqued. "Do you mean to say that the *sleth* is also a visi-scope?"

She nodded. "It's all right," she answered, taking my hand and getting up. "It was all coming to this. It will be interesting to hear what Sanal has to say."

When we came "home," just over the hill, both Sanal and Drganu were waiting for us. They had a way of studying us both that angered me. It was like prying into a private world that belonged to only the two of us.

"So you have seen us," I said, hotly. "It's just as well. I'm going to marry Kria…" An inane sort of puppy defense, but it was all I could think of at the moment.

"Come in," said Sanal. "I want to talk to you." Which was obvious.

We all went inside.

Sanal sat down and studied us a long time again before he spoke. "You realize, of course," he said, "that this is the first case of personal attraction between Earthman and Vanyan. Have you considered the possible consequences?"

Since the question was directed at me, I answered, "There are always consequences. We are in love. The consequence is—we want to get married."

"I know. I know. But you are not aware of the facts in regard to our race…"

I stood up, impatient, fists suddenly clenched. "Then let me in on it," I blurted out. "What's the big secret? Do you go into chrysalis at fifty and turn into bug-eyed monsters?"

"Raymond," admonished Kria. She sounded like my wife already, but I liked it.

"On the contrary," replied Sanal, gravely, "you might say that our hidden secret contains the reverse of an unhappy ending. I only wish to warn you that we do possess a racial secret, and that you must never ask us whence we really came, for if we told you the truth it might spoil your marriage with Kria—yet if you waited long enough there would be no need for telling you anything, because the whole thing will right itself, in time."

This was the reverse of the Lohengrin theme. I looked into Kria's eyes, wondering if there were a swan song stored within her that I might have to listen to at a later date.

"Kria," I asked her, "for our sake I'd like to have you answer just one question. Would you call your marriage to me a deception?"

Drganu and Sanal exchanged serious glances, then looked at Kria.

"Sanal has warned you," she answered. "The end result of our marriage will be perhaps even more than you have wished for. Therefore, I see no deception."

"You know," I said to the three of them, "I think we're going around in circles. Kria and I want to be married."

Drganu and Sanal smiled and got to their feet. Kria gave a little cry and ran to me. My arm went around her, and Sanal placed his hand on my shoulder.

"Congratulations," he said, forgetting for the moment the Earthly custom of shaking hands.

I grasped his hand and shook it, and Drganu offered me his. I gladly accepted them as my new "in-laws."

"Regarding a home for you," said Sanal, "we will have to apply to the Council for that. Or did you have in mind taking up residence back on Earth again?"

"Well, I guess I can't stay on Mars too long without renouncing my citizenship, so perhaps Kria and I had better plan on going to Earth—after we are married."

The three Vanyans stared at each other.

"But—" said Kria, "darling, we *are* married."

I think I gaped at her.

"You see," said Drganu, "in our civilization the graver the decision one makes, such as this one you two have made, the closer it is attached to honor. If the decision is sacred, so is the honor that seals the bargain. Ceremony would merely be a mockery of that which words should not attempt to express."

"Of course I will see to it that this is registered with the Council," said Sanal.

"Wait a minute," I interrupted them. "If I ever want to take Kria back to my own world and present her as my wife, I'll have to satisfy the requirements of our own laws. There has to be a legal ceremony and a proper registration of this."

"That might be arranged," said Sanal. "Already certain government officials from various countries of Earth have set up what you call 'consular' offices here, for the purpose of legalizing Vanyan visits to Earth and keeping track of Earth citizens on Mars. You might—"

"Come to think of it, I really have been out of touch with my own world. If such procedures have been established here already, I'm staying here illegally. I'd better make contact with the United States consul, if there is one here, and reinstate myself as a citizen. Then at the same time I can look into the matter of a wedding."

CHAPTER SEVEN

DRGANU accompanied Kria and me to the U. S. Consul's office in the Palace of the Council. The three of us entered the office laughing over some little joke of Kria's, all of us conversing rapidly in the Vanyan tongue. The consul looked up at us and seemed to suppress a frown. He was a middle-aged man, somewhat overweight, of a reddish complexion that reminded me of high blood pressure—and he was obviously not fond of this job, which removed him to such a great distance from baseball, bars and Bromos. Seated next to him, however, was another type of Earthman. I saw plainclothesman or F.B.I. written all over him. Tall, gaunt, pale of complexion, with a prominent if aquiline jaw and with a legal file cached away behind each of his pale, penetrating blue eyes. Both men had been conversing but as we entered they fell silent and surveyed us as though we were Indians coming off the Reservation with a water rights complaint.

They sat there waiting for us to speak, so I began. "I am a United States citizen," I said. "My name is—"

"Since when?" interrupted the Consul.

That stopped me, but I saw a light began to glimmer in the narrowing eyes of his companion.

"We have no record of a Vanyan becoming a citizen—"

It was then I realized that I should have renovated my Earthman clothes. I was dressed as a Vanyan, or undressed like one, and I had come into the office speaking the Vanyan tongue with what to them must have been perfect fluency.

"Wait a minute," said the plainclothesman. "That English is too good. Who are you?"

"I am Raymond Sanders, of Los Angeles, California."

The Consul tore his eyes from Kria long enough to raise his brows at me. The plainclothesman snapped to attention.

"Ye gods," he exclaimed. "I just got here and my job's done. I came here to trace you."

"Why?" I said.

"You're a U. S. citizen. You disappeared. The story was that the Vanyans kidnapped you."

I laughed. "On the contrary, they sort of rescued me during the anti-Vanyan uprising. I have been living in a Vanyan household ever since, and now I want to get married. This is Kria, my fiancée. And this is her brother, Drganu."

The Consul half rose to his feet. "You *what?*"

"I said we want to get married. I want to know how to legalize it according to Stateside laws—or Earthside laws, to coin a new term."

"But—" The Consul was apparently at a loss for words.

"Hold it," exclaimed the plainclothesman. He looked us over carefully, and I almost saw cogs whirling swiftly in his brain. "Could you excuse us for a few moments?"

Drganu and I and Kria stepped outside into the great halls of the Palace, proper.

"Your world is very complicated," remarked Kria, holding onto my arm.

"It seems to tie itself up and get strangled in its own complexities," put in Drganu.

I could have given them a lecture on the subject, but I was busy wondering what was going on in the Consul's office. Something bothered me, vaguely, like a dark premonition, but I soon threw the feeling off, embracing the simpler and cleaner philosophy of the Vanyan. Honor and idealism were impregnable fortresses. I had only to stick to my guns, without subterfuge, and the battle would be won.

Within three minutes, the Consul, himself, appeared at the door of his office. His attitude had changed remarkably. He seemed to be vitally interested in our case. With a pleasant smile, he ushered us back in. The plainclothesman merely sat where he had been before. There was a somewhat baleful expression on his face, which I did not like.

"I think," said the Consul, "that everything can be straightened out. First we'll legalize your residence here and then we'll get down to the business of the marriage…"

We were married by the Consul next day, after I had received a provisional passport, a Vanyan resident's visa and a Vanyan alien's carnet of identification. Drganu was best man, Sanal gave the bride away, and Mr. Motter, who turned out to be a special U. S. agent attached to the United Nations in some way, was a witness. The legalization of our marriage was almost overwhelming.

Then they told me about the string that was attached to the whole business. Or rather, Mr. Motter did. And it wasn't so much a string as a ship's hawser.

He asked to see me privately and the Consul gave us his office. When we were alone he came up to me and shook my hand gravely.

"Congratulations," he said.

"Thanks," I answered, "but you don't seem to be referring to the obvious."

"I'm not. I'm referring to your unique position to be of great service to your country and to your native world."

"Oh, oh."

"Sit down. I want to talk to you about that."

I needed to sit down, all right. And I was also trying to contain my temper. If what I was thinking was true—

"You have resided on Mars longer than any other Earthman," he began, with enviable smoothness. "You are also a trained linguist and have evidently mastered the Vanyan tongue as well as come to understand their way of life. By the medallion you were wearing yesterday I see that you have been accepted as a member of a Vanyan household. And now this marriage between you and a Vanyan woman completes the picture."

"*What* picture?"

He saw my belligerence but he was prepared to take that in stride, too. These special agents didn't acquire their posts for nothing. That was often the difference between them and the usual type of character we have representing us abroad. That's what special agents were for, I reasoned. They were fill-ins for places where the chips were down and the going was rough.

"Why did you voluntarily seek a U. S. Consul here on Mars and attempt to reestablish yourself as a citizen of the United States of America?" he asked me.

I shrugged. "Habit. Gregarious instinct. The need for a sense of identity, I guess. I have to be some kind of a citizen. I don't prefer to be a man without a country."

He impaled me with a stare. "Is that all your U. S. citizenship means to you?"

"Look, I don't duck draft boards. I'm just as good a citizen as anybody else."

"I know. And you've been a taxpayer, too. But, as a professor attached to the American educational system don't you think you should adhere to a more clearly delineated patriotic policy?"

"I'll put it this way. Patriotism is like religion. It's kind of personal. When Pearl Harbor happened—"

"I know. I know. You volunteered. Well that wasn't nearly as important as what you can do now. Then a people were in danger, as well as cherished ideologies. But now the entire

Earth is in danger, and it hasn't much to do with ideologies, unless you could tack an *-ism* onto the word, Freedom."

"If I picked a label for your speech I'd call it 'razzmatazz.'"

"Please don't be facetious, Sanders. If you don't believe what I tell you, take it on authority. While you've been dreaming around the hill country with your fiancée, things have been happening."

"Such as?"

"So damn much benevolence from the Vanyans that we can already see the pattern behind it all. It's a gigantic booby trap."

"I'm still listening." I really was. I had only gotten married. I hadn't gone deaf. If the Vanyans really were up to something, which I still doubted, well—again there was instinct. Preservation of my own kind. I wanted to know what the Government claimed to know, and here was my chance.

"Consider all the weapons and technological gadgets they've given us. Suppose I told you that they all have a common denominator in the form of a remote control unit? True, those controls are supposed to be for our own use—" He leaned forward to drive his point home. "But there's nothing we can see to prevent them from controlling everything we've got on Earth—from up here, on Mars."

I sat there and studied him, trying to be calm and collected in the middle of incipient apoplexy.

"You have no proof of that possibility," I stated, finally.

"Would you like to prove that we're all wrong?"

That was a clever way of putting it. I couldn't turn my country down—or the whole Earth, my own native planet. On the other hand, I liked the Vanyans tremendously. Here was a chance to prove them villains or friends, and I could hope to prove the latter.

"In other words, you'd like to deputize me as an agent."

"Exactly. You would be representing the Government of the United States—the O.S.S., to be exact—as well as the United Nations."

"What is it, specifically that you want me to do?"

"Remain here in residence on the pretext of taking your honeymoon here. But get around and see if you can find us a clue to their real intentions. Actually, the ideal discovery would be the master switch for those remote controls."

"Ideal? It would mean interplanetary war."

"If that's in the cards, we naturally want to be in a position to strike the first blow."

"Uh huh. Well, I think you're wrong, but if you're right—I'll tell you."

Motter got to his feet with a wan smile on his face. Again he extended his hand. "I guess you're all right, Sanders," he said. "And that's why I say—congratulations."

"Yeah."

I did not feel too happy. I was a spy against my wife's people. Nice...

CHAPTER EIGHT

SO IT was that Kria and I started taking our honeymoon on Mars. I had double reasons for traveling, so by the authority of the Council we were issued a small version of the interstellar type disc, and we managed to get around. Kria was still my third order teacher, and as I had expressed a sudden interest in Vanyan technology she personally escorted me to various strategic spots.

There were no security regulations covering atmospheric plants, or their atomic power stations. I even went through Research Center and Communications—interplanetary communications. I studied their methods of production, learned the intricacies of their weapons.

But there was no master switch—so far. I made weekly reports to Motter, and he was disappointed at my lack of concrete progress, I was not. But I kept my eyes open, as directed.

One day in Sanal's house I was introduced to an important Vanyan—a first order Master teacher by the name of Ralsyan.

He was supposed to be centuries old but he looked about sixty—a healthy sixty.

He was very much impressed with my mastery of the Vanyan language and invited me to witness a tour of first order students under his guidance. Kria and I went along in his "sky island" school, in the company of about twenty Vanyans who were almost of Sanal's age. And one night in a lonely region of Mars I was permitted to stroll with Ralsyan alone in the desert and converse with him.

"Perhaps you can tell me something that I have long hesitated to ask anyone else—even Kria, my own wife," I said to him. "You are a wise man and can consider certain vital questions in the absolute sense."

"I should be glad to help you if I can," he answered.

"All right. Then tell me this. Why are you Vanyans so willing to give us Earthmen all your technological secrets—your method of space flight, your weapons—everything? You don't even seem to be much concerned about defense against the possibility of attack. After all, your total number is infinitesimal compared with the population of my own planet. Our industrial capacity is tremendous in comparison with yours. In another couple of years—"

He laid his hand on my arm and smiled. "Now that you have acquired a knowledge of our tongue, perhaps I can explain it to you. I know exactly what you mean, of course, and as a Vanyan I appreciate your concern."

We walked on across the sands in the light of Phobos and one artificial sun satellite. Earth stood out in the sky like the biblical Star of the East.

"You see, as immortals we abhor the thought of death by killing more than anything else. To lose one Vanyan life would be cataclysmic to us. In cases where wisdom has been obtained—which lies beyond knowledge and mere intelligence—the loss would be very great, indeed. So we have only one form of protection against violence from our neighbors. It is the firm knowledge that they will *not* attack us."

He held up his hand as I was about to interrupt, and went on. "The cause of war is a difference in potentials, which causes discontentment and suspicion. We have attempted to reduce the difference in potential to zero, by making our neighbors as strong as us. We could not tolerate the idea of maintaining constant defenses against possible attack. We can only know that our neighbor has good intentions when he is able to attack and does not. Then we can be assured we are at peace."

"But—that's leaving yourselves wide open."

"Perhaps—"

"It doesn't make sense. You tell me you abhor the idea of death by violence, yet you take a mad gamble by giving us all your weapons, and we can out-produce you a million to one."

He shrugged. "There is the parting line between mere rationality and wisdom. You must wait until you acquire wisdom."

"I don't know about that. The way I see it, you people have no instinct of self-preservation at all."

Ralsyan laughed. "If you only knew," he exclaimed, cryptically.

There was the first dangerous remark I had heard. Here was the first hint of a hidden weapon. My ears felt like rabbit's ears. But how could I get him to let me know what he was hiding?

"I'd like to know," I said.

He patted my arm. "Some things cannot be told," he replied. "You will have to wait. Someday it may be revealed to you."

This harkened back to the cryptic remarks made by Sanal on the day I declared my intentions of marrying Kria. To say that I was assailed by a sense of frustration would be putting it mildly.

Now I *was* discontented and troubled. Could my Government be right, after all? Were the Vanyans wolves masquerading in sheep's clothing?—to use a cliche. But no. There was such a thing as sensing the intentions of another. The Vanyans were intrinsically benevolent, I could judge them by my own, gentle Kria. I would have staked my life and gambled a world on the conviction that there was nothing deceitful or malignant in the Vanyan nature.

But how was I to prove this now?

"I have another question. You people are able to redesign any world to suit your own physiological needs—anywhere. If you value your lives so much, how come you haven't established yourselves on a more isolated planet? Why set up your civilization here so close to Earth and give us the means of reaching you through space?"

"That is related to the basic nature of our purpose in life," he answered. "Of what use is wisdom or knowledge if it cannot be applied? Happiness is derived from striving toward higher goals, and Man's goal is always knowledge and wisdom. But not wisdom in a vacuum. We have deliberately sought contact with a race that could use our help and guidance. It's the way we prefer to live, evaluating our accomplishments in relation to expanding achievement. Therefore you might say that Earth is a sort of catalytic agent to our endeavors. To live for ourselves alone would be anathema."

Here was almost an incomprehensible vista of benevolence. I gave up, for the time being. But I present this conversation as further evidence that the Vanyans were as close to being gods as it is possible to be in mortal life. Study it well, and remember—Earth stabbed them in the back. YOU destroyed them!

A FEW days later, Kria and I had the intention of going "over the hill" again to watch the sunset, by the waterfall. She was still in the sunray mist bath, or Vanyan version of "shower," when I called her, so I walked on ahead with her promise to meet me there soon. I did not bring along the *sleth* as on previous occasions because my mind was troubled. I was even wondering how I might question Kria about her people without arousing her suspicions, yet I was angered by the thought that this cloak and dagger intrigue had entered the picture in the first place.

I had no sooner arrived at my favorite spot near the pool below the waterfall than I discerned the lone figure of a man ascending the slope of the hills from the direction of the Palace of the Council. Long before he arrived at the pool I knew it was Motter, Earth's special agent, who had actually been masquerading as the U. S. Vice-Consul on Mars.

When he came within earshot he said, "I thought I'd come up here to take a look at the sunset and the sunrise. It's the only place I know of where you can watch both simultaneously."

"And you came to get another report," I told him.

"A double sun phenomenon and a strategic report affecting the fate of a world, all in one spot," he grinned. "Can you blame me?"

He offered me a cigarette, but I refused it just as though I were a native Vanyan. He smoked and we both watched the true sun sink and the first artificial sun rise. Deimos and Phobos were both near the zenith, and Earth was a gleaming diamond in the darkening sky. After the real sun sank, the combined light of the two moons and the synthetic sun produced a brilliance comparable to full moonlight on Earth.

"Well?" he said, finally. "Anything new? You went on a little trip, I hear, with a first order Master—name of Ralsyan. He's big timber among the Vanyans and second only in the Council."

"You really get around, don't you?" I retorted.

He shrugged, waiting. His pale blue eyes watched me.

"Okay," I said. "I did pick up one thing." I told him in detail my entire conversation with Ralsyan that night on the desert. When I came to the cryptic part of it where Ralsyan said, "If you only knew,"—Motter raised his brows.

"So that's the way it stands," he remarked. "Well, maybe we were right, after all, Sanders. When I first gave you your assignment, you might have been chagrined to know that we are well prepared to meet the Vanyans in combat. Now, however, perhaps that fact will be of some consolation to you."

I remained silent, and finally I did ask him for a cigarette. I puffed on it rather furiously, more troubled than before.

"Look," he added, "I'm going back to Earth for a few days. I think the home office would be interested in Master Ralsyan's remarks. In the meantime, you'd better concentrate a little harder on getting vital information. Don't forget that the Vanyans might be able to snuff us out with a flick of the wrist, and our only protection may be to strike without open provocation—unless you can show us that we're wrong."

Just then, he staggered and put a hand to his forehead.

"What's the matter?" I asked him.

"Damn headache," he said. "It's the planet. Some of us get *saroche,* you know. Altitude sickness. The atmosphere isn't quite built up to normal yet."

As I made no comment, he finally added, "Guess I'll go back now. This is getting me down."

I watched him in troubled silence as he staggered away in pain down the hill. But I did not watch him for long. Suddenly, I, too, staggered. But I did not hold my head, I was merely astounded by the sight of the *sleth* as it appeared abruptly out of thin air within ten feet of me.

On its surface I saw the angry face of Sanal, and I knew that he had been listening to our conversation. I also knew that the *sleth* could be rendered invisible.

"I made him go away," said Sanal. "Will you please return here at once?"

There was something in his tone and facial expression that intimated that I really had no choice in the matter.

"I'm coming," I told him. "I'd like to explain something to you."

"I think that is in order," he answered, coldly. "Come quickly."

As I walked back over the hill, trailed by a very silent *sleth,* I wondered if I should regret having taught Kria English in exchange for lessons in her own tongue. And at the same time I realized that she must know about all this, because for Sanal to know she would have had to serve as interpreter.

She was there with Drganu and Sanal when I arrived at the semitransparent "sky island" that was Sanal's home. Again I thought from the looks of her she should have been crying. But then the dark thought assailed me that Vanyans had no tears. And superstition asked the question: Is the race human that cannot cry?

She lowered her eyes, refusing to look at me, and it irritated me. "Well?" I said to Sanal. "I'm here." It did not look like this was going to be an old fashioned evening at home with the folks. It had more of an air of the Inquisition.

"You are a spy against your wife's people," accused Sanal, in even tones. "Why?"

I told him. And I added, "I'm glad it's come up, Sanal. Let's get down to brass tacks. You know I want to help establish permanent peace between our worlds as much as you do. That's why I agreed to play it their way. I wanted proof that you were friends, not enemies. Now what's all this secret business? What are you hiding? For example, many scientific institutions on Earth have politely requested an exchange of biological information relative to comparative physiology between our races. In short, they would like to study an X-ray of a Vanyan. This you flatly refuse. If your structure is slightly different, why should that matter?"

Drganu appeared to tense, as though with anger, but he said nothing. Kria looked at me then and I saw the old mystery in her eyes. It was lost gods crying in a bottle at the bottom of the sea. A message from afar—untranslatable.

Sanal got up from his chair and paced the floor. "That is our business," he retorted, bluntly. "But it has nothing to do with the safety of your world. *Nothing.*"

"Then why won't you tell me?" I almost yelled.

All three of them stared at me. There was a prolonged silence.

"Listen to me," said Sanal, at last. "If your world destroys us, it will lose more than we. You had better do something to prevent them from attacking."

"There's another point," I argued. "You have no instinct of self-preservation. During the anti-Vanyan uprising on Earth you were calm as clams. Now you face the prospect of total annihilation with the bland statement that we will lose more than you. Why?"

"Don't ask me that, because I won't tell you. But I want to tell you this. I shall be forced to bring all this to the attention of the Council immediately. However, to bring this out into the open would definitely increase interplanetary tension. We will handle the situation secretly, from our side, if you'll do a little counter-espionage for our side."

"What?"

"You became a spy for Earth merely to prove to your own people that we were friends. Now I want you to be a spy for us for a reason that is equally constructive. Please realize that our weapons are not the kind that cause death. We cannot tolerate killing. We could not harm you. But if you tell us Earth is ready to attack us, we might be able to prevent such an event—without bloodshed."

"But—what about your magnetic disintegration? That could snuff out a world."

"Its end use is related to physical obstacles. We dig great shafts with it and level mountains or clear our path of meteors and other debris during space flight. The disintegrater is not intended for killing."

"But it could be used as such."

"*We* could not use it for that purpose, but *you* could."

All this time I was doing private thinking of my own. I actually wanted to see what Earth was up to. I wanted to talk to the authorities and see how bad the situation was getting. If I could pretend to spy for the Vanyans, it would keep their knowledge of my activities under cover. I could play the game both ways and with my own deck of cards.

"Suppose I go to Earth," I said, "and look things over for you. I'd have to have a logical excuse—some vital secret to bring back. Can you think of something that would appear to be a vital secret yet which wouldn't harm you if you revealed it to me?"

"Yes," said Drganu.

Kria and Sanal looked at him wonderingly.

"One thing you did not examine very closely in your tour of our world was the *sleth*. I believe it would be valuable for Earthmen to be able to duplicate it, and you could offer the secret information—of which you only became aware tonight— that they can be made invisible."

"That's it," exclaimed Sanal. "I think we can give you plans for the *sleth*, but I'll have to take it up with Council. The *sleth*, you know, emits various types of rays, which could be considered as weapons. Your own people would look upon it as a rare acquisition, indeed, which, in fact, it is."

So it was decided. I knew I was playing both ends against the middle, and I didn't like it. To have denied my espionage against them in the face of concrete evidence, which they had picked up by means of the *sleth* would have really created an obstacle for our side. Actually, playing their game was subterfuge on my part, but my objectives were sincere both ways. And that was what made it so difficult.

I tried to make up with Kria, but she resisted me.

"There are things here more important than individuals," she said. "I love you, Raymond, but I am bound to things beyond myself." She walked toward our room.

I began to follow, but both Sanal and Drganu laid a hand on my arm. I might have shaken them off, but there was a strange expression in their eyes, which detained me.

"Among ourselves," said Sanal, "we are telepathic—and more. We feel the other's suffering. Your only recourse now is to prove to her that your marriage—can continue."

That did it. I flared up. "Where I come from a man's wife is his property! It's a mutual situation, actually, but even one's own relatives have no right to interfere. I have certain prerogatives as her husband. If I want her to come to Earth with me, I can take her when the times comes—or she can stay for good!"

"You wish—to take her to Earth with you?"

"Not now. But I'm just saying, she's my wife, which is a very personal business."

"That is understandable, but among our kind one's world, one's society, the entire welfare of the race, is a personal business, too."

I went to "town" that night, via the teletransportation system, and stayed with the U. S. Consul. Motter had already left for Earth. I availed myself of the Consul's private liquor stock and asked him if he could fix me up with an Earthside suit of clothes...

CHAPTER NINE

IN THREE days I was on my way to Earth with a set of Vanyan plans for the *sleth*. Inasmuch as I had a chance to go in a ship piloted by Vanyans rather than Earthmen, I was supplied with a little case containing shots of the serum they had given me before for the purpose of enabling me to withstand more than ordinary maximums of acceleration and deceleration. Which was to come in handy later.

In Washington Motter traced me down immediately and I told him about the *sleth*. To make it look good I added that although the *sleth* was strategic stuff, I had used it as an excuse to come home and get a better briefing as to what was going on. Again—both sides against the middle. But it worked. He took me in on the inside.

The situation was worse than I had thought. Public opinion was in favor of action against the Vanyans. Aside from the United Nations, the U. S. Congress was in a dither. U. N. decisions were slow in coming, and the President was faced with the necessity of thinking in terms of U. S. safety, regardless of

U. N. decisions. Moreover, there was a sort of tacit agreement that Mars fell outside the scope of U. N. machinery as far as aggression or war was concerned. In other words, the Vanyan Government was not a U. N. member and therefore Mars was a sitting duck for anyone who wanted to take a pot shot at it. In fact it seemed the U. N. was *hoping* somebody would make a move so as to take the hot potato out of their hands.

I was present in Washington at a secret hearing on the Vanyan situation—strictly from the point of view of our own government. As an authority on Vanyan affairs and in the Vanyan way of thinking and the Vanyan language, I was questioned from time to time, but in all cases I perceived that I was regarded as a minor cog in the machinery. At the last minute it was decided to bring in a U. N. representative and go over the situation.

Before my eyes I suddenly saw the definite plans for an attack taking shape, and I demanded the floor. Grudgingly, they yielded it.

"I have it on authority," I said, "that the Vanyans are incapable of killing. I suggest an alternative. Call them in and explain the grounds for your fears and tell them the only way the situation can be relieved is for them to move somewhere else."

This proposal was met with a general ripple of laughter. The U. N. representative, an Englishman named Spaulding, answered me.

"As a citizen of a nation possessing a long history in colonization," he said, "I can appreciate the possibility of a man's going native and wishing to speak for the aliens among whom he has long resided. But there is something in legend pertaining to the dangers of eating the lotus too long. Pearl Harbor was a pointed example. I am afraid we shall have to reject your opinions as being distorted by your personal attachment to the Vanyans through your marriage with one of the heathens."

"An uncalled for insult," I retorted. "Rather than reverting to stereotyped form, I'll overlook the insult in consideration of its source."

The chairman of the committee rapped his gavel smartly and glared at me.

"But don't destroy the Vanyans," I warned. "You will be the losers—not they."

"Is he nuts?" queried one committee member.

To make a long story short, it looked like an attack was imminent, and I could do nothing about it. I walked out, stamping my heels. Motter came out after me and took hold of my shoulder.

"Sanders. Watch yourself."

I jerked loose and walked away from him. Which was all the provocation he needed to put a spy on my trail from there on out. I expected that and acted accordingly.

The fellow who was tailing me must have been confused when I went to the Lincoln Memorial and stood around like a tourist reading the Gettysburg Address and gaping at the moonlit Potomac. I was really having a mental wrestling match with two sets of emotions. There was my country and my world, which I felt was not in danger, in spite of official opinions on the subject. Yet as an assigned agent employed by the Government it was not for me to question, but to do, I suppose. Then on the other hand, there was my wife and her people, whom I loved and trusted. Moreover, idealism came into the picture in regard to Earth's human society. I felt that the Vanyans could benefit us beyond measure and that we were on the verge of killing the golden goose.

Question: Should I warn the Vanyans? And if the Government was right, after all? Well, take it from there and you'll know what was going through my head.

I read the Gettysburg Address about a dozen times, but that didn't help. Far out in the sky beyond the Potomac was a little red light that was Mars. It was gradually losing some of its red as the mighty machines of the Vanyans gradually released the oxygen from the soil and veiled the planet over with a thickening atmosphere. Science, knowledge, wisdom—benevolence. About to be destroyed.

Question: If Earth destroyed Mars and was actually wrong in doing so—then what? A terrible loss to Mankind. I was convinced that historical blunder was being made. Moreover, fifty thousand wonderful people were involved.

I spoke their language. I thought in their language. I lived in their thoughts. This was an extra soul, which fought with my own.

Decision was mercifully taken out of my hands when a Vanyan disc suddenly swooped down in front of the memorial building. I caught the sound of scurrying footsteps as the agent tailing me ducked for cover. I think they paralyzed him.

Two Vanyans walked up the steps of the memorial building and addressed me in their own tongue. I was wanted back on Mars immediately. One of them carried a paralysis generator. Since it was more graceful to enter their disc on my own feet, I went with them.

How did they find me? Now that it looked like the chips were going down they were showing more of their cards. Personal direction finders. Mine had been set up shortly after my arrival on Mars. The Vanyans were benevolent and wise, but they were also smart. At least they weren't lotus eaters, themselves, even if I might have been accused of being one by the U. N. representative.

We were not long under way when the fireworks started. A communication was received by my "escorts" to the effect that I was to be returned to Earth at once. But inasmuch as the directive was issued from the Government of the United States, they did not obey it . They were under orders from their own government to bring me in.

The ship's commander came to me and asked me if I had any acceleration serum for myself. When I asked him why, he turned on his three dimensional visi-scope and I pretty nearly fainted.

Following us was not a ship, or a squadron, but every flying disc we had—an unsuspected fleet of them. They were far astern but coming fast. I felt very sick as I realized what had happened. My capture alerted the attack. They could wait no longer. This was it.

"It wouldn't make much difference if I didn't have any serum, would it?" I said to the Vanyan officer. "You wouldn't wait around here for my sake, would you?"

He smiled. "We feel that you are partially a Vanyan now. You deserved that much consideration." Without further comment, he turned and walked toward the control room.

I knew what was coming, so I brought out my little case and gave myself a shot of serum. And just in time. As I flung myself onto a couch, the lights went out.

Inside my head...

I drifted between unconsciousness and fitful dreaming— awful delirium in which I saw atom bombs crashing into Mars and making tall mushrooms over the wreckage of my wonder world.

"The fools," I remember shouting once, referring to the Vanyans. "They wouldn't put up defenses. They'll be obliterated."

And of course I know I must have called out Kria's name many times. Destruction or no destruction, she was my wife. I loved her and I didn't want her to die. Now the veneer of civilization was peeling off down to primordial instinct.

"To hell with everything," I shouted. "They won't kill her!"

We maintained a good lead all the way, and in fact got ahead of the Earth fleet. When we swept in alongside the Palace of the Council at Tharsis, I knew I only had about an hour in which to act if anything was to be salvaged.

I went with the guards directly into a Vanyan Council. I saw the U. S. Consul and other Earth dignitaries scuttling out of the building in haste, entirely unmolested. Evidently the warning had come through. They were on their way to the Earth-built ships—ships that had been built on Earth by Earthmen, thanks to a Vanyan supply of a peculiar element that went into the makeup of the relay units controlling them. The Vanyans' own gift was being turned against them.

When I came into the Council Chamber I looked around for Sanal and Drganu and Kria. None of them was present. I dashed to the speakers' podium and yelled at all of them in Vanyan.

"Tell me the truth! Will you defend yourselves?"

A grave body of Masters looked back at me. They shook their heads negatively, Ralsyan, my one acquaintance among them, spoke.

"And it is your loss," he said. "Not ours."

"But you're not just going to sit here?" I shouted.

"It is too late to do aught else. We know what we sought now. The answer is: Earth is not ready for the higher way of life."

I shook my head, trying to clear it of dizziness. "All right. Then why was I recalled to Mars?"

"That you will discover in due time."

"The time is due right now. Listen, I can't understand your attitude and I'm not waiting..."

I ran to the nearest guard and took his paralysis generator from him. Before they could recover from their surprise, I paralyzed the entire assemblage. I did not have to leave the room in order to escape. There was a first rate teletransporter there and I knew Sanal's call number.

So it was that in less than half a minute I stood in Sanal's private "sky island" once more, paralyzer in hand. Sanal and Drganu and Kria were there. They had been watching me in the three-dimensional viewer, and now they were on their feet, forewarned. Kria hung her head and ran to her room—*our* room.

"I want all three of you to come with me," I said. "This idea of sitting idly by and waiting for the destruction is insane. Now you'll do it my way or I'll *force* you to do it."

"We appreciate your concern for us," said Sanal, "but it's too late. However, in regard to your own safety—"

"To hell with that," I blurted, out in English. "Kria!" I ran to her room and took hold of her. In fact, I took her into my arms and hugged her. *"Kria,"* I exclaimed. "You know I love you. Why do you run from me? Come on. There is still time to go. I can't leave you here to die…"

Again there was that lost, far away look in her eyes and the longing in her to be able to cry. She suddenly gave in and her arms went around me, desperately. "Oh my love, I don't matter. It is you who must save yourself," she gasped.

"Are you *all* crazy?" I exclaimed. "Come on! You're my wife and you're going with me." I pulled her and she came, as though struggling against her own will, wanting to and wanting not to.

Sanal and Drganu blocked my path with a neutralizer of the paralysis weapon, making it ineffective. However, my two hundred pounds were not neutralized. I plunged through them. They were resilient, but they couldn't stand against me. I found their teletransporter and fought them while I dialed another frequency—the one that would put me at the Research Laboratory. Kria and I stumbled through.

"Raymond. Raymond," she complained. "This was not meant. You don't know what you are doing…"

"The hell I don't," I yelled, and we raced for a Vanyan disc outside the lab.

Then I stopped, suddenly, to ask her, "Tell me once and for all, Kria—*is* there a master switch, a master control of some kind, which could make Earth's copy of Vanyan gear ineffective? You people wanted me to find out if Earth was going to attack. Now you *know* they are. Are your people going to sit here and die?"

"Raymond, the attack strikes too swiftly, and the speed of light—" She shook her head, refusing even then to reveal secrets to me. "It is too late—but not for you. You were brought here to—"

"Come on," I interrupted her. "I guess it's my way, after all."

Earth's representatives had left. There were only a few Vanyan discs available, totally unguarded. I pulled Kria into one and made her guide me at the controls...

Racing Earthward into the teeth of the armada, I sent out a call to the attackers, identifying myself so as not to get blown out of space before I started. In our three-dimensional scope we could see the approaching ships. Ahead of them, and near to us, was a cloud of ponderous projectiles already launched and coming fast. We began to maneuver out of the way.

"Flagship to Sanders," came an officer's voice. "If that's you, keep clear and hold course for Earth at half speed. We will pick you up. You are under arrest on suspicion of treason."

"Treason?" I yelped into the mike. "Somebody is—"

"You were a counter-spy for the Vanyans. You may blame yourself for triggering this attack."

"But I had nothing to do with it!"

"Ha! You made a brazen rendezvous with a Vanyan ship right in Washington—how stupid can you get. But there's no time now for argument. Follow instructions."

"Damn Motter and his spy," I muttered, as I turned off the transmitter switch. That I had planned no rendezvous with the Vanyans I knew, but it would be hard to prove otherwise.

Kria came into my arms. She did not want to talk. She merely wanted to be held close to me. We remained that way for some time, watching the fleet approach Kria's adopted world. Watching the projectiles approach, carrying their atomic warheads.

"Kria," I exclaimed. "Now is the best time to analyze you and your emotions. Under normal circumstances, this would be monstrous of me—*but I've got to know about you.* What are you thinking? What are you feeling?" I shook her gently. "Tell me—now."

We both looked at the three-dimensional picture of Mars and saw filtered flashes of light trace a pattern across that area where

the Vanyan "city" was located. There were flashes farther removed, also, where power plants were located. Then the
surface darkened slowly under the shadows of man made,
mushrooming clouds. And all of a sudden we saw bright, jagged
lines appear across the planet's surface as huge earthquakes were
summoned into being and great gashes were cut into the
staggering little world.

"The disintegrators," I exclaimed. "For the love of God.
The bombs were enough."

Kria shuddered, tried to hide her face. "You are children,
giant children," she said, "flailing about in darkness."

I tried to lift up her chin, and when she looked into my eyes
and saw *me* crying, it was too much. She ran from me and threw
herself onto an acceleration couch. She actually suffered
because she could not cry. I left her alone.

I was too overcome, myself, to give her comfort. I stood
there looking at the destruction and I yelled at the three-
dimensional color image of it. I can't repeat what I said because
most of it would seem like gibberish. But I am not ashamed to
say that I bawled, openly and uncontrollably.

It was about a day later that the Flagship overtook us and I
was commanded to draw alongside the other much larger disc.
As the capturing crew secured our airlocks for boarding, Kria
rushed to me, alarmed.

"What is the meaning of 'treason?'" she asked me, having
heard the commanding officer use the word over the receiver.

When I explained it to her, she asked, "But how can they
accuse you of that? You are not guilty."

"Thanks, sweet. But can I *prove* it."

Her eyes were wide with concern, and there again I saw her
looking at me from afar off, as though out of other worlds of
her own. The old mystery, which would never be solved. I had
given it up.

"What—is the penalty—for treason?" she asked.

I shrugged, saying nothing.

"You mean—they will *kill* you?"

"If I can't prove myself innocent. But take it easy—"

She clenched her fists and stamped her foot in anger. "Kill! Kill! Kill!" she cried. "Is that all your barbaric race can think of?"

"Honey," I said, trying to calm her. "Now there's no need to—"

"They shan't kill you. You cannot die."

"Why?" For reasons, which I could not have explained to myself, I wanted a specific answer to that question. There was more than personal emotion behind her insistent statement.

"Because—because—there is a reason. I can't tell you."

Before I could argue about that, the inner door of our airlock opened, and armed M.P.s attached to the U. S. Navy Airforce stepped into the control room. They were armed with business-like, understandable, old-fashioned automatics.

"Stop," cried Kria, holding up her hand. "This man is innocent. You will not take him prisoner."

The M.P.s struggled to overcome their surprise at finding one Vanyan alive. Also, they must have been surprised at her English. But then their leader grinned.

"Okay, beautiful," he said. "Keep out of trouble. You're under arrest, too."

Kria did not budge. She stood there facing them, and all of a sudden I saw the M.P.s change their expressions. Their mouths dropped agape and in their eyes was both wonderment and fear. They became rigid and their guns dropped from their fingers.

I shouted at her, asking her what she was trying to do, knowing all the while that now she was *really* showing her cards. With sheer mental power she seemed to be capable of paralyzing them.

It was in that moment that a new detachment of guards entered the room and shot her down. I screamed, throwing myself at them, but they pumped bullets into her and she slumped to the floor. I punched hard, but something descended on my skull and I went out cold…

I HAVE not seen Kria since then, but I am told I may see her after writing this story. I am told she still lives, and I thank God.

You all know what happened from that point onward. The Vanyans not only allowed us to destroy them rather than lift a finger to harm us. They made sure that we would not harm ourselves, because they knew in that last terrible hour that we were not yet ready for interplanetary civilization.

Even in their posthumous revenge, however, they were benevolent. They had set up the hidden master switch on one of the Martian moons, it is presumed. Those robot controls were set to go off *after* the last Earthman had arrived safely home. Mind you, they could have destroyed us at any time. They could have taken revenge while the fleet was still out in space. But they did not.

After we were all on the ground, the propelling apparatus on the discs quietly dissolved, as did all our supplies of the Vanyan element that made such ships possible, and their weapons. Those were incapacitated also, never to be used again. The Vanyan answer, gentlemen. After you killed them, their voice spoke out of the tomb of space and said, in effect, *"You are not ready."*

And I agree. I shout to their noble spirits and proclaim them godlings—a golden, benevolent benefactor whom we have slain.

My fate matters little. It is *yours* with which we should be most concerned.

CHAPTER TEN

THEY told Ray Sanders he would not be able to see his wife until after the court-martial, but they assured him she was rallying slowly and had a good chance to live through her injuries. This pacified him to some extent, and it also motivated his desire to prove his innocence.

They let him testify, but as he continued referring the court to his story, which had been published all over the world, there was nothing new that he could offer in his defense. In regard to the Vanyan rendezvous in front of the Lincoln Memorial, it was only his word against theirs.

The Press was worried, but the Administration was not. Public opinion was largely on Sanders' side. Washington was being besieged with messages from all over the world. Some countries even threatened diplomatic reprisals if Ray Sanders received the death penalty.

But then the prosecution took over and X-rays of Kria's bullet-ridden body were presented as proof that the Vanyans were inhuman. They were a synthetic race. In a word—androids…

Swiftly, the judgment followed. "Therefore, Raymond Sanders, it is the decision of this court-martial that you have been found guilty of treasonable negotiation with an inhuman enemy who stood ready to conquer and perhaps destroy not only your own native country—but this entire world."

The Press was released with the news, and Congress and the President watched the reactions.

The headlines fulfilled their fondest expectations: SANDERS WIFE INHUMAN!—SANDERS CONVICTED!—FEDERAL EVIDENCE BREAKS SAND-ERS—VANYANS PROVED MONSTERS!—X-RAYS PROVE KRIA FAKE HUMAN—U. S. SWINGS AXE!

The sympathetic world turned antagonistic overnight. The Government gained new prestige. They had been right, after all. Congress convened briefly, and the President signed the death penalty.

Then he authorized Sanders to see Kria…

The Press was excluded from that meeting. Sanders, a visibly broken man, went alone into her hospital room. He was with his Vanyan "wife" a full hour before he was called out by his custodians.

He came out a different man. He was straight and tall again, and there was a new light of defiance and triumph and even joy in his eyes.

"I want to talk to the Press," he exclaimed.

"Too late for that now, Sanders," the police officers told him.

"But I've got to talk to the Press."

"Come on." They pulled him along with them.

"The President," he yelled. "At least let me talk to the President."

In his jail cell he raved and swore and even appealed to fellow prisoners for aid, but his totally incredible story branded him as an insane man. There was a sympathetic shaking of heads.

"The poor guy. He's off his rockers."

"I guess I'd be, too. He gets shot tomorrow morning."

The next morning, Sanders even argued with the officer in charge of the firing squad. "You don't know what you're doing," he pleaded. "Give me one more hour. This is vital. I demand to speak to the President."

The officer tried to be patient, but finally he lost his temper and called the guards. They took Sanders and stood him against the wall.

"No. I don't want a blindfold," he told them. "I want to watch the sky."

He stood there looking up into the brightening sky, and several times he called his wife's name.

"Ready...!" barked the officer to the firing squad.

"Kria!" yelled Sanders.

"Aim...!"

That was as far as they got. A few guards testified later that they observed a gold-emblazoned disc in the sky. It paralyzed the firing squad and the officer in charge. It lowered itself swiftly into the prison yard and Sanders ran to it. It took off with him, and he was never seen again...

IT WAS then that the President of the United States decided he would have to have a talk with Kria. He, too, went into her room alone, while his bodyguards waited outside.

She lay there like any other rapidly convalescing patient, but she was far more beautiful than the normal run of women. Synthetic or not, she was an object of the Chief Executive's pity—belatedly.

"I want you to tell me what happened," he said to her. "Who rescued your husband? I thought we destroyed your race."

"You did," she replied, sadly. "But *my* race did not matter."

"Then—to whom did that mystery saucer belong—the one that rescued Ray Sanders?"

Kria smiled wanly. She indicated a chair. "Sit down, won't you? I think I can tell the story now."

She talked for a long time. She described for the President a truly human race of immortals who faced the necessity of making contact with us, of finding a world within a solar system such as ours on which they could continue their existence in accordance with their basic philosophies, as explained by Ralsyan to Sanders when he was on Mars.

"But immortals come to treasure their lives, not so much for themselves as for the knowledge and wisdom they have acquired. They could not risk contacting you directly, so they created us—their android extensions—to contact you first."

"Do you mean to say—that all the while your race was renovating the planet, Mars, your human counterparts waited somewhere out in space to determine what our reaction would be?" asked the President.

Kria nodded. "That is well expressed," she answered. "They *are* our counterparts. For each of us there is a human duplicate, in form and mind and personality, with whom we were in mental contact at all times. Through us they could sense everything we sensed here."

"Wait a minute. You mean—somewhere, there is a *human* copy of you? One who knows as much about Sanders as you do—who perhaps loves him, actually—*humanly?*"

Again, Kria nodded. "Yes, she loves him, and she is with him now—for all time. It is she who rescued him. In fact, she ordered him brought to Mars just before the attack, in order to pick him up there, so as not to appear in her ship in Earthly skies and thus reveal her secret. But your attack was too sudden. Limited by the velocity of light, she could not get here in time from the mother ship. Ray Sanders, alone, of all Earthmen, will join the true Vanyan race in search of a new home and a new race of people who, perhaps, will deserve their guidance more than you."

The President shook his head. He fell silent. After all, he *had* made a historical blunder. The truth might even cause his impeachment.

"You—ah—say the true Vanyans preferred to keep this a secret. Why have you told me?"

"I had to tell someone. It's all past now. They are gone."

"Well, we might as well keep this secret, just between you and me. The world would suffer greatly to know it was guilty of a great crime, after all."

"I don't care what you do."

"We'll say that some fanatic rescued him in a ship that looked like a disc; that we shot it down over the ocean. It will be simple enough to bury this whole story."

"Do what you wish."

The President, greatly relieved, looked at her kindly. "Why so sad?" he asked. "You are immortal, human or not. Think of the many years ahead of you—the things you'll see transpire here on Earth. Why, you might even land a movie contract, with your looks—"

Kria shook her head. "You don't understand," she replied.

"What don't I understand?"

She looked into his eyes and said, "You see—*I* love him, too."

THE END